"I longed to be friends with every character   ing, honest stories. Whenever I thought I h   suddenly opened into a moment of queer   been so sexy and gay."

—Marie-Helene Bertino, author of BEAUTYLAND

"Funny, sharp, surprising, and bizarrely relatable, readers can't go wrong with this entertaining and moving collection. Gay is good, and bad gays are even better."

—Marissa Higgins, author of A GOOD HAPPY GIRL

"The newest addition to the dyke aching genre, this is a desperately needed unhinged collection for the gays and theys."

—Chloé Caldwell, author of WOMEN

"Chaotic, sexy, and binge-worthy as hell, *Be Gay, Do Crime* is an EVENT."

—Ruth Madievsky, author of ALL NIGHT PHARMACY

"A collection that is truly firing on all cylinders. The stories are propulsive, compelling, and incredibly enthralling. Immensely enjoyable. I couldn't put it down!"

—Kristen Arnett, *New York Times* bestselling author of MOSTLY DEAD THINGS

"This irrepressible, riotous, and very gay collection of stories from some of our best emerging writers charms and entertains, leaving the reader veering in a getaway car between laugh-out-loud and gasp-out-loud."

—Sarah Thankam Matthews, author of ALL THIS COULD BE DIFFERENT

"Audacious, outrageous, alternately tender-hearted and razor-sharp … With fearless exuberance, the authors of these stories lean hard into all that is messy and magical about queer existence, honoring the joy of defiance and the legacy of communities who must defy both social norms and the long arm of the law to survive."

—Kai Cheng Thom, author of FIERCE FEMMES & NOTORIOUS LIARS: A DANGEROUS TRANS GIRL'S CONFABULOUS MEMOIR

BE GAY
DO CRIME

SIXTEEN STORIES OF
QUEER CHAOS

EDITED BY

MOLLY LLEWELLYN AND KRISTEL BUCKLEY

DZANC BOOKS

db
DZANC
BOOKS

2580 Craig Rd.
Ann Arbor, MI 48103
www.dzancbooks.org

BE GAY DO CRIME: SIXTEEN STORIES OF QUEER CHAOS.
Copyright © 2025, text edited by Molly Llewellyn and Kristel Buckley. All rights reserved, except for brief quotations in critical articles or reviews. No part of this book may be reproduced in any manner without prior written permission from the publisher: Dzanc Books, 2580 Craig Rd, Ann Arbor, MI 48103.

Library of Congress Cataloging-in-Publication Data Available Upon Request

First US edition: June 2025
ISBN 9781938603310
Interior design by Michelle Dotter
Cover design by Betsy Falco

Printed in the United States of America

10   9   8   7   6   5   4   3   2   1

CONTENTS

THE MEANING OF LIFE
MYRIAM LACROIX • 1

IT'S A CRUEL WORLD FOR EMPATHS LIKE US
SOULA EMMANUEL • 19

REDISTRIBUTION
TEMIM FRUCHTER • 33

WILD ALE
S J SINDU • 46

PEEP SHOW
ALISSA NUTTING • 66

OF COURSE, A CURSE
KAYLA KUMARI UPADHYAYA • 82

WILD AND BLUE
AURORA MATTIA • 100

BAD DOG
ANNA DORN • 112

TWO HUNDRED CHANNELS OF CONFLICT
MAC CRANE • 132

"FUCK YOU" MONEY
FRANCESCA EKWUYASI • 151

MAKE LIFE GREAT AGAIN
PRIYA GUNS • 169

TOOTH FAIRY
MYRIAM GURBA • 178

BLACK JESUS
VENITA BLACKBURN • 194

DISTRACTION
MAAME BLUE • 198

GRAND BEAVER CABIN
EMILY AUSTIN • 215

OPERATION HYACINTH
SAM COHEN • 235

EDITORS AND CONTRIBUTORS
• 262

You have to remember that it is impossible to commit a crime while reading a book.

—John Waters

We make our own choices, we pay our own prices.

—Violet, *Bound* (1996)

THE MEANING OF LIFE

MYRIAM LACROIX

They'd planned on getting beer from Toby's, but instead they got a baby, and they were not unhappy about it. Myriam and Allison hadn't talked about kids yet, but finding one seemed to be a sign that it was time. Besides, being lesbians, this spared them the trouble of adopting or getting one of their friends to have sex with them.

They found the baby in the alley behind their apartment building, close to a gutted couch and confetti and some blood. There'd been a fight outside Toby's—on stand-up comedy night, of all nights. That was Toby's. They were inspecting the couch, wondering if they could turn it into some sort of art installation, when they noticed little feet kicking at the inside of a flannel cocoon. Allison wiped her glasses and Myriam kneeled, poking the bundle.

"Look how serious this baby is right now," Myriam laughed. She traced its droopy cheeks and sullen brow. "I like, love this baby."

"That baby's a critical thinker," Allison agreed. "I'd hang out with that baby."

Back at their apartment, they gave the baby a bath in the kitchen sink. They rubbed it until it was clean and warm and happy, then dried it with a dish towel and took turns smelling its head. It smelled like green apples from the dish soap.

They wrapped the baby in a sweater and gave it a tour of the apartment. The narrow kitchen, with its lemon-slice wallpaper. The Boggle corner. The broken kids' toys Allison collected from the alley to use as instruments, and the bathroom, whose walls were covered in red-lipstick poetry because Myriam wrote in there and frequently felt oppressed by the page. The baby loved the apartment. It gurgled and touched and put everything in its mouth.

They made their new baby a bed next to their bed by stuffing blankets inside a Rubbermaid bin, but they couldn't get themselves to put it down. They pressed it between their skins and fell asleep, warm as hams.

☙

Jonah, because they'd never met anyone with that name. They had no idea what Jonahs were like, and they liked the element of surprise. They were not going to be the kind of parents who call their baby Mozart or Beyoncé. In fact, they immediately agreed they would never wish any real-world success on Jonah. That was how people ended up with stomach ulcers, or making bad art.

They called Myriam's mom first to tell her the news. They told her a desperate woman with no eyes inside her eyeholes begged them to take her baby and raise it as their own. They said that because they knew Myriam's mom wouldn't understand, she'd pester them about not making any efforts to find the parents.

"Babies are expensive," she pestered anyway. "How're you gonna pay for diapers or dentists or, worse, orthodontists? With Allison working at that call center?"

Myriam's mom thought that because Allison had short hair and wore men's shirts she should be the breadwinner. She understood nothing about lesbianism, and she understood nothing about them.

"If you don't try to be more supportive, we're gonna tell Jonah he only has one grandmother," Myriam said. She hung up.

Allison's parents offered to host a late baby shower, and Myriam and Allison invited all their friends. Myriam wore her gold latex minidress, and Allison put on a gold chain to match. They dressed Jonah up in a little white-and-gold dress they'd taken off the baby Jesus doll at the Salvation Army.

Myriam and Allison's friends decided that Jonah was a very cute baby, which meant he'd be an ugly adult. Allison and Myriam didn't mind. Ugly people had more incentive to tell good jokes, or develop an amazing sense of fashion.

They all sat by the pool in lawn chairs with Allison's parents occasionally refilling the chip bowls, and nobody swam. Myriam and Allison's friends were not the swimming type. They wore thick makeup and boots that took a long time to lace.

"You have to let me do a photo shoot with Jonah," their friend Ash said. "Anne Geddes meets Marina Abramović's *Balkan Baroque*—an homage to Jonah's dark provenance."

Ash was the best thing to have come out of Myriam's general arts undergrad, and Myriam told them so.

"To the best chosen family in the world!" Myriam cheered. "And to our cute-ass baby!"

They all raised their glasses and took big gulps of their drinks. Myriam was drinking lemonade in case her breasts started making milk from being around a baby, but Allison got sloshed. About five beers in she climbed onto the diving board and started screaming the lyrics to a song she'd written for Myriam.

"Until our asses hang like sandbags! And our pussies smell like kelp! Say you'll love me, baby, or I'll be needin' help!"

"Okay, okay, I'll love you forever!" Myriam shouted as Allison inched closer to the edge of the board. She rolled her eyes and laughed, blushing behind her hair. "So dramatic!"

Allison jumped in anyway and Myriam waded in after her, wrapping her arms around Allison and kissing her with full tongue. They made out in blue-lit water until Allison's mom yelled that the pizza was here, then they wrung out their clothes and rejoined their friends. On the pool deck, Ash was passing around one of their signature joints, and Kamran was giving Jonah an undercut with tiny leopard print on the sides of his head. Allison started playing a synth she'd found in her childhood bedroom, and her best friend Nate drummed on patio furniture. They played space-age versions of lullabies that everyone danced to, undulating their hands against the dark night sky.

Around sunrise Allison's dad drove them home, and Allison puked a thin string of puke on the family van's carpet. Back in their room, Allison and Jonah fell asleep right away, but Myriam stayed awake, wondering about the meaning of life.

Myriam and Allison had met when Myriam was in university, at a show in a run-down punk house in East Vancouver. Allison had just finished playing a set and asked Myriam if she thought her last song was "derivative." Myriam had never heard that word, but the way Allison asked her, with sweaty hair and an electric vulnerability in her eyes, made Myriam want to have sex with her right away. Two years later, they were so in love it felt like living inside a dream, only some nights Myriam got nervous. She'd grown up with her single mom, moving every time her father made a new threat. She couldn't turn love into a story that made sense, and would get into these existential spirals.

Myriam looked at Jonah, whose toes were curling in his panda socks. She didn't agree that babies gave a meaning to life. Nuclear families were a concept made up by the same people who wanted you to get full-time jobs or sell your art for money. Still, when she lifted Jonah from Allison's heaving chest and held him in her arms, she could feel the exact dimensions of her happiness, its weight and humid breath. It wasn't a dream.

Myriam couldn't stop smelling Jonah's neck. At the store, on the bus, while changing his diapers. His baby smell was intoxicating, like the smell of permanent markers or very fresh flowers. Allison found a knitting kit in the dumpster and started making Jonah lots of little hats and tunics, all from the same purple wool. Myriam learned to cook. After her shifts at the café, she'd come home and soak bread in milk and sugar to make soft pudding that Jonah could eat. She stewed apples with cinnamon, for vitamins and because it made their apartment smell like a candle store. She thawed frozen peas and puréed them with the heel of her hand.

Some nights Myriam still wondered about the meaning of life, but then Jonah would yawn and put his hand against the side of her head, tangling his fingers in the curls as his eyes slowly closed. Allison would pull them both into her chest, which, despite being flat and ribby, was the most comfortable chest in the world. The questions would float away, making way for sleep.

Things were like that, when Jonah was a baby. Soft, warm, easy. They spent all their free time playing—dress-up and tickle fights and spin the baby's bottle. When one of them got feelings they'd practice primal screaming and make up dances to it, spinning around until they were so dizzy they fell limply onto various surfaces in the apartment.

Then, one day, when he was two, Jonah got an ear infection. Myriam and Allison had avoided going to the doctor until then, but this time there was no way around it. Jonah's upper lip and chin were permanently caked with snot from crying all the time. His little child body felt like a hot-water bottle. They took him to the walk-in clinic by their house and claimed to have lost Jonah's health card.

"No problem," the receptionist said. "I'll look him up in the system."

"Fuck the system," Allison thought to say. "The system is oppressive and one day the world will return to its natural state of anarchy."

"Just have a seat, please."

The doctor was a short old guy with really long eyebrows. He was grumpy with them, told them that even anarchist parents had to make sure their child had health care. He sent them off with a handwritten prescription for antibiotics.

In the lobby, they thanked the nice receptionist and promised her that they were going to try to accept organized society. When they turned around, Jonah was throwing magazines on the ground and a lady in a pinstriped jacket was looking at him funny. Deep creases were forming in her makeup from how much she was frowning. Allison picked up Jonah and apologized to the lady. As they left the clinic and turned the corner into the alley where they'd found Jonah, they heard the lady yell: "Hey, where'd you get that baby?"

"We got the baby in the normal way of giving birth to him!" is what they should have answered, but instead they started running. That was a bad call. The woman charged them like a provoked pit bull and caught up to them almost instantly, grabbing Allison by the sweater. She was breathing hard and her face was red like a demon's. At first glance, she'd looked like the kind of lady Myriam and Allison would never talk to: a business executive or a paralegal, someone who lived in a condo with chrome appliances. From up close, though, they could see that the skin under her makeup was leathery, that her too-tight bun was held together by a purple elastic threaded with silver tinsel, that her skirt suit wasn't so much navy as the tired color of a varicose vein. She was a fraud, which meant that she was one of them, which meant that she was no more entitled to having a baby than they were.

"Where'd you get that baby?" the lady asked again.

"You can't have him," Allison said. Another faux pas. She may as well have said finders keepers.

Myriam got a feeling like a cold glass of water down the back. This was the same feeling she'd gotten as a teenager in her Montreal suburb, when she'd sense a manager trailing her through the aisles of a department store and her messenger bag was full of crop tops and flavored lip gloss. She yanked the woman's bun back and the woman collapsed like a folding patio chair. She grabbed Allison by the arm and they ran. When they looked back, the woman was trying to sit up on her knees, a palm on the back of her neck. Her eyes didn't know where to be in their sockets.

Allison pulled Myriam into the yard of an apartment building that wasn't theirs. They snuck around to their own building, half a block down. Myriam was pretty turned on by how clever Allison was, throwing the woman off their tracks like that. When they got back to their apartment, they calmed their sweet baby and didn't waste one second after he was asleep to start fucking like astronauts who just came back from a mission and actually survived and took off their spacesuits and were suddenly irresistibly bare and fleshy, floating around their tiny tin-can room. They loved everything about this situation. They loved having a baby, yes, but they also loved fighting together against a nemesis. They loved breaking the rules in the name of their love, and they especially liked getting away with it.

When Jonah woke up from his nap, they put all the pillows, cushions and blankets they owned on the living room floor and lay down on them. They poured chocolate chips into their palms and ate them with their pinkies up, as if they were tiny appetizers. They cut up some picture books and rearranged them however they wanted. When Allison had to leave for her evening shift, she kissed their baby on his face for five minutes, then she kissed Myriam deep and put her hands in Myriam's underwear, stroking her bum.

☙

"She's out there," Allison said when she came back later that night. "She's just sitting out in her car. I had to come in through the back."

Allison's nostrils pulsed open and closed like little jellyfish: she was worried. Myriam took her by the hand and pulled her onto the couch, wrapping her arms and legs around her from behind, like a backpack.

"She'll go away," she said in Allison's ear. "When we wake up, she'll be gone."

☙

She wasn't gone. She was there as they ate their Corn Pops, did their morning aerobics, listened to their morning podcasts.

She was still there when Myriam came back from work around dinnertime. She was there when they went to bed. The following morning, they parted the blinds and there she was, wiping something off her windshield with a napkin.

She'd spend the whole day on their street, sitting in her old gray Camry. Sometimes she'd step out and circle some buildings, or she'd get on her knees in the middle of the street and say please, please with her hands clasped over her heart. She'd drive off late at night and be there again the next morning.

At first it was fun to sneak around like spies whenever they left the house, but, after a few days, the woman's presence started getting to them. They left the apartment less often. They kept the blinds closed. They stopped taking Jonah to the park, and if he cried too loud they all huddled in the bathroom, stuffing towels under the door so the sound wouldn't seep out into the street.

It was almost two weeks after their trip to the clinic, and Allison and Myriam had planned a parent meeting. Until now, parent meetings had meant coming up with fun new art projects, or sharing intel about where to score free baby stuff. Not this time.

They'd thought the woman would have given up by now, but they were starting to worry she never would. The day before, she'd gone into the alley, written down GIVE ME BACK MY BOY in blue chalk and stood over it, screaming like a burning witch.

"Maybe we should move," Allison said. She was sitting at the Formica table, playing the same ominous notes over and over on a toy keyboard.

"And leave our apartment? The best apartment in the world?" Myriam said, pacing the kitchen. "I don't think so. Anyway, we'll never be able to get Jonah's drawings off the floor, and we can't afford to lose our damage deposit."

"Well, we have to do something," Allison said. "You know she could actually take our baby, right?"

Myriam picked up a rag in the kitchen and started wiping the counters, which was disgusting because they never cleaned them. Allison's song faded away, and for a moment Myriam imagined that she was alone in the kitchen, that this was her apartment, that there had never even been an Allison or a Jonah. In a world like that, her mind wouldn't spin at night with unanswerable questions about the universe. The questions wouldn't be worth asking.

"Hey, it's okay," Allison said, putting her arms around Myriam because tears were falling down her cheeks. Whenever Myriam cried Allison's voice got soft and hesitant. She sounded so helpless. "I didn't mean to scare you."

"I don't know what I'd do if I lost you or Jonah," Myriam said, crying in Allison's neck. "Everything would be so terrible."

"That's not gonna happen," Allison said, squeezing Myriam protectively. "Whatever we have to do, we won't let it happen."

Myriam blew her nose into one of the Easter napkins they'd gotten at a discount.

"What are you saying, bun?" she said. "Like, we kill her or something?"

Allison rubbed Myriam's back, considering.

"I don't know," she said after a while. "I don't think I'm ready to take a human life. We could do blackmail, though."

"You mean get some dirt on her?"

"Maybe. We do have the advantage. She can't see us, but we can see her."

And they could see her right then through a crack in the blinds, sitting in her car and mouthing the words to some unknowable song, deep half-moons carved out under her eyes by the yellow streetlight. They could feel her presence like a mop bucket weakly but relentlessly slopping all over their shoes.

∽

Allison asked her parents to babysit and borrowed a coworker's car for the night. She and Myriam parked three cars behind the old Camry and hid under a musty wool blanket on the backseat. When the sexual tension of being on a mission got to be too much, they played a game where they made each other cum and had to stay very still and quiet. By midnight, they were so exhausted they almost didn't notice when the Camry's taillights turned on. Allison climbed into the driver's seat with her hood down to her nose and Myriam joined her, sinking low in the passenger seat. They followed the Camry slowly, from a distance, through the dark streets of their neighborhood. The woman pulled into the driveway of an old brick bungalow only a dozen blocks from their apartment. Allison had to parallel park and wasn't very good at it, but the woman didn't seem to notice. She walked around the side of the house and down a small staircase, into the basement. Myriam and Allison snuck across the wet grass and crouched on either side of a small slit of basement window.

༒

Dina poured the milk first, then filled the top third of the glass with Kahlúa. She stuck her finger deep into the glass and swirled until it was homogenous brown—adult Nesquik. The first gulp pulled her back into herself, into her clothes, into her basement apartment with its humming refrigerator, bluish ceiling lights, the beautiful Christmas tablecloth she'd inherited from her grandmother and used year-round because it was so *sturdy*, the reds and greens and oranges so *rich*.

"Who's winning?" she managed to say.

"It's a tie," Ken said, looking at the television. "Did you find your kid yet?"

"Don't you go calling him my kid, Ken. He's your kid, too."

"Fine, fine, sorry I asked," Ken answered. "What's for dinner?"

"There's chicken in the fridge. You could just get off your ass and warm it yourself," Dina said, opening the fridge and peeling Saran Wrap from a dish of chicken covered in cream of mushroom. She scooped two chicken breasts and two dollops of mashed potatoes onto plates, microwaved them one at a time.

"Your job called. They're wondering when you plan on going back. 'Soon,' I told 'em. Didn't seem to believe me. Go figure."

"I'll go back when I have my boy. If they don't like it, they can shake a can of Coke and squeeze it up their tight asses."

Dina didn't want to go back to work. She couldn't stamp another passport application, force another customer service smile, put on another stiff skirt that left deep red grooves in her sides. For the first time since she'd lost her boy, she felt alive. After all the scenarios she'd imagined—Lucas being eaten by alley dogs, or chained up by psychopaths who made him drink his own urine—the thought that two young dykes in ripped denim had found and claimed him seemed like a joke. Knowing that the only thing standing between her and her Lucas was a couple of anarchist idiots filled her with hope. She knew they were hiding inside one of those cheapo apartment complexes. It was only a matter of time before they gave themselves away, and she'd be right there when they did.

Besides, sitting in her car all day allowed her to connect with herself, to think her thoughts and figure out how she really felt about things. The answer was that she felt like life had decided to make the space above her head its toilet seat. She looked like shit, felt like shit, probably smelled like shit and, irony of all ironies, hadn't herself taken a proper shit in at least two weeks, making her acutely aware of all the shit piling up in her gut every time she took a bite of buttered bagel, ate a bowl of minestrone, got up in the night to eat an Ah Caramel! in fucking peace. There must have been at least six chicken breasts sitting in her gut at that very moment, and there were about to be seven. Dina took a steaming bite of mushroom chicken.

Realizing that she felt like shit was a bit better than feeling like shit but being too dissociated to realize it. Now, if she started to punch her steering wheel, she knew why she was punching it. If she started to slap herself in the head, looking up to the sky and asking God what the point of life was and why didn't he just blow her head off with lightning, because it would actually be less cunty than taking her baby—she could reassure herself that she'd only called god cunty because she was in a difficult place, emotionally. And who wouldn't be, in her situation? The same scene had been replaying in her head for almost two years. Bringing baby Lucas to comedy night wrapped in a flannel blanket because babysitters were expensive and she couldn't stay in that damned basement one second longer. Why should Ken get to have all the fun? Ken mouthing off at Toby's, as usual, shouting "Get off the stage, faggot!" to some kid who, it turns out, really was a faggot, the kind with a tear tattoo and boxing-gym arms. The kid had taken Ken out to the alley and punched him until his face didn't look like his face. The kid kept hitting and hitting— Dina had never seen so much blood. Then he'd started dragging Ken down the sidewalk by his shoe, saying homophobic fuckers like him didn't deserve to live. That had scared her, really scared her. She didn't much like Ken herself, but the idea of living without him made the ground drop under her feet. She'd tucked the baby in a corner of the alley and gone after Ken. "Help!" she'd screamed like a twit. As if people hadn't already made the decision to stay out of it. She'd tried to pull on Ken's leg, get the kid to let go, but the kid had kicked her off like a dog. She'd fallen to the ground and hit her head on a fire hydrant. The rest was fuzzy.

She'd come to on a stretcher in some hospital hallway, doctors and nurses running around her like clean chickens. She'd walked right out of the hospital, hailed a cab she couldn't pay for and gotten out at Toby's to find the alley empty, with nothing but blood and confetti where her baby should have been. That night, Ken had come home from the hospital and the two of them had beat the shit out of each other. They'd looked pathetic, swinging at each other and missing half the time, dizzy from concussions and pain medication. Still, it was the first and only time they'd hit each other, and they'd made it count.

The next day, they'd wept together in bed, disinfecting wounds and icing bruises. The day after, Ken had gone back to work, proudly parading his black eyes and casts, and seemed to forget about Lucas completely.

"They're not gonna do anything," Ken had said when Dina called the police. "Why should they care? You're not pretty enough to be in the paper."

He was right. The police put out an amber alert, but after a month they stopped calling her with updates. Eventually, Dina's grief turned to numbness and time went by like a really strong wind, sweeping her up and carrying her like an empty bag of chips.

Dina finished her chicken and brought the plate to her mouth, licking it clean of sauce, getting every last smear of mashed potato.

"Can you not eat like a pig in a goddamned barn?" Ken said.

She was done, anyway. She went to their room and took off her jeans. As she was taking off her bra, she noticed shuffling outside the window. She looked up to see the two dykes with their hands over their eyes, cringing as if they'd bitten a lemon. God, her tits weren't that bad! They were holding up pretty well for forty-two. She threw on her oversized Labatt t-shirt and bolted out of the apartment, lunging across the grass and landing on the girls. They screamed and swore and tried to roll away, but Dina grabbed them both by the hair and mashed their faces into the muddy ground.

"Give me back my baby boy!" she roared. "Where are you hiding him? That's MY boy!"

"We're not telling you anything!" the more feminine one screeched.

"That's what you think," Dina said. She yanked them up by the hair and dragged them into her apartment. "Get the duct tape, Ken. These are the little bitches that stole our baby."

Dina pushed the girls down on kitchen chairs and Ken came to tape them up.

"What do we do?" Ken asked. "Should I take out my knife? Bleed it out of them?"

"Girls, what do you think? Is it worth losing an ear to keep playing house with my boy?"

The girls didn't move.

"Looks like these little rug munchers aren't too attached to their ears," Dina said.

Ken got his pocket knife out of his leather jacket and walked toward the girls.

"Last chance, girls. Are you gonna tell me where you're hiding my boy?" Dina asked.

The girls shook their heads and squeezed their eyes shut. One of them started humming. Ken got closer to the boyish one and grabbed her ear, brought his knife to the back of it and started pushing down. Blood began dripping on her shoulder.

"Jesus, Ken! Don't actually cut their ears off!" Dina pushed him off the girl, who was crying now, snot dripping over her mouth tape.

Dina couldn't believe she'd married such a monster. He'd looked thrilled at the thought of hurting these two dumb-looking girls.

"Whatever," Ken said, and went back to the couch to watch the hockey game. "Come on! Just shoot, you prairie sissy!"

Dina got the first aid kit from the bathroom. She cleaned the back of the girl's ear with gauze and alcohol, put a band-aid on the wound. The girls were sobbing, their whole bodies trembling.

"Alright, alright, let's not be overdramatic," Dina said, her own eyes filling with tears.

One tear escaped, then another, and suddenly she was curled up at the girls' feet, wailing. One of the girls reached out her foot and started stroking Dina's back with her toes. Dina hadn't been touched like that since she was a child, before her mother had passed away. She put her head on the feminine girl's lap and wept even harder. The girls made a muffled "aww" sound through the duct tape on their mouths.

"I miss my boy so much," Dina blubbered.

The girls made the "aww" sound again, tilting their heads.

"Will you give him back to me?" Dina asked, wiping her nose with her hand. She reached up to peel the duct tape off their mouths.

"No," one girl said.

"No way," the other agreed.

"But maybe you could come over for a visit sometime," the feminine one said. "Allison, what do you think?"

"I'm not sure if we can trust her," Allison said. "Ma'am, you left a baby in an alley. A dangerous alley with garbage and sharp objects. Myriam and I aren't sure you're the kind of person we want around our child."

"It wasn't my fault!" Dina protested. "My husband got into a bar fight, I thought they were gonna kill him!"

"Okay, but why would you raise a child with the kind of person who gets into bar fights?" Allison said. "Honestly, this guy looks like a grade A asshole. Is he seriously watching hockey right now?"

"That's really inappropriate, considering the circumstances," Myriam agreed.

"Suck on that puck, you hick faggot!" Ken yelled.

Dina looked up at the girls, whose young faces suddenly seemed so wise, like two lesbian angels who had come to tell her the good news, or at least call her out on her shit.

"You're right," she said, "my husband's a dink. Did you know he gave our son beer one time? In his bottle? So he would go to sleep already?"

"Oh my fucking god," Allison said.

"Why are you even still with him?" Myriam asked.

"Honestly, I never thought I'd be this kind of woman. I never thought I'd have to wipe chip crumbs off the couch three times a day, or hide my face at the bar because my husband asked the bartender if the happy hour special included her jugs. But before I knew how I got here, this was my life, and it was the only thing I had. It felt like leaving my life would be admitting there was nothing good about it, that I would be better off having nothing than having the few things I did have. It sounds dumb, I know."

"No way, that totally makes sense," Myriam said.

"Yeah, that's a rough spot to be in. Don't be so hard on yourself," Allison said.

Dina thought of her father, who viewed softness as a thing to press your thumb into. She thought back to those first few months with Lucas, how she'd stiffened when he cried. One day, when Lucas was a big, tall man, he was going to fuck up really badly. She thought how perfect it would be if these two eccentric girls were there to look at him the way they looked at her now. *Don't be so hard on yourself.*

"Come stay over at our place," Myriam said. "Our couch is a total cloud."

"Mind if I pack my things first? I don't think I'll be coming back here," Dina said.

"Take your time," Allison said. "And make sure you grab that tablecloth. That's a quality tablecloth."

☙

Dina happened to be really good at Boggle. She agreed that the apartment had a great vibe. She also loved how much of her son was in the apartment. She could scan the floors and see the evolution of her son's artistic talent, which, if she was honest, was nothing to write home about—people, alligators, houses, there was no telling what anything was. The girls told Dina she could stay as long as she wanted—in fact, they wouldn't mind some help with the rent.

While Allison went to pick up Jonah from her parents' house, Myriam and Dina hung out in the living room. They made rum and Cokes and talked about the meaning of life. It was hard to say what the meaning of life was, they agreed. Maybe nature, or friendship. Definitely not money, but maybe art or scientific discoveries.

When Allison brought Jonah home they introduced him to Dina, but Dina was crying so hard she couldn't talk. She started hyperventilating but stopped suddenly when everyone spread out around the apartment, threw their heads back, and began screaming primally toward the ceiling. At first Dina considered tossing her son over her shoulder and running, but then a scream ripped through her, as if it had been waiting in her throat this whole time. The scream lasted so long. When it ended, everyone fell to the floor and Dina started fake-snoring, which made Jonah laugh and try to tickle her awake. She kept making these loud sleeping grunts but everyone could see through it because her mouth was quivering, trying to suppress a smile.

They helped Dina unpack her things and decided they should all have a sleepover in the living room. Jonah fell asleep in Dina's arms, and the three moms stayed up late talking in hushed voices. Myriam and Dina asked Allison what she thought the meaning of life was, and Allison said she thought there was no meaning to life—she identified as a nihilist.

"For me, looking around right now, I'd say it's love," Dina said.

"I'm with Dina," Myriam decided. "Love."

"Interesting theory," Allison conceded. "I guess if there was a meaning to life, maybe it'd be love."

IT'S A CRUEL WORLD FOR EMPATHS LIKE US

SOULA EMMANUEL

THIS TIME AROUND, Fern devotes particular attention to the hair under your nose. A sadist at the clinic and really, it's hard to imagine anyone else working there would relish the opportunity to blast heat at the upper lip, site of the toughest hair and the most sensitive skin, a sensuous and erogenous spot of taste and smell and touch.

It feels hot and sharp, like someone is holding a lighter under your nose. It is intimate, the close examination, the awkwardness, the early-morning sniffles.

It is a quiet part of your routine, for now, one which you hope will beget a new routine entirely. Every four weeks, on a Friday, at 8 a.m., you go to a place halfway between a dentist's surgery and a tanning salon to get laser beams blasted at you.

A face is cleansed in the same way a lawn is mowed: over and back, systematically, like it is terrain rather than identity, place rather than person. You fancy yourself as a place, one in the grip of a kind of revolution, where the natives are restless and the rulers' fists no longer iron but mere flesh and bone.

Then, after seven to twelve minutes, it is done, and there are raised red bumps where your old self used to be. This is normal, Fern says, and you are booked in for the following month, subject to the follicular cycle you vaguely remember from biology class. The hair chooses its own time to die; all you can do is respect it.

Fern is peroxide blonde and lives with a fiancé in Kildare somewhere. She asks if you are doing anything for the weekend, as if it isn't obvious by you taking the Friday-morning graveyard slot that you are not.

Yes, Fern, I'm going to be applying aloe vera at nightclubs and sex dungeons through the greater Dublin area, because I am a fun person and not a gremlin vacillating between personhoods like a rickety bridge.

Thank you, Fern, see you soon, Fern, have a lovely weekend, Fern.

☙

People stare on the street, at the big bank on the green, on the big bridge over the river, but it's a pitying stare, not a hostile one. They assume you must have experienced an allergic reaction of some sort, and in a way, you did, a reaction to manhood. You are horribly allergic to it. It brings you out in all sorts. One thing it does not bring you out in is yourself.

☙

The office has polyester carpets and almost no natural light. It has given you five static-electric shocks in the seven months you have worked there: two from the radiator, two from a bolt on your swivel chair, and one, oddly, from a hole punch dropped on the floor.

You would struggle to explain your job. You put things where they need to be. Things are sent to you, and you put them. You are a putter, and the world is your golf green. Elsewhere in the open-plan office are the bringers, the describers, the deliverers, and the managers, who mostly drink green tea.

These are hot desks, so in theory anyone can sit anywhere, but in practice everyone sits in the same spot every day. You take your place, the paranoiac's perch, with your back to the wall and your eyes scanning for who knows what.

This is a useful spot, because it allows you to imbibe the routine of the place: who comes in with bicycle helmet in hand, who is and is not good with layers during Dublin's many not-quite-hot-not-quite-cold days, who makes a porridge breakfast for themselves immediately after clocking in.

"Oh, [name]," Brian, the man next to you, one of the older members in a company with poor retention, says to you, "you've got a rash on your face."

You like this company, because it is transitional, and you are transitional. It is faceless and impersonal, and you? Guilty as charged. And you love the banter. Even if you weren't paid to come in here, you'd probably do it anyway, just for the banter.

"Yes, I know," you say. "It must be the cold. It's Baltic out there." Baltic is a word people who are good at banter use. You picked it up from them and now you use it too.

"My sister had a rash like that on her arm. It could be dermatitis. You should get it checked out."

"Thanks, Brian. I will."

I am doing things you have never attempted, Brian. Why would I want your advice?

You're clocked in, so you look for something to do. So, it's straight to the news.

CEOs warn of threat posed by AI
Democratic Republic of Congo threatens to fall into anarchy
U.S. Capitol evacuated after bomb threat

Just a lot of airy guff about things that might never happen. A threat is not news. It is a tickling sensation that is not a sneeze.

Plan B: you set to the in-tray.

Behind the banter shroud, people are bashful. People are exceptionally good at not drawing attention to the things they do not wish to draw attention to. The rash is widely ignored, at the coffee station where the woman calls everyone *my friend*; at the midday staff meeting, where your team leader stares down from a screen like a movie villain; and at lunch, because you go for a walk, to get some space, to get some air.

☙

Henry is a great deal more intelligent than people give him credit for. He has to be, given he spends so much of the day left to his own devices. He has achieved all manner of higher-order abilities, from grudge-holding to voice recognition. He can even count to three with sufficient prompting. You once swore he even helped you with a word game on your phone. He opened his mouth and out heaved the correct answer.

PROXY. How does a cat know proxy?

You live alone with him, in a two-and-a-half-room apartment that is impossible to heat. Not because of high ceilings or large windows- not at all! - but because you cannot afford to heat it. He is an indoor cat. The last thing you need are dead birds and quadriplegic mice. He keeps himself busy, probably busier than you. That's what you always say to him.

He is gray and white, with soft features and inquisitive, decisive eyes. There is just the slightest hint of Jeff Goldblum. Henry is six years old, and the average life expectancy of a cat is thirteen and a half years, so you reckon you have some time left. You are sharing yourself with someone worth sharing with.

And he is not like your co-workers. He glares at the redness around your face and he will not stand for it to be explained away.

You decide to write an email to the clinic.

> *Dear all,*
> *I am sorry to bother you and I hope it is no trouble but unfortunately I have a rash on my face which has persisted after my laser session this morning. Although I am not a great fan of my face (ha ha!) I would like to get this remedied. Please reply at your earliest convenience, and sorry for the inconvenience.*
> *Best wishes,*
> *[name]*

Send.

There is an immediate response.

> *Thank you for contacting us. Due to the volume of correspondence, please wait five days for a reply to your message.*

❦

The great advantage of administrative busywork is that if done efficiently, it affords a great deal of mental space for quiet rage. You still look like someone has walked over your face, has done a little Michael Flatley jig on it. It makes you feel like a candle in the middle of a room, radiating heat and light, ambient but unmistakeable. You've spent your whole life recoiling from visibility, but now look at you. It's almost impossible not to.

There is a brief hush in the office, staffers shutting their brunchholes in anticipation of opening them again shortly.

"Don't miss out, they'll all be gone soon," the head of finance says, placing a case of twenty-four donuts in the middle of a table in the small canteen off to the side—but you know that's not true, because your workplace is full of chronic dieters and gluten-intolerants.

Isn't it funny how the creation of beauty requires a certain meanness?

You wait until the crowd disperses and end up with something sticky and powdery.

As you leave with your donut wrapped in a bit of blue roll, the CEO passes by. You had never met a man like him before you were introduced at your job interview. He is the kind of man bank advertisements are made for. The kind whose entire self-perception is built around the commuting he does and the parenting he doesn't, but wishes he did.

Intelligence is knowing where you'd like to be in five years; wisdom is recognizing that *not dead, hopefully* is an unacceptable answer at a job interview. You are not wise, but he employed you anyway.

"Oh, that's a nasty red mark. Do you play rugby?" he says. He doesn't remember your name. He seems like a rugby man himself, beef and cauliflower, a bit misshapen. Rugby son turned rugby dad. He probably went to a school with a driveway, whereas you went to one with a car-park.

You say you don't play rugby but you got a scratch from your cat.

"Your cat must be a tiger," he says.

Pretty much. That's what you say. Pretty much.

Aren't you funny?

༄

Midway through chewing on the donut, your phone buzzes, and as if to snap you out of your sugary indulgence, it's an email from the laser clinic.

Hi [name]. We are sorry that you are experiencing after-effects from the laser treatment. However, redness on the skin is a normal consequence of the laser and should be managed using the aloe vera gel. If the issue persists for another week, please get in touch.

Then there is a ping on the work instant messenger.

Sorry, [name], but please don't forget the conversation we had about looking at your phone during working hours.

But you don't care. You are blissing through the day, phone or no phone. You have always wanted to be the kind of person who is triumphant with a grievance, and now look at you!

❦

The flat gets moldy in winter, but you found a bleach that cleans it right off. The unfortunate consequence is that the place smells decidedly of chlorine for a while afterward, which necessitates leaving windows open, which only makes you and Henry colder. The flat has two and a half rooms—the bathroom has no natural light and the fan sounds like an extended smoker's cough—and the landlord said you can't plug in a kettle and a toaster at the same time without tripping the switch entirely, a problem you have avoided by not having a toaster.

At least Henry grows fur to keep him warm. He grows fur while the walls grow fur. You have to pay for all your own clothes—and brand new ones at that, a slave to fashion, among other things.

The flat's bathroom door also needs to be kept open while you are in the shower, because the light over the mirror, which is the only one in the room, has been broken for five weeks, and the maintenance guy has not yet come to fix it.

This is your chrysalis. This is where the magic happens. In the inner-urban equivalent of an unmarked grave. But you don't complain.

It is a Thursday evening, cold and still. You are inspecting the moment for its potential rewards. You have washed your hair. It takes longer to dry than it used to.

You look the place up on the online map, using the address you have by now committed to memory. It is on a junction of two streets, next to the headquarters of an insurance company. You have never noticed this from street level, but it is a very small building compared to those around it, like a child in a family, a loose cannon.

Across the road, in a large building that also contains a casino and a tanning salon, there is a tourist shop selling Irish trinkets to Spanish students and cashed-up Americans to a soundtrack of diddley-eye tunes. The shop has a webcam sticking out of one of the upstairs windows, which displays the entire street. It is dark now, but through the lit streets the front windows can be seen. You look at people moving in and out of the front door, at staff members moving displays in silhouette. It is a month to Christmas now; they have displays up encouraging people to go in before the holidays. There is a curious sensation to it, to looking at this formidable, awful place in miniature, the way it looks like a toy town, like nothing at all.

So near and so far, it is, so nothing and yet so everything, so diminutive and yet so responsible for a small but significant portion of your problems. You endeavor to deepen your voice, in the hope that it will give you a kind of ambient authority, although it's been so long that you can barely do it without sounding like you are doing a bad impression of yourself. You find the phone number and you dial, careful first to turn off caller ID.

But you don't complain.

It's like *Dilbert*, the comic strip. You imagine that if they knocked down the front wall of the building, what would be left would resemble a series of *Dilbert* weekdays, agonized dialogues and just-so scenarios. They might not be funny, but the guy who does *Dilbert* stopped being funny years ago.

The rash is diminishing, but it is beginning to flake. You can see it, inspecting yourself in the mirror of the office gender-neutral toilet like a menial worker sexing chickens, always staring at one part, never contemplating the whole. This place and its incompetence are going to follow you around for the rest of your life, just like everything else. You will never be beautiful. You have stewed in your upset about the situation for several days, but you have done nothing, wondering if there is some delayed response coming. But nothing happens.

At home, you rehearse calls in front of the mirror. You need to show you are more than just a disgruntled customer. But the thing about the clinic is that every room is the same: they all have the ambiance of a waiting room, even the ones that aren't waiting rooms. They all have that gauzy haze. You are not anaesthetized in the clinic, but you might as well be, given the way each wall and each door and each face blends into another.

You could tell them what color the plastic flowers in the waiting room are.

They are purple.

Aren't they?

The woman on the other end of the line, a different woman to last time, says she doesn't take you seriously. "Whatever you say," she says.

You look out at the street on the webcam again, at the pedestrians moving past, cars emerging from a multi-story car park. The odd taxi, but very few buses, because this part of the city is too good for them. A man leaves the insurance company beside the clinic. He looks prosperous. He is wearing a suit.

You think about men and their tendency to overreact. There must be loads of men working in that insurance company. They will take you seriously.

And you dial.

The man on the other end of the line—yes, somehow you knew all along it would be a man!—hangs up immediately after you give your little speech. You are not sure what to think.

You carry on looking at the camera footage of the street below. And now it is finally happening, people are evacuating the building. You have such power in this moment, the power to move people, if not emotionally then at least physically. Within ten minutes there is a crowd of people on the street, about fifty of them, with others walking away, perhaps to get coffee. You have liberated them from the drudgery of work. Out they go, like raindrops from a great cloud.

Insurance is organized gambling. That's what you've always reckoned. Just a way for the wealthy to beat the odds by predicting the misfortune of others. As you look at the crowd gathered on the street, all you can think about is the money the company will be losing as a result. It is wondrous, a great fatberg in the pipes of the system. It is divine, and it makes you wonder how it is that you have held out for so long.

It is suffering that makes us all beautiful.

You can see Garda cars on the scene, but where are the army? Surely the army will be invited? More and more people are there: bystanders, employees from the other offices on the street, and there they are, the staff of the laser clinic and their customers, standing on the street like condemned women, and they are almost all women.

It ends up being the third story on the evening news. Nobody has a clue who was responsible, which is reassuring to hear. The

Gardaí are requesting information about it, inviting anyone with information to make themselves known, but you've made enough phone calls for today. The fuzz think it relates to gang activity, or perhaps something to do with a drug deal. Incredible: gang activity. You have made yourself plural in your connivance. The authorities think there are many of you.

The story appears on social media.

Buildings in Dublin evacuated after threat

There is a picture of a police line. You do not remember seeing that.

You reply to the story:

What is the world coming to?

You: the world is coming to you.

It becomes a habit. Not every day, because that would be too much, but every week, every second week. You look through the street where the clinic is located and make call after call: a pharmacy, a bookshop, a shoe shop. It becomes a kind of therapy. Some people listen to the dawn chorus; some people watch the waves rippling on the shore; you watch the people of Dublin standing around wondering what they are doing in the whirlpool of waiting you have created for them.

☙

"You should press the mark with a glass," Brian says, while opening his emails at 8:15 in the morning one Monday. "That's what it says in the ad."

"I don't think it's meningitis. If it was, I'd be dead already."

"You never know."

"I think I know. I think therefore I am therefore I definitely don't have meningitis."

Another day. Nose to the grindstone. The reorganization of one set of distractions into another set of distractions, and their dispatch to an even bigger distraction located in an industrial park on the other side of the world.

Spring has arrived like a marathoner's second wind, and you sense it around you, in the lightened moods of your co-workers, in the gentler light that dribbles through the blinds in the mid-morning. There are probably lambs frolicking somewhere.

People talk about their favorite podcasts. They talk about *Dancing with the Stars*. Their children's mucus. Their children's milk teeth, candy and literal. Their children's caustic and witty remarks. They talk about the little treats that make life worth living: a gin and tonic on a Saturday; a couple of Linda McCartney sausages on a Sunday. That is them: treats go in and obedience comes out.

You used to be a cog, but now you throw yourself across the workings. You impede the system while remaining embedded in it. You are like a spy.

You are happier. You have cried every second day for the past three months. That in itself is a sign of progress, a sign that something is being purged from you. There is an ill feeling in you still, but it is eroding gradually. You are a real person who feels things, and isn't that what you have always aspired to be?

If you can't handle me at my worst, you don't deserve me at my best.

That is how you view it, in the apocryphal words of Marilyn Monroe. You are cutting off toxicity.

You decide to go out for lunch. To a nice little Vietnamese place on a back street, fifteen minutes from your office, between a betting shop and another betting shop. It's run by a short man who always wears gloves, like Jackie O. He's got great lighting fixtures and abstract paintings on the wall and attracts an eclectic mix of office drudgers and wanky arts students. He does a scalding bún bò huế, and you'll have a solid twenty minutes to eat in between journey and return.

You get a seat at the bar next to the window, which is uncomfortable as all hell, presumably so you won't be able to sit there for too long. But while you are there, it begins to rain copiously. Great big pissy strings of rain fall from the sky outside your window, which within minutes resembles a glass shower door, foggy and damp.

Soon your time is up. You want to stay indoors but you can't. Not with the beckoning siren call of whatever it is you do for a living. But then you overhear a man and a woman talking as they leave the restaurant, putting up their hoods and girding their umbrellas.

"They've got him," the man says. "The guy who's been phoning in threats around the city. That's what the news says. They've made a breakthrough in the investigation."

They've got him?

How could they have got him?

And just who is *he?*

You hastily do away with your lunch, placing it into the refuse box before leaving. You walk through the sodden streets wondering if at this very moment there is a man apprehended in a Garda station for the calls you have made. You are completely unprepared for this: the rain and the injustice. You are soaked in them. It is an acute responsibility you feel, walking past one of the big old city center churches into which no one ever walks; over the river, brown, scuttering; on the bridges, quiet for this time of day.

You look at your phone to get the time, and behind dozens of droplets there is an email from the laser clinic.

> *We are pleased to inform our customers that the Gardaí believe they have found the individual responsible for making nuisance phone calls.*

You turn back and go home. It's too long to walk but you walk it anyway, soaking yourself through. The workplace will have to go on without you. There will be discussions of the latest episode of *Joe Rogan*. There will be a flying visit from the head of HR, which leads to a forty-five-minute chat. It will all be happening but you will not be part of it. You dart past the city, past schoolchildren with their coats held over their heads, past forlorn dogs on pointless walks. Cars make trails behind them, snail-paced, snail-like.

When you get home, Henry is at the window, as if keeping guard. You chat to him. It's a funny old world, isn't it, where beauty and kindness are always at odds with one another. This terrible fascism of the self that makes us beautiful deprives from us the essence of humanity. Thank goodness we have each other, you say. We can keep each other honest.

You get up and put on the kettle just in time to hear a knock at the door.

REDISTRIBUTION

TEMIM FRUCHTER

AT THE FAMOUS WRITER'S house, the lights were always on. This wasn't privileged information. Anyone at all could see it, walking past at dusk, when all the other kitchens and living rooms pooled with golden light that illuminated dinner prep or cartoons or cocktails. People in the neighborhood didn't seem to care for curtains, or at least the people who had something to show off.

But at the famous writer's house, it was every room. Each window was a bright block, revealing high shelves of books or mysterious abstract sculptures or assemblies of lush plants. It wasn't the only large house in the neighborhood, but it was the only one that never went dark.

At night, M took walks. She liked her neighborhood at night. It was stately, but the lit houses gave it a kind of warmth, the curtainless people in their bayed windows seeming almost as if they were inviting her inside. Come for appetizers? Or a soda? Stay for pot roast? Or curry? Her favorite windows were the ones through which she could see people, little animated domestic scenes. Someone chopping at a counter, or the backs of two heads on a couch, a pair of gesticulating arms coming from one of them.

But not at the famous writer's house. Always all the lights, but never any people.

She thought she remembered reading once that the famous writer had kids. Were they grown kids? Kid kids? Or somewhere in the middle? She was also certain the famous writer had a famous ex. But did she have a current, famous or otherwise? M liked the feeling that the famous writer might be something of a recluse in plain sight, an ill-hidden secret in a brightly lit house for all their neighborhood to keep. Whenever M walked past, she fantasized about somehow making her way inside that house. There would be something glamorous, she thought, about getting closer. About being invited inside.

It should be noted that the famous writer was a handsome woman. Not beautiful, really, but extremely handsome. Tall and broad-shouldered, thick eyebrows and cheekbones that looked a little bit photoshopped. M did not know this from seeing the famous writer in person, only from looking at the famous writer's photo in the jackets of the many novels she'd written over the decades. The famous writer might be getting on in years, but in photos, she looked ageless. Or maybe timeless was a better word for it.

☙

M's life, meanwhile, was, to put it politely, in shambles. She'd been doing the paycheck-to-paycheck hustle for as long as she could remember, but a couple of her gigs had petered out, so now it was more like paycheck-to-almost-paycheck. Rent for her apartment—the third floor of a Brooklyn Victorian she was going to stay in until she died unless it killed her first—wiped out most of her income. But she was a *creative*, she kept insisting, if only to herself, as though this justified all the rest of it. The truth of it was, while she was indeed a writer, she had not written much in recent memory. She'd published a couple of essays and one short story several years back, but now was mostly stalled out, save for the lackluster sentence or two she periodically typed into a Word doc just to remind herself she could. Her sister wasn't speaking to her, though this was not uncommon. M and her sister fought viciously once a season. They always reunited, but the lonely aftermath of these fights was the worst. And perhaps most devastating of all, Jack had just left her.

M had grown accustomed to being left. She had behaved less-than-virtuously in a string of relationships. In this one, she nitpicked. In that one, she was controlling. In monogamy, she wandered. In polyamory, she was unethical and greedy. She had, in fact, never been the one to leave, though it was on her bucket list. *Leave someone for once.* It was right above *Rock climbing in actual nature* and below *Bake a fancy pie that doesn't look fucked.*

But Jack had been different. Jack had once dipped her under a moony sky, just like they were dancing in an old movie, and told M that she wanted to be with her *for a very long time.* No one had ever wanted to be with M for a very long time. M usually fucked things up way before the very-long-time phase. But Jack was generous and funny and charming and, somehow, instead of finding M's questionable behavior only insufferable, found it charming, too. Until, of course, M slept with one too many other people, and said one too many mean-spirited things, just to see how Jack would react. Usually, people left M with a dramatic bang of the door or a stream of screaming expletives. Jack, though. She left with a sad smile and a gentle kiss right in the center of M's forehead. *I can't do it anymore,* she'd said. This was too much, even for M, who thought she'd seen every single angle of the wrong side of a slammed door. She'd lost an entire day, evening included, to crying.

On their first date, Jack had insisted on paying for M's dinner. *No,* M had said. *We're queer, we're not beholden to that chivalrous masculinity shit, let's split it. Oh,* Jack had replied, sliding her credit card into the leather folder the server had left on their table. *Not like that. It's just that I make more than you. I simply believe in wealth redistribution.* M was only slightly embarrassed she hadn't thought of this herself. Did she know the difference between communism and socialism? Only vaguely. Did she consider herself a socialist? Marginally. But did she know what any of this actually meant, in practice? Clearly not like Jack did. She decided right then that Jack had more wisdom and integrity than anyone she'd ever dated. She proudly accepted Jack's wealth redistribution every time they went to dinner.

M did know something about redistribution, though. In fact, she'd been engaged in a kind of cosmic redistribution for several years now.

As soon as M began to realize she'd become the kind of person who might be regularly dumped, she understood she was going to be at a deficit. The breakups, she thought, were the world taking something away from her. So she decided to start taking something back from the world, just to even the score. Just one theft, every single time, to bring things into balance. It came to feel almost evolved, like a ritual.

She started small. When Jenna dumped her, she stole a silk scarf from the woman whose children she'd occasionally been babysitting back then. She didn't know if the woman figured it out, but she was never asked back. When Lee dumped her, she stole a pair of earrings from a boutique. It was risky, but it was a small item, slipped easily into her bag. But when Melora dumped her, she was especially angry. It had been a vitriolic breakup, and she'd felt excessively defensive. She'd been working for a florist then, making deliveries, and one day, out delivering a bunch of extravagant wedding bouquets to a big house on Long Island, she took a small piece of original artwork from the garage where they'd left the flowers. It was art, but it had also been leaning against a dirty wall in storage, so she thought it might take them some time to realize it was gone. The painting was kind of ugly, lots of dark blobular squares, but it was still something unique, and M liked that about it. She had enjoyed the thrill of taking something likely irreplaceable and the elevated chances of getting caught. But no one had caught her. She'd never heard about it. In spite of her generally dirtbag luck, she sometimes felt a little bit invincible.

❧

So far, she had mostly evaded consequences. After Sabrina left, she'd attended a party at an acquaintance's house and stolen a limited-edition Marilyn Monroe figurine from her collection. M was sure she'd gotten away with it, but then the acquaintance called her, saying she was so sorry for the random call, but she was baffled by the disappearance of this favorite of her vintage things. She knew M had been at the party, and did she remember seeing it? No hard feelings, said the acquaintance, if it simply shows up on my doorstep. M fingered the figurine's plastic contours as she said nope, sorry, she didn't remember any such thing.

❧

The famous writer was indecently rich. She was among the very small percentage of writers who got notoriously rich simply by writing. Four of her seventeen novels had been made into movies, two of them Hollywood blockbusters. M did not even love the famous writer's work. She did not hate it, but of the three of her books M had read, she'd liked only two, and felt fairly neutral about the other. Unmoved. Nonetheless, she could understand that the famous writer was talented.

Still, M felt strongly that the famous writer's palatial estate was wasted on her. She started to think that if she herself could sell even one novel, she would buy a house, too. It might be a much smaller house than those of her neighbors, but she would use it well. She would entertain. She would decorate. She would be responsible about turning off the lights.

In the few days since Jack's very recent absence, the famous writer and her house had become even more of an obsession for M than it had been prior. This was not unusual for M. *My toxic trait,* she'd cracked on the internet one recent night, *is taking my obsessions seven steps too far.* It was a joke, but also, it was a sincere confession. M was not great at letting things go.

But she was ready now, as she hadn't been a few days prior, to steal something. For Jack. From the universe, as payment for Jack's departure. For this one, though, she knew she had to go big. Here, she hadn't just lost sex, or even affection. She'd lost integrity. She'd lost redistribution. She'd lost *a very long time.* The fucking universe owed her big.

෴

Shockingly, the opportunity presented itself almost immediately. That night, on M's anxiety walk through the neighborhood, the famous writer's lights were off. She swore she could not remember a single time the lights in that house were off. It was quarter after eleven, a time by which most of the houses in the neighborhood had finally gone dark, but never the famous writer's. You could walk by at one in the morning, as M had on a couple of particularly insomnia-ridden nights, and every single light in that house would still be blazing.

The famous writer, she thought, had to be out of town. She felt like someone had given her a present. M stopped where she was on the sidewalk, staring down the house like an opponent in a fight, or like someone who had just dared her to do something outlandish in public. It was almost too obvious, she thought: This was as close as she was ever going to get to an invitation. And what bigger get was there than something from the famous writer herself? Jack had always teased M for her fixation on the famous writer's house. *You might need a new hobby, my love,* Jack would say, and her tone was kind, but now, when M replayed it in her mind, it curdled with condescension. She had not, in fact, acquired any new hobbies, but her old hobby was about to pay off. She steeled herself and decided to accept the dare. She truly had zero to lose.

She moved closer to the house, slowly and gradually. On this block, all giant houses and affluent residents, you never knew who had cameras or who might be surreptitiously watching out an upstairs window. She got to the front porch, walked slowly up its steps, and all the way up to the front door. She looked around her, looked up and out. No sign of anyone watching. The handle to the front door was large and wrought iron and looked very old. It was, of course, locked. She made her way around to the side of the house. There was a side door, which she tried, and which was also locked. Then she unlatched the wooden gate and walked around to the back.

She marveled at the hidden paradise the fence had been obstructing. Where some people had one garden, the famous writer seemed to have several gardens, each beautifully landscaped. A cobbled path threaded them together, leading to an in-ground pool and an adjoining hot tub, and then to a patio where luxe outdoor seating flanked a stone table. There was a sliding door out to the patio. M tried it. The door slid open, and M walked inside.

M could not believe it. She was standing inside the famous writer's house. She slid the glass door shut. In the dark, she couldn't see much, but worried that turning on any lights might call attention to the house. She turned on her phone flashlight, which she shielded with her hand.

She was standing in a room she'd seen many times only from the outside. Around the periphery, she could see several giant plants with dark, shiny leaves. A large oak desk on one end, and a big leather armchair in the corner. In the middle of the floor, an asymmetrical shaggy rug. M wondered what, exactly, the purpose of this room was. She moved from this room into a spacious entryway, the ceilings unnaturally high for any living space in Brooklyn. She'd seen pictures of this home in an online magazine about New York architecture and home décor, but it was strange and different to be seeing it for herself, in three dimensions. To be able to touch things, as one simply cannot do through a stranger's lit window.

She touched her way around what seemed to be a living room. A soft leather sectional couch so big and deep, it was all she could do not to fall rapturously onto it, to feel its skin on her cheek. A chair covered with a wool throw blanket that felt scratchy but in a high-quality way. Her eyes had begun to adjust to the dark, with help from the light coming in through all the curtainless windows, and she saw walls covered in expensive-looking artwork. There was some kind of sculpture in one corner. Several bookshelves. An ornate fireplace, its mantle tastefully dotted with small plants and knickknacks. M moved into the dining room, out of whose walls little sconces jutted, and at whose center, under an opulent vintage crystal chandelier, was a long, beautiful, live-edge dining table with a jute runner all along its middle. At one end was a beautiful glass bar cart, fully stocked.

M heard a sound then, jolting her out of her reverie. She couldn't simply rest on her laurels here; the famous writer's lights might be out, but who was to say she wouldn't be home any minute? Who was to say she wasn't somewhere in the house right now? She would decide what to take, and then get out of there. The trouble was, of course: how on earth did one decide in a house like this? She guessed one didn't; one needed to choose arbitrarily. She returned to the living room, the mantle full of knickknacks. Those would be portable, she thought. Easy enough. She already had her work cut out getting out of here without anyone seeing or suspecting. She shone her phone along the mantle, selecting a slender and expensive-looking pair of candlesticks, which she dropped into her tote bag.

She started back toward the sliding door, but something stopped her. Jack had left her. Jack. Who'd promised never to leave. And here she was, in the famous writer's home, the one who had so much money she didn't even need to think about her electrical bills. This moment—this house, M thought—owed her more. She felt a surge of rage then, a righteousness about all that she was owed, and swept her arm along the famous writer's mantle. All of the sculptures and knickknacks fell to the floor with a satisfying crash. At least one item shattered. M felt a stab of embarrassed regret that she swallowed. Who cared? The famous writer had more where that came from.

M walked into the kitchen. She opened several different cabinets until she found a tumbler. She held it under the chrome refrigerator's ice machine until it released two perfect ice cubes, then returned to the bar cart, where she opened an expensive-looking bottle of scotch and poured an obscene amount of it into the tumbler, filling it nearly to the top. She stood there, sipping at it until the sharp, smoky taste of it neutralized in her mouth, until she started to feel a little bit heady.

Then she went up the stairs to the second floor.

Upstairs, M found a hallway that seemed wider and longer than any Brooklyn hallway should be. The doors along the hall were wide open, so M could see clearly into each. She chose one and entered an enormous bathroom with an embarrassingly large soaking tub. There was no window in the bathroom, so she turned on the light, which was orangey and warm, nothing fluorescent for miles. The white tile was so clean it gleamed. M imagined her own bathroom—the grimy old tub, the faded pink tile, the dirty grout, the dust motes that seemed to gather and appear out of nowhere. How did one keep a bathroom this clean? Almost without thinking, she turned on the water in the bathtub. She plugged the tub and lit one of the tall candles on the corner shelf. She set her drink down next to it. As the water ran, the room filled with steam, and M breathed it in. It relaxed her in a way she hadn't relaxed in several days, even as she stood, very illegally, in someone else's empty home. She took off her socks and shoes and peeled off her jeans and underwear. She pulled her sweater over her head and unfastened her bra, feeling her chest breathe again as it dropped to the floor. Then she climbed into the bathtub, sinking into the still-running hot water.

As she lay there, she thought about Jack. Jack's steely dark eyes, Jack's strong, stout arms, Jack's way of walking into a room like she owned it, but gently. M grunted with frustration, sinking back against the edge of the tub and deeper into the water. The motion made several pleasant splashing sounds, and she relaxed again. She only had to expel Jack from her mind. Think about someone else, she thought. Immediately, she imagined the famous writer in this very bathtub. The famous writer's long legs propped up on the edge and crossed at the ankles. The famous writer's gorgeous breasts aloft on the water, just as M's were now. The thought of this made M instantly hard. She put her hands on her own breasts, pinching her nipples under the water's surface. She closed her eyes, thinking of the famous writer. She let her hands wander down her body, eventually fucking herself as she thought the famous writer might: with an almost cruel patience, torturous, and then, at last, permissive. She came so hard and so loud, she worried a neighbor might have heard. For a long moment, she lay still in the tub, but heard no sound in response to her animal scream, so she got out. She drained the tub, blew out the candle, and wrapped herself in one of the famous writer's fat towels. She walked back out into the stately hallway.

In the room right across from the bathroom, where M's dirty clothes still lay piled on the floor, was a beautiful study. A wooden desk looked out a huge window onto the street, and the shelves were lined with books. A laptop computer was shut on the desk. M opened it. It was, of course, password protected, and she didn't have the patience for all that, so she closed it again. She sat down at the desk and started flipping through the famous writer's notebooks. Much of it was unreadable to M, especially in the dark, but she felt thrilled peeking into the famous writer's work behind the scenes. This, she thought, would be something to write about. She deserved that, too. Enough for the famous writer, who M thought had written plenty. She dropped one of the notebooks, chosen at random, into her tote bag. She picked up a fancy-looking pen and dropped that in, too.

She padded down the hall again. A plush rug ran along the center of the hardwood floor, and M enjoyed the feel of it under her feet. She peeked into several other rooms. At least one looked like it could be a child's room, though not a young child. Perhaps a teenager. There was another that might be a guest room. And yet another that seemed to be simply for games and television.

Finally, at the very end of the hall, she found it: the famous writer's bedroom. It was a chamber of pure luxury. The walls were painted a dark blue so creamy M wanted to lick it, and hung with a few very large pieces of abstract art. There were notably no photographs. Not of the famous writer, nor of anyone else. A huge, gold-framed mirror hung above a low, wooden chest of drawers. And in the center of the room, a king-sized bed covered in pillows and a velveteen golden duvet.

M dropped the towel, enjoying how it felt to stand in the middle of the famous writer's bedroom stark naked. She wondered why she didn't feel nervous. She started to think she should, and then she started to think that she actually might, but was simply too numb to access the depths of that. Whatever, she thought, taking another very long swig from her tumbler of scotch, which she placed on a blown-glass coaster by the famous writer's bedside. Then she climbed into the famous writer's bed. Climbed, because it was extremely high off the ground. She slid underneath the impossibly soft duvet, the impossibly soft sheets, onto the impossibly soft pillows. She lay there, staring up at the dark blue ceiling with a kind of wonder that made her feel like she was staring up at something celestial, instead of just a ceiling.

She didn't know how long she'd been staring before a cold fear began to overtake her. It was sudden, and staggering. She didn't understand what she was doing here. She didn't understand what she had been thinking. She missed Jack so much she could feel the ache physically, right in the middle of her chest. Maybe it was time to do things differently. Maybe she could still bring Jack back to her. Maybe she could apologize to her sister. Make this all better somehow. She lifted her wet head up from the pillow, realizing she'd gotten the pillowcase wet, too. She sat fully up, looking across the room at the towel on the floor. She only had to get back to the towel, back to her clothing, to retrace her steps, to get out of there. But she was so comfortable, so scotch-drunk, so tired. It was so late; it hardly mattered if she left now or in a few minutes. She squeezed her eyes shut, laying back on the famous writer's damp pillow.

It was in this way that M fell asleep. She dreamed of the famous writer. In her dream, she was also in the famous writer's bed naked, but the famous writer was standing over her, also naked, except for a giant pair of blue hoop earrings. *Are you warm enough,* asked the famous writer in the dream. *Yes,* said dream-M. *But I would be warmer if you got into this bed with me. Hold on,* said the famous writer. *Let me just get Jack.* Dream-M tried to refuse, but she found she couldn't speak, was plastered to the famous writer's bed. The famous writer returned with Jack, who was also naked, except for a gold chain around her neck. *Hi,* said Jack, looking a little bit shy and wearing an expression that made M want to cry, to hold her, to say she was sorry. To say she would do better now. That she would take only what was hers and nothing more.

But then Jack's expression changed. *We know what you've done,* Jack said, her voice cold. *We know what you've done,* echoed the famous writer, hissing. *You won't get away with it.* Jack and the famous writer both got into the famous writer's bed with M, flanking her, both naked, both looking very hungry, and not in a good way. M felt that she was about to be devoured, and while she was scared, she was also ready. Dream-Jack disappeared then, and it was only the famous writer mounting M, straddling M with all of her weight, looking down on M from on high, her fangs bared. In her dream, M prickled with both full-body excitement and profound dread. *I'll pay you back,* M said in the dream. She wasn't sure if she meant it as a promise or a threat or a plea. The words hurt her throat as she spoke them. She said them again, just to make sure she hadn't imagined it. *I'll pay you back.*

She was startled awake, then, by the sound of the key in the door, by the sound of the front door swinging open, by the sound of the rustle of bags, by the sound of a woman's voice, by a garbled *Oh my god, what,* and then, much more clearly, almost like the sound of music, by a terrified *Hello?*

WILD ALE

S J SINDU

My wife Adria and I are supposed to be in Europe, driving a tiny rental car from Amsterdam to the South of France, then ferrying to the Greek islands. Instead, we're self-isolating inside our third-story walkup, a month into lockdown. Adria tries to tell me it's better this way, but then again, she believes that crystals can bring luck or doom depending on the moon's cycles.

"Something terrible could've happened on our trip," she tells me. "One of us could've broken a bone. We could've been arrested. We were probably saved."

"Sure," I say. "Our stuffy apartment is so much better than Mykonos."

Last month we had friends over to taste some beer I'd brewed. We smoked weed and played poker, and when the guests went home, Adria and I screamed at each other like usual before going to bed wrapped up in our drunken rage. If I'd known the country would go into quarantine shortly after, I would've tried to have a better time. Instead I fumed at our university colleague Dennis—a newly tenured professor who specializes in the literature of David Foster Wallace—who hit on Adria every chance he got. After the party, I accused Adria of inviting his flirting, and she called me a jealous tyrant.

It's a cold, bright weekend morning, and Adria is drinking her coffee and reading her daily horoscope—Gemini sun, Sagittarius rising, Virgo moon—and I'm researching the Wild Ale Challenge, a Midwest home brew competition I've decided to enter. We sit facing each other on our green velvet Chesterfield, our legs intertwined, next to the large picture window in our living room. Adria's pillowy hair catches the sun, bending light over each dark coil. She reads my horoscope—Sagittarius sun, Virgo rising, Aquarius moon—and tells me I need to watch out for bodies of water and that maybe I shouldn't take a bath tonight.

The April sun shines brilliant, but somehow there're tiny hailstones going *tink tink tink* on our windowsill. On the street below, no pedestrians, few parked cars, one biker wearing a blue medical face mask. A large pickup truck drives by with the Chicago Bears logo painted on its back window. In the truck's bed lie protest signs saying STOP THE TYRANY! and OPEN LLINOIS!

"What selfishness," Adria says.

"They spelled *tyranny* wrong."

We both turn back to our phones. I surf past a bunch of social media posts with the hashtag #wildalechallenge. Three weeks ago, I brewed an almond-coffee stout. Base of two-row and Munich malt, with 45 crystal, 150 crystal, roasted barley, chocolate malt, and debittered black malt. Magnum and crystal hops at 60, 30, and flameout. Wyeast 1056. Fresh brewed coffee, almond extract, and roasted blanched almonds in secondary. It'll be two weeks until I can drink it, but by all estimations, it should be good.

My next beer will be a wild ale. In the Wild Ale Challenge, you're supposed to make beer from foraged ingredients. The only thing you're allowed to buy is your grain bill. No hops. No yeast. No nutrients. No flavorings.

Down below on the street, a truck honks and someone shouts something, the words garbled by our window.

"Chili pepper IPA's ready to drink today," I say.

Adria idly scratches her eyebrow, then smooths the hairs back into place.

"IPAs are an important part of beer history," I tell her. "Did you know they were invented by the British during colonial times to survive the trip to India? The hops served as an antibacterial agent."

Adria doesn't acknowledge my factoid. On our first date during grad school, this is the kind of historical trivia I'd awkwardly toss across the table as I clutched my brown ale in a smoky dive bar in Florida. Back then, Adria's eyes would light up in the dim grittiness.

The noise on the street gets louder. When we look, the Chicago Bears truck has stopped and a blonde woman is shouting down the owner of the bodega across the street.

"I want my morning croissant!" she yells.

"Online orders only." The bodega owner is calm but resolute, his arms crossed, his mask on, blocking her from going through his front door.

"This is tyranny!"

Adria sighs and rubs at her temples. "I don't know how much more of this I can take."

"I miss those croissants," I say.

Adria gives me a look like I'm a cockroach sitting on her favorite cake.

I scroll through more #wildalechallenge posts. In a few weeks, I'll ship out four bottles of my finished beer and get feedback from the judges and, maybe, win a medal. I've spent weeks tweaking my recipe, trying to nail every single weight measurement down to the hundredth decimal point.

I close my laptop. "I'm going to try the chili pepper IPA."

"It's ten in the morning, Cam." Adria takes another sip of coffee. Her mug says HERS, part of a HERS AND HERS matching set we got for our wedding. The woman on the street gets in her truck and drives away.

"It's five o'clock in France," I say.

I pour a sixteen-ounce bottle for myself. A bit too much caramel flavor, but the pepper extract shines through nicely. It reminds me of our bicycle brewery tour in Denver during our honeymoon road trip across the US. We got caught in the rain and danced in the street with strangers, and every brewery had a chili pepper beer on tap. I make a note in my logbook not to add crystal 60 malt next time.

☙

By lunch, I've had three chili pepper IPAs and Adria's in a state. She hasn't moved from her position on our Chesterfield for over an hour. She rests her chin on her hand and stares out the picture window at the empty street below. The wind whips up the accumulated hail into white snakes on the asphalt.

I sit next to her and shake her gently.

She turns to face me like I've roused her from a deep sleep. "I wonder how many couples will get divorced during the pandemic," she says.

I imagine the millions of couples around the world, all cooped up with each other and no escape. "Why would you say that?"

"You're drunk," she says, cringing from my breath.

The bones of her shoulders jut out more sharply than they did a month ago. She's been forgetting to eat, lost in a time fog.

I'm glad the world is losing shape around me. "It's time for lunch. You need to eat," I tell her.

"What's the point?"

I go to the kitchen to heat up leftover pasta and push the bowl into her hands.

She stares at three pieces of rigatoni speared on her fork. "Your brewing station's taking over the kitchen. It's getting so claustrophobic in here." She stares some more at her pasta until I feed her, and even then, she only chews a couple of bites before shaking her head.

"It's just because you've been cooped up. We don't have to quarantine so strictly," I say. "We could invite over Dennis and Rhonda for some beers."

"What the fuck is wrong with you?" Adria rubs her eyes with the heels of her palms. "And you hate Dennis."

"I don't hate Dennis." Despite what she says, I know Adria's attracted to him. I can feel it like static in the air when they're around me. But at this point, I'm willing to put up with even that for some damn company.

"He's a sweet guy," she says, and I grind my teeth. "You just want him over so you can show off your manly brewing skills and display me like a trophy and feel masculine."

"That's not true." I want her to keep talking so I can dissect her voice for any clues as to how she really feels about Dennis. Despite her assurances that she's done dating men, doubt clogs my throat. "You think he's sweet?"

"Stop, just stop. I can't do this."

"What do you mean by *this?*" The beer makes me reckless. Already I'm itching for another.

Adria covers her face with her hands and sobs. I think about comforting her, but my body vibrates with anger. She was the one who brought up divorces.

"You're such an asshole," she says.

I finish the pasta and have another beer. She goes back to staring at the empty street.

The fourth IPA calms me. I go to my favorite home brew site—still shipping through the pandemic—and add $3000 worth of equipment to my cart: the fully electric Bluetooth-enabled Grainfather brewing system, which can handle up to six gallons of brew, and which I can control from my phone with multi-step mashes and custom brew times; the SS Brewtech seven-gallon stainless-steel conical fermenter with yeast dump valve; and a glycol temperature controller that can heat and cool up to four fermenters at a time. Three thousand dollars is more than I make per class I teach for the university. I close out of the tab without checking out and drink another beer.

Lightheaded and guilty about our fight, I wobble to Adria's crystal box and pick out two pieces of orange carnelian, which she's told me inspires and motivates. I place these crystals next to her on the couch.

I check on my Mason jars. I'm trying to cultivate wild yeast for my entry in the challenge. Two weeks ago, I filled Mason jars with boiled water and dry malt extract and set them outside on our balcony to collect yeast. One smells like plastic. One is growing what looks like a mushroom. I throw those out.

Adria thinks my home brew obsession is a manifestation of my inner frat boy. When we first met, she was into my butchness, but now she says I remind her too much of the "douchebag cis men" she used to date. She won't listen when I try to explain. I love brewing because at its core, it's simple: water, grain, yeast. With the world in chaos, I find calm in the pristine science of gravity readings, equipment sanitation, and hops schedules. When I brew, I can control everything. Or, nearly everything. Right now, with my ragtag DIY mash tun and my repurposed stock pot as a brew kettle, I can't keep temperatures as steady as I need to. I can't ferment at a perfect sixty-eight degrees or crash cool my beer before bottling. For that I'd need my dream $3000 system.

I make a great show of changing into my fleece-lined leggings, coat, hat, and gloves, but Adria doesn't seem to notice.

"I'll be back," I say, and put my face mask on.

Outside, I strip my coat off and stuff the hat and gloves into my pockets. I want to feel the cold sink into me. I also take off my mask, because wearing it makes me feel like something heavy is sitting on my chest.

Wind rattles the streetlights as I pass. Avoiding the handful of others on the sidewalk, I stroll to the park down the street and pick dandelions and yarrow, which showed up after a week of good weather. I need to collect them before they die from the snowstorm predicted for tonight. I pluck whole plants—roots, leaves, and all—and stuff them into my pockets. The park is empty except for a young runner and an old Asian couple doing tai chi, all with face masks on. When they see me, the Asian couple moves away, and the runner mutters, "Mask up, asshole," under her breath. I want to tell her she's not going to catch the virus in a mostly empty park, but I still feel bad.

A truck drives by, the same one I saw earlier with the Bears logo on the back window and protest signs in the bed. The middle-aged blonde woman who yelled at the bodega owner rolls down the passenger-side window and leans her head out. The truck slows to a stop in the middle of the road.

"Reopen the country!" she shouts to the four of us scattered across the park. She looks directly at me like I'm on her side. "Sacrifice the weak! The virus is a hoax!" Her face turns red from the effort.

The runner slows down to watch us. The tai chi couple turns our way. The woman waits. I wish I hadn't taken off my mask.

"Stop watching Fox News!" I shout back to her, holding a handful of plucked dandelions.

The driver of the truck is an acne-faced boy wearing all orange. He could be any one of my first-year English students at the university.

"Stay the fuck home!" I say.

The woman yells, "*You* stay home, dyke!"

The truck drives away.

※

The next day, while it snows, I brew my wild ale recipe using the dandelion greens as a hop substitute and yarrow as a way to add flavor and depth. For aroma, I add stinging nettle I found growing wild by the river where I walk every day without telling Adria. I use the same grain bill as a rye-wheat beer I brewed last summer that Adria loved: rye malt, Durst pilsner, pale, 80 crystal, flaked rice, wheat, and rice hulls in a multi-rest mash. The stock pot I have isn't big enough, so I have to brew in two different pots. One boils over, the flaked rice making the wort too sticky.

Called by my screaming, Adria runs into the kitchen and finds me sitting on the floor, my head in my hands.

"Wort boiled over," I say.

Adria puts her fists on her hips. "I thought something bad had happened."

Anger rushes up inside me. I jump up and dump the whole boiled-over pot into the sink. Immediately I regret it. I've gone from five gallons to three gallons.

I lean over the sink and watch the last of the perfectly good wort spiral into the drain. I think about the Grainfather system, how this would never have happened if I had it.

Twenty minutes and a chipotle stout later, I wash and pluck the dandelion flowers and nettle, sanitize them by dunking them in boiling water, stuff the petals and leaves into three glass carboys, and siphon the cooled wort on top. I aerate the wort and pitch yeast from the Mason jars. I drink my chili pepper IPA while I brew, but I don't need the booze—brewing is the only time I don't feel like I've got glue in the veins of my heart.

By the time I'm done cleaning up, I've had a few more beers and my walk is wobbly. My anxiety about our fight yesterday, combined with losing half my brew to equipment failure, makes my stomach churn. Now that I'm not brewing anymore, it's hard to breathe right.

When I'm done, I find Adria in our shared office—her hair and makeup done, a silk button-up shirt over her sweatpants—video conferencing with her students. When the university went online and Europe was canceled, Adria agreed to teach a new critical theory class over video. She's placed carnelian, amethyst, and rose quartz on her desk outside of the camera frame. Her face has that plastic smile she wears whenever she's trying to convince someone she's happy.

I've agreed to teach two creative writing classes for extra pay, but without face-to-face, real-time anything. I told my students it's to respect their other obligations during this time, and even dropped the buzzword *asynchronous pedagogy*, but the truth is that I can't hold any thoughts in my head except for beer recipes. I can't imagine lecturing like Adria does. I'm behind on grading, and I haven't written anything in weeks except for brewing notes in my logbook, though I'm supposed to be finishing my novel.

"When you read the assignments for next week," Adria says into the camera, "remember that Schinkel is responding not just to Benjamin but also to a large body of social science where researchers have focused on the causes of violence rather than autotelic violence."

I stand out of the video frame and watch her. We've been together for six years, but I've never gotten to watch her teach the way I have this month. She made me read that essay about autotelic violence. Violence without a direct cause or goal. Violence for the sake of violence. I remember the woman in the park, her absolute conviction and panic. My palms itch. Maybe this pandemic has made us all into assholes. At the very least, it's made us into cornered animals, hissing and spitting at the faintest shadows.

"Any final questions before we wrap up?" She notices me lurking nearby. "Oh! Look, here's Cam." She says it in a fake upbeat way that makes me cringe.

I step closer and wave to Adria's students, whose cameras are turned off in a gallery of blank gray boxes on her laptop. My usual short hair is getting shaggy around my ears, and I have dark bags under my eyes.

"It's a wild time we're living through," she says to her students, "so please remember to be kind to yourselves. Eat well. Don't leave the house. I'm here if you need me."

Adria closes her laptop and takes her earbuds out. She changes out of her nice shirt and into her usual stained tank top and worn-down sweater.

I can't help myself. "Don't leave the house?" I say. "Isn't that a bit extreme?"

"Most of my students' parents won't self-isolate," she says. "They keep going to work."

"Adria, *my* mother won't self-isolate." My mother and I aren't on the best of terms, but we still talk every week. "She said she was going to one of those protests."

Adria stares at me, her mouth open. I can feel the tirade coming. If I don't distract her, she'll try to lecture me on how to talk to my own mother.

"I finished my wild ale," I say. "Want to know what I used?"

Adria cuts me off before I can tell her about the yarrow.

"We need to pay the credit card," she says. "I just got the statement."

"Okay." My heart skips a step.

Adria puts her hands on her hips. "*Six hundred dollars* on brewing supplies?" she says. Her voice is calm and dangerous.

"I needed grain. And you know liquid yeast is better than dry. And shipping is expensive."

"You're going to brew us into poverty."

I reach for her arm, but she snatches it away. I can't take her look of disdain.

"Then leave," I say. "Leave if that's what you want to do. Go fuck Dennis or something."

Adria is struck dumb. She flaps her mouth open and closed. She takes a big, rattling breath and closes her eyes. "You can't spend six hundred dollars on beer," she says. "We can't afford it."

Just to torture myself, I picture her with Dennis. I picture them laughing, Adria sitting on his lap.

"I can spend whatever the fuck I want," I say. I plop down at my desk, open my laptop, and load the home brew site where my cart still has $3000 worth of brewing equipment. "I want this stuff, I need this stuff," I say. Part of me is floating near the window, watching myself unravel. "You spend hundreds on crystals and have I complained? No." I know I should stop but I can't. The image I've conjured up of Adria and Dennis—now both naked in bed—blurs my vision. I squint at the screen, click "Check Out," and enter our credit card information. Each form element I fill in makes me breathe a little easier.

"What are you doing?" Adria screams.

From the window, I watch myself turn toward her and flip her off. I watch her incredulous face, her body tilted sideways, leaning on one hip.

Then I click "Pay Now," and it's done. In a few days, I'll get the brewing system of my dreams.

☙

Every day, the same Chicago Bears truck drives by midmorning. The blonde woman leans out the passenger-side window to yell at whoever is on the street or in the apartments. The weather warms up enough that we have the windows open, so we hear her. Several times, Adria yells back at her, after which the woman calls us godless heathens and the truck drives away. Adria hasn't talked to me since the moment I ordered my new brewing system. I keep wondering if she'll ask me to call them and cancel the order, but she hasn't. Instead she shuts me out. She's frozen solid.

I've split my wild ale into three one-gallon containers, each with a different yeast. Every day, I sniff the air locks. I unwrap each container from its towel and look for the krausen forming on top of the wort, a sign that fermentation is healthy. But the krausen is slow to form, and when it does, it doesn't look as foamy as I expect.

"I just can't stand it," Adria says after the fifth encounter with the Bears truck woman. Her first words to me in days, and I note that her voice is normal, as if for a moment she's forgotten. She massages her forehead with the tips of her fingers.

"People do strange things when they feel helpless," I say, quoting one of Adria's lectures.

"Thanks for the psychology lesson, Dr. Losh. Why don't you go check on your beer?"

I check on the beer. Five days after brewing, a pale film has developed on top of one of the batches. White, coin-sized bubbles form and don't pop. The air lock smells like vinegar. I move that container away from the other two. I crush a campden tablet and swirl it into the white-filmed beer, hoping to deter the infection.

"I think one of them's infected," I tell Adria.

She's lying on the couch with her laptop, scrolling through endless social media feeds.

"Hmmm," she says.

It's better than silence, so I push forward.

"Have you eaten?"

"Hmmm."

"Yes or no, have you eaten?"

"It's my stomach, my body. Stop micromanaging it. I'm not your beer."

I kneel by the couch and touch her hand. She startles as if I'd just screamed into her ear. She puts her hand on my cheek.

"I miss you," I say.

I do. I miss her like I missed salmon for the first six months after we went vegan. My body craves her. It's not just the silence in the house. Without the routine of our classes, our dinners out, our hikes, our walks by the river—she feels so far away, even when we're getting along.

"Let's just take one walk," I say. I lay my head on her stomach. "We can go down to the river."

"The horoscope said you should avoid bodies of water."

I laugh without meaning to, and she pushes my head off her.

"I'm sorry." I mean it. I'm too sober. I need a beer, or I need her touch. "I'm sorry. I want to be close to you. Please."

Adria considers me for a moment, and I think she's going to tell me to leave her alone, but instead she hugs me and pulls me onto the couch on top of her. She runs her fingers through my hair.

"Remember when you made AdriAle for my birthday?" she says. "I loved you so much for throwing me that party."

When we were still in grad school, I brewed a raspberry sour, though I cheated on the fermentation by adding lactic acid in secondary. AdriAle and the party I threw went far toward getting Adria to fall in love with me.

We fuck on the couch. She scratches my arms so hard she leaves marks, and afterward we lie there until my fingers dry, crusted and pungent.

※

A few days later, two more trucks join the Chicago Bears one, and the caravan stops for a while on our block. Six people get out and circle their parked trucks, honking and waving their signs—We demand haircuts! The lockdown is killing us, not Covid! Don't ruin my golf season!

Adria and I stand at our open kitchen window with our hers and hers coffee mugs—hers with actual coffee and mine with ground dandelion root tea, which is supposed to promote liver health. All down the street, neighbors stick their heads out of their windows or watch from their balconies.

"I saw a Facebook event yesterday," Adria says, fiddling with the citrine crystal she's wearing on a gold chain. We're talking again, as if things are normal. She hasn't brought up the brewing system. "They're building up to a big protest tomorrow. Calling themselves the 'unheard majority'."

The doorbell rings, startling both of us. Since the quarantine began, we haven't had anyone ring our doorbell except for the rare package. Adria looks fearful, so I put on my mask and go downstairs to the door. It's the brewing system, delivered in three gigantic boxes at the bottom of two sets of stairs.

I drag one of the boxes up the stairs, my body rising in temperature with each step.

"What's that?" Adria asks as I haul it through the door. Her voice says she already knows what it is.

"Do you want to help me with the other boxes?"

Adria says nothing, but she comes down and helps me bring up the other two packages. The boxes take up a third of our living room. Adria stares at them from the kitchen, her hands wrapped securely around her coffee.

"Sixty thousand people are dead in the US," she says, "and you spend $3000 on a fucking home brew system."

"Those things have nothing to do with each other."

Adria slams her HERS coffee cup into the sink, where it shatters and spills its last dregs. I'm itching to open the packages, but instead I put my arms around Adria, and we stand there as the blonde woman and her friends down on the street shout, "This is China's wet dream!"

☙

Even though Adria's anger radiates throughout the apartment, I'm too excited to care. Instinctually, I have the urge to protect my childlike elation, to wall it away from her fury.

I open the boxes. Adria retires to the office. I run an extension cord from the living room to the closet where I put the fermenter and glycol chiller. I set up the Grainfather in the kitchen underneath our rolling butcher block island, displacing the onions, potatoes, and various pots onto the countertops.

After it's set up and sanitized, I transfer the two gallons of good wild ale into the stainless-steel fermenter for a temperature-stable second fermentation. This is when the flavors will really develop. I turn on the glycol chiller and sit there watching it run for a long time, imagining what the ale will taste like. A sweet note because of the dandelion. A bite because of the nettle. All held up by a smooth rye base. If I win this home brew competition, I can justify spending all this on the Grainfather. If I win, I can quit teaching, take an online brewmaster course, and join a local brewery. Spending my days elbow deep in grains and yeast will keep me at peace, keep the claws of the world from wrapping themselves around my throat.

☙

Adria shakes me at five in the morning. I wake, half in my dream where I was putting together a recipe for a black tea porter.

"The apartment smells like feet," she says.

I rub the sleep out of my eyes. She's right. The smell is overpowering. Saliva gathers at the back of my throat, my stomach contracting like I'm about to puke.

It takes me a few seconds before I know what's wrong. The beer. The wild ale.

I stumble out of bed and almost crash into the wall, but I catch myself. My knee rams hard into the steel bed frame. I clutch it and hobble to the closet where my fermenter is.

As soon as I open the closet door, the smell hits me, and I have to pinch my nose closed as I grope for the pull light. In the sudden brightness, I struggle with the lid of the fermenter.

When I finally get it open, the beer inside is full of unmoving white bubbles, each the size of a knuckle. The white film crawls up the sides of the fermenter, down into the beer, and all over the dandelion petals, nettle leaves, and yarrow. My knee throbs with pain. The smell is so strong I can't breathe. Something inside me breaks open like a seed, and it's not until Adria pulls me out of the closet that I realize I'm crying.

I sob into her shoulder, drenching her pajama top with tears and snot and drool. She holds me, though. When I stop crying, Adria says, "We have to get that stuff out of the house. I don't want to know how many fungal spores are floating around."

We open all the windows to the frigid night air and take the fermenter out onto the balcony.

"Shouldn't we throw this out?" Adria asks.

Even though the batch is ruined, even though it's too late to save,

I can't bear the thought of dumping it.

I hug the fermentation vessel. The infected beer is still warm under my hand.

"I can't," I say, and press my face against the steel of the fermenter. Adria rolls her eyes.

Down below, the quiet, dark street sleeps before its big protest day. I imagine the blonde woman with her Bears truck, her supporters at her side, all of them lost in the frenzy of their belief, shouting at the world for daring to put the health of others before their own small freedoms. All this while Adria and I burn our freedoms under our crushing sense of collective duty. I hit the side of the fermenter in frustration, and I keep hitting and hitting and hitting until that anger transforms into an idea.

"I want to put this stuff to use," I say.

Adria crouches by me. "What use?" She sounds exhausted.

I tell her my plan, expecting her to object, but apparently I've worn her down. A smile creeps over her face. And just like that, it feels like we're back to before, when our love sat deep, knowledge under my doubt.

So we work, Adria and I, in the early morning as dawn breaks pink and raw on the horizon. We're out on the balcony in our winter coats, house slippers, latex gloves, and masks that somewhat shield us from the nauseating stink of toe jam. We work until the sun warms the backs of our necks and Adria has taken at least five coffee breaks. By the time the trucks arrive for their planned protest, we're ready.

This time, word's gotten out. That Facebook event Adria saw has attracted at least twenty trucks, all parading down our street. They park in the middle of the road without hesitation. A swarm of people exits. The woman in the Chicago Bears truck has a MAGA hat and a blow horn, through which she shouts, "The revolution has begun! Socialism sucks!"

Our neighbors on the street open their windows and come out onto their balconies. The fancy RAM 1500 Limited has double speakers in its bed and starts to blast out NWA's "Fuck tha Police."

"What a weird choice of song," Adria says, drinking coffee out of the other HERS cup.

The protesters on the street chant, "We're here, we're right! Reopen the country!"

"That doesn't even rhyme," one of our neighbors shouts from a nearby balcony.

The woman with the blow horn points it at him. "You libtards have no idea what's happening to this country." She catches sight of Adria and me watching and wags her fingers at us. "God's brought down this wrath!"

The protesters start to chant, "We want BBQs! We want prom!"

I reach down into my five-gallon plastic fermentation bucket filled with what Adria and I spent the morning preparing: small muslin hopsacks packed with infected yeast, dandelion petals, and nettle leaves, all soaked in rank wild ale.

I chuck the first hopsack at the truck blasting music out the back. It lands with a satisfying *thunk* on the windshield, leaking greasy white film all over the glass.

Adria aims one at the blonde woman with the blow horn. It misses her but lands at her feet, splashing her espadrilles and shins. There's chaos among the protesters as they try to figure out what's happening.

Above the booming music, someone shouts, "Dr. Losh?"

I freeze with another hopsack in my hand, ready to throw. Only my students call me Dr. Losh. I search the crowd, and then I see her. Maggie Carlson. My star student. She and her girlfriend are standing on one of the truck beds, pointing at me.

I lower my arm and toss the hopsack back into the bucket.

She waves at me, and I wave back. She and her girlfriend are holding a sign that says, WE WANT TO GRADUATE.

The NWA song ends, and Toby Keith's "Made in America" comes on. One of our neighbors starts playing Rage Against the Machine's "Killing in the Name" from their apartment, trying to drown out Toby Keith.

"Throw your bombs!" a neighbor shouts to us.

I stand still and try to block the view of the stink-sack-filled bucket from the street. But the neighbors don't need us to continue the attack. An older lady three doors down throws a couple of tomatoes at the trucks below, splashing a white paint job in splotches of red. Someone chucks their morning oatmeal, which plops onto a woman's head. She screams, but in the commotion, no one seems to notice. The food lands on protesters, on their trucks and signs.

Adria's hand fumbles for mine, and when I look at her, turning away from the chaos, her face is alive and wild with something I haven't seen in her in a long time.

"Autotelic violence," she says, her lips quivering into a smile.

Protesters clamor for cover, their chants forgotten, their shirts stained with rotten fruit. Many get back into their trucks and roll up their windows. My student Maggie and her girlfriend cower under a nearby awning, both splattered with eggs. Yolk glistens all over Maggie's mousy brown hair.

Adria leans back and grabs another sack of infected beer. I hesitate, but only for a moment. Buoyed by the happiness in Adria's face, I take a hop sack, and together we hurl them onto the protesters, where they splatter with stink.

I lose track of Maggie and her girlfriend, but then I spot them, running away from the commotion, pulling each other along.

We continue to throw until the trucks start their engines. The street is covered in smashed food, and I wonder, briefly, who'll clean it up. The roar of our neighbors overwhelms the din of the trucks driving away. When the Chicago Bears truck rounds the corner of the block, our neighborhood erupts in cheers.

Adria leans on the railing and laughs. She laughs and laughs. Her skin shines with sweat. I peel both our winter coats off and hug her close. I bury my face in her shoulder. We sit on the balcony with our feet dangling off the edge, listening to our neighbors go back inside their homes, glorying in the smell of rank wild ale.

PEEP SHOW

ALISSA NUTTING

I DO MY BEST not to stare at Sabine at work. Actually, that isn't true: I do my best not to *get caught* staring at Sabine at work. Though on certain days, if I'm feeling downright bratty, I need to get caught. But only by Sabine. I grow more and more brazen in my glances until I see her roll her eyes and shake her head, seemingly in frustration at her computer, an elegant way of camouflaging a response to me: *Fine, I see you, stop already.*

Or maybe that's all in my head.

For Sabine, I'll try to be as honest as possible telling this story. I say that even as I imagine her correction: no, I'm telling this story for me. An act of narrative trepanning, writing the words to ease the pressure of guilt inside my skull. She'd say my telling this has little to do with her, and even less to do with honesty.

Sabine tends to be right. So maybe it's better to start with lies.

Our boss Levi lies about our office's open floorplan; he says we have no walls to "enhance collaboration." But it's so our bodies and monitors are visible at all times to anyone walking by. Meaning you can't take out your cell phone or check your team's stats for fear of being caught. In fact, sending a personal email has to happen on your break, on your own device, outside the building, just like smoking a cigarette.

There used to be a few individual glass booths with desktop computers next to the break room, for personal use if you weren't on the clock, but Levi removed them due to pornography use. Or so he said.

Levi is a garish, horny nerd with a shit ton of money; plus he's hyper-connected to every major player in the tech industry. Some things I've overheard coworkers say about him:

"Our company is in Miami instead of Silicon Valley because Levi has a pathological need to dress like a DJ at all times. That's it; that's the entire reason."

"He smells like cologne and STDs. Not the actual smell of an STD but the way an STD would smell if it anthropomorphized into human form."

But there's also a reason that Levi gets away with this, and more: "Damn, that pervert can code."

Levi is, unfortunately, a computer programming savant. Since I'm attempting truth here, I'll admit there have been times, studying printed dumps of his output, when I come across a section so artful that I've actually teared up. At its elegance, yes. But also at the unfairness. Why place such a brilliant gift in such a foul human package?

In his natural form, Levi is a white, almost translucent Midwestern transplant like me. But he thinks his weekly spray tans perform an alchemy of racial ambiguity. "I'm telling you," he likes to brag, "chicks in the clubs assume I speak Spanish."

Levi also forbids romantic relationships between employees. We're too small for it to be a big problem—the company is his AI programming startup; there are only a few hundred of us. When I first got hired, I figured the no-relationship policy was just his way of making sure female employees who sleep with him won't expect a commitment. Then Isha from accounting and Callum from design got engaged. And immediately fired.

Perhaps sensing everyone's collective outrage, Levi called a session of "church," his name for meetings with the entire company.

"This isn't me denouncing love," he stated. "It's me *respecting* it. When you're here inside these walls, this company has to be your highest purpose. I ask that you be as passionate about our mission as I am. And if you're working here and your wife is working here, and she has a problem? Love's going to ask you to prioritize her over your job. You don't want to be in that position. I'm doing you a favor."

Even before Sabine, I never would've gone so far as to sleep with Levi to get a promotion. Partly because I'm not straight; partly because I find him abhorrent; partly because I've seen it backfire. If he sleeps with you, then he has to go out of his way to prove you aren't benefiting from it. The last woman I knew who did it, Liset, left after he passed her up for another candidate. Though I'm sure he gave her a stellar recommendation letter.

Before she quit, Liset told me Levi spray tans his penis, too, and he told her he has to get hard before he does it. If he sprays it when he's flaccid, his boner will have white stripes.

But I'll admit that I do fem up for the office. I avoid disclosing anything that would compromise an assumption of me as straight-presenting. I even laugh somewhat flirtatiously at Levi's jokes. Why leave a harmless competitive edge on the table?

One answer, perhaps, which I realized only in hindsight, is that my acting so hetero with Levi meant Sabine didn't consider me dateable for a very long time. Maybe if we'd been together longer before The Incident, she wouldn't have quit me so fast. Maybe if she hadn't begun the relationship already having reservations, I would've had more runway.

But our getting together felt fated, and when it finally happened, immediate. I was watching her eat lunch by herself across the cafeteria. She was reading a book, and when she smiled at a line I smiled too, involuntarily, and she happened to look up and see. Her grin was epic, reading me and my desires fully with a sort of amused outrage. As if to say, *You know I can see your face and that we're in public, correct?* "Sorry," I mouthed. What else can you say when you're caught? "Sorry?" she mouthed back, which seemed like an invitation to come explain myself.

When I sat down, it felt like we were already on a date. I was giddy in her presence. We could read each other's expressions so well, so wordlessly. She was laughing and shaking her head. "You look like a cartoon right now," she said.

"Are you single?" I asked this in a near-whisper. Not just because it was best if no one overheard us. I could really barely speak.

"I might be," she said, with an intonation that conveyed a few concerns. "This is all a surprise. When I've seen you in meetings, you seem…"

"To have no self-respect?" She smiled and visibly relaxed a bit at my self-diagnosis. "Yeah," I admitted. "I leave my dignity at home to try to get promoted faster."

"How's that working for you?" Her eyes glimmered. I loved the rhetorical purity of her question, even though it meant I could only shrug, a sheepish admission that I still hadn't been chosen by Levi for any of the select teams, still hadn't been promoted.

"Okay," I agreed, "if my work persona asks you out, you should say no. But this is non-work me asking you out, and I think you should say yes."

"That's cute," she said. "How you tell yourself they're different."

I believe my jaw dropped at this.

Then she started laughing again, and I laughed too, telling myself she was joking but also knowing maybe she wasn't.

"To be fair," she finally said, "I mean…I don't kiss up to him the way you do. But I do let him call me Rihanna." She explained that he does this not simply because she's Black and a woman; it's a little more twisted than that. The "nickname" came about in her interview, when she told Levi her parents immigrated to central Florida from Haiti before he was born. "Haiti, huh," Levi had said, "like Rihanna. I'm gonna call you Rihanna."

Sabine says she's still not sure whether his ignorance is real or feigned, some kind of mind game, which Levi loves. "Was he testing whether or not I'd correct him and say she's from Barbados? Did I get the job because I smiled instead of telling him he's wrong?"

With Levi, you can never really know.

❦

Six months later, we'd settled into a basic cohabitation at my place, though Sabine kept her place and continued getting her mail there. On paper, our job couldn't see we slept together every night.

We drove to and from work separately. And when Levi threw "parties" at his mansion for the programmers (attendance was compulsory), we drove separately as well. Every party included a tour to show us any new home updates, major purchases, etc. We all had to follow him through the house listening to him talk like he was a museum docent.

Prior to the first quarter party, Sabine bet me $20 that he'd say, "And this is where the magic happens" when we entered his bedroom on the tour. I'd bet he wouldn't, since there weren't any new hires since the last party. We'd all seen his bedroom multiple times (some of the female employees even more extensively than others); we'd all heard him use that line multiple times. Would he really say it again?

We try not to stand too close to one another even at these events, but I couldn't resist walking behind Sabine on this tour. "And here's where the magic happens!" Levi boomed. Requisite laughter followed.

"Well done," I whispered.

"Oh no," Sabine said, to no one in particular. Then I followed her line of sight and saw it: a small wiry dog in a cage in the corner. This was new. As the tour continued on, Sabine briefly broke our own rules and looked at me. "He showed us the talking toilet but didn't say a word about the dog? That poor thing. I bet it's in its cage all day. I wish we could save him." Then she scurried to catch up with the group and didn't give me another look again for the next hour and a half, at which point she left.

Sometime between her saying it and her leaving, I got the idea that I needed to steal the dog for her. It would be a valiant act. A rescue. She'd admire my daring.

I pretended to go to the bathroom, then snuck back to Levi's bedroom, moving silently in the dark, on the lookout for any blinking lights that might indicate a security camera. I didn't know if the dog would fit inside my large purse; didn't know if it would bite or resist. But when I opened the door to its crate in the dark room, it allowed me to scoop it up and place it inside my bag like this was a daily occurrence.

I tried to do quick, waving goodbyes, making steady progress toward the exit. But just as I'd almost reached the front door, Levi called out after me. "Not so fast," he said. "Come back here."

I swallowed. Could I pretend to be a lot drunker than I was? Would I have to perform some untoward act on Levi to keep him from calling the cops on me? Would he accept a topless handjob? Oral or vaginal sex seemed like they'd be equally traumatic with Levi. There was no lesser evil in that situation.

As I walked back toward him, I tried to clutch the bag close in case the dog wiggled. My pulse was roaring in my ears. There was a moment I thought I might vomit all over Levi's ten-thousand-dollar sneakers.

"Here. Take this." Levi handed me a bottle of quite fancy champagne.

"Wow," I said. "Thank you. Great party."

⁂

At home, Sabine's reaction was not the gushing admiration I was hoping for.

"You realize you probably just ended us, right?" In my head, I'd decided that at worst, I alone would get caught and exposed. But Sabine was right: if Levi put me under a microscope, it followed that our relationship would probably come to light as well. "You risked our jobs and us being together for a dog? You know Levi will probably keep you and your long blonde hair and fire me, right? He'll say he's sure I put you up to it."

"Shit," I said, digesting this. "I'm sorry. I didn't think. I wanted to make you happy."

"You wanted to feel loved," Sabine said. "Acting careless isn't thinking about my happiness."

This was accurate. My mind started racing for ways to fix it. "Maybe I can go back and say I left my phone? Try to sneak him back in?"

Sabine picked up the dog, considering. "Either Levi's got security camera footage of you taking the dog or he doesn't. If he does, you could return him and still get shitcanned."

"I really didn't see any cameras. I looked."

"Well. For now, what's done is done." Sabine nodded toward the champagne bottle. "We might as well drink that and hope you got away with it."

"I promise I'm very ashamed," I said. "But do you find the new criminal me a little sexy?"

She just sighed. But later, in bed, she lifted my pajama top and poured the slightest bit of champagne down it; I laid back as she licked its path down my torso and parted my legs, then drizzled just a bit there, too. I gasped at the feel of its cold bubbles followed by her hot, firm tongue, was about to lean back and close my eyes when I saw him: there was the dog, eyes locked with mine, staring at me like this was a show he'd paid for.

For reasons I couldn't yet articulate, I began moaning louder, gripping my breasts and squeezing my nipples as I writhed against Sabine's mouth, all while keeping steady eye contact with the dog. I guess I was testing something. Would he look away, maybe even show confusion at the increasing volume of my cries? But he did nothing except stare.

The next day at work, I felt like I was going to faint going through the metal detector. I was certain its alarm had somehow also been outfitted to pick up on recent dog theft. At my desk, my hands shook as I typed my password into my computer. It seemed likely that it wouldn't work; that I'd call IT and say, "I can't log in," and they'd direct me to HR, where police would be waiting.

But that didn't happen. Instead, Levi came out and announced a new ten-person project team. When he called Sabine's name, I had to clench my teeth to avoid smiling, both with pride and relief. He'd hardly pick her for a team if he suspected even her passive knowledge of his missing dog's whereabouts, right?

Except then he called my name. Right after hers.

Sabine's poker face is legendary. She didn't look bothered or freaked out in the least. She successfully "introduced" herself to me along with the others. But I had what felt like a series of nineteen consecutive panic attacks throughout the day. I sped home, beating Sabine there by nearly fifteen minutes even though we left around the same time.

"He *definitely* knows," I blurted. The dog ran to her and began jumping at her legs. "Picking both of us? Saying our names right after each other? It's too exact to be coincidence—"

"Both of you need to calm down and give me a moment," she said, shutting and locking the door. I realized she hadn't even put her bag down.

"Sorry." I walked over and took her coat and hung it up while she took off her shoes and put on slippers.

"It is absolutely coincidence," she said. "And I'll tell you why. Wine?" I nodded and sat on the couch as she brought back a bottle and two glasses, running through her very logical theory with a near-absent level of anxiety I can only describe as wildly arousing. "Let's play out what you're saying. He knows. And since he picked both of us, he doesn't just know you stole his dog; he also knows we're lovers. How would he know that?"

She handed me a glass of wine, which I chugged. "What if he doesn't know we're lovers," I finally conceded, "but he knows I stole the dog. You've been picked for a team before. Maybe the message was only to me." I poured another glass and started to chug it, but Sabine pulled it out of my hand.

"Try some deep breaths. If he knew, you'd be fired. You're okay."

"Maybe...he thought my stealing it showed initiative? In a fucked-up way?"

Sabine chuckled and started running her fingers across my throat. "I think there's only one kind of female initiative Levi likes... and it isn't that."

I smiled and put my fingers overtop hers, intertwining them. "What kind does he like?" I asked, quietly, playfully.

"This kind," she said, lifting onto her knees and straddling my lap. I reached behind her and pushed her close to my face, breathing hot air against the crotch of her pants, then began to unbuckle her belt. I looked up at her, making a show of sucking two of my fingers until they were slick, then pulled her underwear down, my fingertips barely touching her, until she got frantic enough to lower herself onto them. I wrapped my other arm around the left side of her waist, and placed my face against the right side, gripping her tightly, pushing steadily then stopping till she whimpered, then slowly starting again. When her legs began to shake I slid under her, dragging the tip of my tongue across her front until she was seconds away, then I took out my fingers and climbed out from beneath her, standing up behind her, moving her legs farther apart with my hands before starting to finger her again from behind. I pressed my cheek against her back, wanting to feel like I was sinking inside her in every way.

That's when I saw the dog. Three feet away. Eyes locked with mine.

Sabine screamed, reaching back and grabbing my wrist, holding my hand still. At first I thought she screamed because she saw the dog looking at us too, but when it continued into a moan then softened, I realized she'd just finished. She laid down to catch her breath and pulled me on top of her; I clutched her with a sinking worry as she kissed my head. "No more paranoia about the dog," she declared. "Okay?"

"Okay," I said. Then, "But real quick—"

Sabine groaned and sat up. "Hand me my wine." I did.

"Why didn't he say a single word about his dog today?" I questioned. "Why hasn't he sent a MISSING poster to the Slack channel for all of us to print out and hang up all over town? Why isn't he on social media offering a huge reward for its return?"

"Maybe we should smoke a joint," she offered.

"I'm serious."

"I am too. He probably got *wasted* at the party and figures one of the seven women who stayed over accidentally let it out and it ran off. He probably bought a new one ten minutes later."

"True," I said.

"But what," Sabine asked drily. "Just say it."

"What if we got picked because Levi can watch us having sex through the dog?"

Sabine nearly spit out her wine. "Stop it. First of all, robots don't pee in your closet." She nodded toward the dog. "This one already owes me a new pair of Oxfords." It felt like an unspoken agreement that we weren't naming the dog yet. At least in my superstition, it seemed like the moment we named him, we'd be caught.

"I don't think he's a robot," I agreed. "But…I dunno. What about an ocular implant or something?"

"These are really words coming out of your mouth right now?"

"He was in Levi's bedroom." Sabine let out a long exhale.

"Uh-huh. So you're saying he made a bionic dog to record sex with unsuspecting women."

"That way he'd never have to worry about them finding the camera." The look in Sabine's eyes after I said this worried me. It seemed like if she could press an EJECTION button on the couch that would launch her out of the apartment, she would. Inexplicably, though, I continued instead of giving it a rest. "I mean, isn't that what Levi would do?" I asked. "If he were him? Which…he totally is?"

Sabine made a show of staring over at the dog. He was absentmindedly licking his asshole.

"Okay," I agreed. "You're right. I'm spiraling."

೧

The next day at work, I got promoted.

"I've been watching you lately," Levi told me. "And I like what I see. Keep doing what you're doing." I'm not positive, but I think Levi then did, in fact, stare at me for what seemed like a few seconds before walking off. I guess I could have imagined it.

I wasn't sure what I believed. Levi's words to me having zero subtext or being all subtext felt equally possible. Sure, my whole Levi-spying-on-us-via-living-dog concept was farfetched. But it also made sense in a simple way that felt true. I decided I wouldn't bring up the theory with Sabine again; it wasn't something we had to agree on. In fact, to her, my promotion seemed to prove the opposite: she didn't think Levi would promote me if he had even the slightest suspicion.

Maybe so. Maybe Levi had no idea his kidnapped dog was now living with two of his employees whose intimate lives just happened to check off both the lesbian and interracial porn category boxes.

Or maybe my ill-advised spontaneous theft had actually put us in a win/win situation.

That night, as Sabine and I began having celebratory promotion sex, I tried to be mindful of the dog's view. I could tell Sabine was getting a little frustrated with my frequent repositioning. I attempted to make the deviations from our usual routine feel organic, subtle: my ass suddenly tilted into the air instead of grinding against her leg, my back arched, my hair down and loose. I wanted to be as casual as I could in making things more visual. But I noticed that the more I moved, the more still Sabine became. The louder I grew, the quieter she got. I was fine with doing most of the work, though.

"Open your legs for me," I whispered. But when I moved my head between her thighs, she suddenly pinned me there, immobilizing me.

"Hold up," she said. I looked at her and was horrified to see her looking at me, then looking over at the dog on the end of the bed, calculating his line of sight with the position of my splayed ass cheeks. "Oh. God." She released me from her grip and sat up quickly, getting under the bedsheet and pulling it up over her chest, like a stranger was in the room with us. "You're acting for the fucking dog."

I watched her eyes despondently move up to stare at the crown molding at the top of the wall. When Sabine's very angry with me, she stops looking at me. That's how I know when something's resolved to a point of satisfaction: her gaze returns.

"From now on," she finally said, "the dog goes out of the room when we have sex."

I scoffed a little. "But you don't even believe that's happening."

"But you do."

I guess I did more than I didn't. But I tried to downplay it. I was panicking a little. I'd already benefited so much from the dog being there, in just a few days. Why did Sabine need to take it away when things were just getting started?

"I mean, I don't actually, but…I dunno, it's like…a confidence boost for me. Like that book *The Secret*. What's the harm if it's getting results?"

"What was happening just now? Were we having sex, or were you putting on a cam show for our male boss in your head? Because that's sure how it felt to me. And I'm not down for that."

"Sorry," I said. "I thought I was…doing both."

"If you stop talking right now," Sabine generously offered, "I'll try to forget you ever said that."

"You're right," I finally conceded. "No more voyeur dog in the room." Now she turned to me and nodded, her eyes meeting mine. I crawled over and kissed her, which she didn't return but did allow.

"You should talk about this with a therapist," she muttered, half smiling but not joking. I kissed her again.

"Can the therapist watch us have sex?" She laughed and I kept kissing her; finally she turned to me and opened her mouth, drawing me closer, but stopped when my hand began to find her body beneath the sheet.

"I'm not fucking you tonight," she said. "You messed that up."

I nodded. "Can we just make out?"

We kissed until we got tired; as we fell asleep, I could hear the soft, wheezeful sounds of the dog snoring.

※

So the new routine became this: anytime things began to get horny, Sabine would pick up the dog, deposit him in the hallway, and shut the bedroom door.

And if Anish, one of the team coordinators at work, hadn't abruptly resigned the next week to go work for his friend's newly funded incubator, I probably wouldn't have interrupted this system. But suddenly, there was a new opening that would be a significant promotion. And myself and four others were called to a conference room and told we were in the running. Levi would be meeting with each of us individually and making the decision over the course of the next few days.

When I stepped into his office, he gave me a look that felt a bit impatient. "This job would be a big move up," he said. "I can't just give it to you based on potential. You need to show me why it should be yours. I need to see it."

"I understand," I told him. "I hear you."

That night, while Sabine was in the shower, I put the dog inside a box with my laptop. Then I called myself on Facetime from my cell, and hid my phone as best I could behind a plant in the bookshelf across from our bed.

When Sabine came out of the connected bathroom, I was already on the bed naked, waiting for her. I patted the comforter. "Come here," I said. "Door's shut. The dog's out."

"I'm sleepy," she said.

I had an answer for this.

"Then let me give you a massage." Soon my touch began to lightly wander, and after a few minutes she was asking for me inside her; it wasn't long until I was straddled topless over her back, fingering her, licking my lips and looking toward our bookshelf, smiling coyly. It would've worked perfectly were it not for a delivery person, or maybe maintenance; someone in the hallway that suddenly drew the dog's attention and made him bark.

I realized too late I hadn't muted the volume on my phone. He's usually such a quiet dog.

"What was that?" Sabine propped up onto her elbows.

"He's fine, probably someone in the hallway—"

"Stop." The dog barked again, and soon Sabine had shaken me off. She followed the barks straight to the bookshelf, where she found my phone. She looked at it like she was reading a text message from another lover, proof I was cheating, then put the phone down and began getting dressed.

"Sabine…I know you're mad," I tried. "But I really need this. It isn't even real. I'm up for Anish's job, and this helps me feel like…I don't know, I have a competitive edge or something."

"I need space. I'm gonna sleep on the couch."

"Why? This is just an imaginary thing. It's not hurting anybody."

"Did you really just say that to me?"

Now I saw an irate Sabine staring right at me. She'd never done that before. Glowered at me directly. I wasn't sure what it meant. But I didn't have to wonder for long, because then she walked to the living room and shut its sliding partition.

☙

The next day, she was gone before I woke up. At work I tried to get her to glance at me all morning, but she wouldn't. At lunch she disappeared. When I finally caught sight of her again in the afternoon, she still refused to look in my direction.

Before I left work that evening, Levi called me into his office. "I've narrowed it down from five candidates to three," he told me. "You're one of them. But the ideal candidate has to demonstrate creativity. An ability to perform even when there's a curveball. Is that you?"

"I can perform," I promised.

When I got home, Sabine wasn't there, and neither were any of her clothes or toiletries. She must've packed up her things on her lunchbreak. She'd left her key on the counter. I tried calling and texting, but she wouldn't answer.

Before bed, I sat down in front of the dog with my vibrator.

This is what I do at night now. The faster I can get another raise, the faster I can rise in this company, the sooner I can influence Sabine getting promoted, too. And then won't she have to forgive me? Admit I was right?

At work, it's easy to pretend we're still together, because we always had to basically ignore each other during the day. For me, this makes it easier to be patient. I wonder if it has a similar effect on her. And I mean this; this is the truth: if I don't get this next promotion and results continue to elude me on my own…if I have to start occasionally bringing one-night dates home in order to get to the next level…I won't be doing them for my own pleasure. Or for any other reason than to get to a place where Sabine and I can in fact *both* benefit. I know Sabine would disagree with this, so I'll note that, in fairness. Her opinion would be different, but here's mine: If those dates happen, I can honestly argue I'll be doing them for us. And if Sabine wants to stay firm and refuse to share the spoils with me, that's her decision. Of course I'll be heartbroken. But it would be ridiculous to turn this opportunity down.

I've got to hope she'll come around eventually.

OF COURSE, A CURSE

KAYLA KUMARI UPADHYAYA

After years of considering it, of threatening to do it, of so many almosts, Naya finally took matters into her own hands and ended the curse.

She woke up before C, which was easy to do, as C tended to sleep until four, which in winter months meant rarely living in tandem with the sun. C, her night creature, her firefly, as Naya often thought of her.

Naya moved from their bed to the kitchen as if an invisible hand were pushing her, making a puppet of her hollowed-out, hungover body.

On the counter, a hat. *The* hat. Same as it ever was, worn in over time, Naya supposed, but it's hard to notice the erosion of something you see so often, shifts steady but subtle. C's clothes were piled beneath a barstool below the counter. Dried blood on the collar of C's white tee. Naya'd deal with that later. In a way, the bloodsoaked shirt felt less threatening than the hat, which wasn't stained, and even if it was, C would make sure it was scrubbed clean, take it to a dry cleaner if that's what it took. Naya once watched her scrub at it with a wet rag and dish soap, handling the hat as tenderly as advertisement hands washing clean those ducks after oil spills.

Naya had been cooking, and when C hugged her from behind

and buried her face in Naya's nest of hair, sesame oil crackled from the pan and onto the hat. The hat, itself a stain, now stained. And then it wasn't. C worked it back into perfect condition. She had a way with her hands.

Naya picked up the hat before she could overthink. She'd held it in her hands before, often removing it from C's head at the end of the night to hang it on the hook where it lived. It felt somehow lighter than she remembered, though, or perhaps that was the influence of whatever invisible hand was guiding her through these movements, because it couldn't have been just her own. If it was, then why hadn't she done this all sooner?

She got a trash bag from under the sink, bagged the hat, all the while avoiding eye contact with an eyeless thing. She walked with her sack out the apartment door, down the hall, descended two flights of stairs, outside to the alley behind C's building, where she discarded it not in their designated dumpster but in the bin belonging to the barbershop next door. She did it all while trying to blur her vision, unfocusing her sight, as if not seeing her own actions could somehow absolve them.

Naya would like you to consider doing the same now, to let your vision go slack. Come on, you know how. In fact, she'd like you to stop reading altogether.

As she closed the bin, she imagined its other contents. The hat atop a mountain of other people's shorn hair. She dry heaved a bit, her hangover knocking hard against her skull to make itself known. She needed a quick cure. The hat disposal crystallized from an action into a feeling, deep in her stomach, curdling alongside the previous night's poisons. She texted Jade, asked to meet at their brunch spot.

❦

They called it C's cursed hat, because that was what it was. Cursed.

C wore it cocked on her head a little crooked, canted to the left so it framed her frustratingly symmetrical face asymmetrically. *I love this hat*, C said on her third date with Naya, or was it their fourth? Naya couldn't recall. Five years in the past, it felt distant, smudged, like mascara the morning after a late night rimming the ditches of her eyes. She said it early on, is the point. The hat and C, they came into her life almost simultaneously, filling one of the various holes Naya felt she'd been born with.

It was a fine enough hat. Solid sky blue. Flat brimmed.

C did not call it cursed.

Naya and C met on Reddit, which always surprised people to hear. Not even a dating app? Not even Instagram? But no, Naya and C were both desperate for a cyber-cruising option for dykes, and most of the dating apps had done them dirty, even the ones making promises of "Grindr for dykes." But r/lgbthistory, that's where the real freaks were.

Naya and C found each other deep within the annals of a thread on the history of lesbian cruising on New York's Riis Beach. Prior to this, they'd independently discovered it was easier to cruise somewhere where it wasn't the explicit purpose to do so, which made sense, ultimately, as cruising historically took place not just in bathrooms and bars but in unexpected places, too. In-between places. If this is starting to sound like an alternative queer history lesson, it's by design. Naya considers herself a queer archivist and wishes this story to be preserved, so she might remember it as real, and presented to others so as to be educational—but not didactic, never that. C considers herself a patron of archival work.

Naya was a community journalist, covering local queer events and issues for a local LGBTQ+ newspaper funded by C, who was independently wealthy as a result of being the offspring of two liberal landlords, who resided in a different state from C and Naya and therefore made it easier for them to ignore the fact of their existence. The newspaper had a modest circulation, buoyed by the fact it was the only queer print publication left in the state.

C started funding it shortly after her first hookup with Naya, during which Naya accidentally let slip some work talk, which was atypical for her sexual encounters, especially because Naya's preferred mini-kink was being gagged, so there was usually little opportunity for conversation once things really got going. But she'd had a tough day at work. It seemed like the newspaper would close *for good* soon, a threat looming approximately once a month. C had said something like *Well I'm looking to add a media property to my investment portfolio*.

When C started funding the paper, it was never explicitly stated she and Naya would transform their loose and liquid arrangement into something more solid. But they both fell into the relationship the way they always had, like it was an inevitability. Naya was drawn to C's almost cartoon character-like consistency. C was drawn to Naya's tits and hair. They both liked some things about each other and loathed others. They both thought of themselves as *difficult people*, though they weren't always good at explaining why. In gay internet lingo, they might be considered a classic black cat (Naya) for golden retriever (C) couple. They both would hate this description.

☙

The night before Naya disposed of the cursed hat, C punched a man in the teeth. Perhaps we should have mentioned that earlier.

He deserved it, technically, Naya could concede. She just wished literally anyone other than her punch-drunk girlfriend had punched him.

Naya found it difficult to archive C's incidents of explosive anger into a legible record of events.

This was partially on account of also being intoxicated during most of the worst of it. Even when Naya wanted so desperately to remember, she also found it much more comforting to forget. This went against everything she believed about preserving a queer historical record, even if it was silly to apply such logic to an interpersonal scenario.

A few she remembers and their frequency:

C dumping her drink on someone (x4)

C cracking her phone on a table (x2)

C turning the volume all the way up on her car radio (x7ish, this was a favorite)

C throwing a dart at someone, swearing she missed their head on purpose (x1)

C breaking her own finger against a table (x1)

In addition to funding the paper, which was not profitable and likely never would be, and having some sort of "investment portfolio," C had a side hustle.

Everyone C and Naya knew had a side hustle on top of their main hustle, which was usually a podcast of some sort or something else Naya previously would have considered a side hustle. Naya wasn't sure what counted as her main hustle or her side hustle anymore. She spent most of her hours working for the paper, but it barely paid, even with the books more stable since C's investment. Her more lucrative work was making beaded bracelets with nonsensical combinations of words on them that people gobbled up. Things like ANCHOVY FAG and SARDINE DYKE and TUNA SLUT and MOMMY SPIT.

C's side hustle was stealing watches. Or was it the main gig?

She slipped them clean off the wrists of men, usually when they were looking right at her. Like the cursed hat, this skill existed beyond the world Naya knew before C slunk into her life. Even as she watched closely, she couldn't figure out how C did it. She was never caught, not on security footage or by bystanders.

They probably all have watch insurance anyway, C explained. Naya nodded. C knew a guy who knew a guy who knew a guy who moved the watches so they couldn't be traced back to her or their original owners.

It requires careful calculations, C told her.

Naya, apparently incapable of the calculations required to steal watches from the wrists of wealthy white men, instead did calculations of her own. She got very good at counting. Not cards, which would have catapulted their relationship to lesbian heist movie status between the high-end pickpocketing and the card sharking. No, she counted drinks.

In the one to three range, C was usually fine. Maybe a little snarky, that same sardonic humor that drew Naya to her at first. Naya thought perhaps if they'd met another way, not on Reddit while cruising but in a bar, that C was the rare white butch who could have negged her and gotten away with it.

⁕

On the night she punched a man in the teeth, C had had thirteen drinks. It seemed an impossible number. A baker's dozen of drinks. The numerology of it all was cliché; *things going wrong at thirteen*.

Naya blamed the hat, of course. She herself had had four drinks, though two of them were doubles, so did that count as six?

They were celebrating, hence the bevy of beverages. The newspaper—Naya's work for it, specifically—had won an award that came with a research grant that would allow Naya to travel to several LGBTQ archives in the country. Naya intended to use the clout, money, and opportunity the award offered to finally break ground on her lifelong dream project of creating a queer and trans archive built on collaboration, collective mindset, and creativity. Naya saw it as a mixture of historical archives and folklore. People would self-submit their own stories to be included in the archives, and they'd then be sorted into various categories in a complex filing and tagging system that so far was only spelled out in the pages of a spiral notebook Naya kept in her desk drawer.

Sure, Naya could have used some of C's watch theft money to do these archive research trips, but she wanted to earn it herself.

C was not supposed to steal any watches. At drink six, she got twitchy.

You're like whatsherface in Bling Ring, Naya said, a little slurry. *You know. I wanna rooooob.*

She hung her arms around C's neck and ducked under the hat's brim to kiss her. She wanted so badly to remove the hat then. It wasn't invited to her celebration.

Let's do picklebacks, C said. She shrugged out of Naya's arms and pinched her ass on her way to the bar.

When Naya felt a hand on her ass again, she assumed it was C's. But it was a man's. He had a sharp chin and orange-brown eyes. A strange shape of blond wavy hair sat atop his head.

Sorry, he said. *Just trying to get around you.*

She wasn't in the way of anything, wasn't even close to the bar.

Sure, Naya said.

C returned with picklebacks. The guy, who looked like his name might be Craig or Greg, looked at her, looked at Naya, looked back at C, and walked away.

Asshole, C mumbled. She handed Naya two shot glasses, and they clinked and shot in quick succession. C set the empties on a hightop next to them. She suddenly had a tallboy in hand.

How'd you carry all that? Naya asked.

Magic gay hands, C said, winking. She grabbed Naya around the waist and pulled her in. They kissed. C tasted like pickle brine, whiskey, and something herby Naya couldn't identify. Bitter. Naya liked it.

Did that guy have a watch? C asked.

Naya pretended not to hear. This was a bar they frequented with friends. It was on the same block as C's apartment. There were a million reasons why it wasn't right to do it here. Naya looked down and saw a new beer in C's fist. But it wasn't possible. She hadn't left her side.

And then at some point, C did leave her side. Naya busied herself on her phone, sent a blurry selfie to Jade, who was saved as Cecilia in her contacts. Cecilia, her older sister who she did not actually talk to. She didn't even know where she lived. Luckily, C, often eager not to discuss her own family, rarely asked Naya about hers. They both had a habit of introducing themselves as orphans. Sometimes, C took it as far as telling people that's where her money came from: inheritance after a freak accident.

The man reappeared. Naya ignored him. He made it so she couldn't ignore him.

Naya, inebriated, never locked into *exactly* what happened. But the man touched her waist and then her shoulder. C appeared and punched him in the teeth, a tremendous amount of blood exploding on all three of them. Naya didn't know a mouth could bleed that much.

They were kicked out of the bar and threatened with charges. All those watches C had stolen through the years, and they'd never been kicked out of anywhere once.

☙

Jade was already seated outside when Naya arrived at their clandestine brunch spot, a place C would've mocked for attracting lesbian influencer types, the walls of neon and fake greenery screaming *content creation*. C was friends with many a lesbian influencer type.

Naya waved. She slipped her phone out of her pocket to switch it into airplane mode, mad at herself for not doing it sooner. She and C shared locations, under the guise of a safety measure in case C got caught. Really, they just liked to surveil each other.

Naya sat across from Jade and reached for a glass of water on the table. She chugged it.

Late night? Jade asked. She herself didn't look rough at all. Her dark brown hair hit just above her shoulders, always looking as shiny as a shampoo commercial bitch. She wore a green hunting jacket over a tight white crop top and vintage jeans. Naya felt mangy in her presence.

I destroyed the hat, Naya said. She hadn't been planning to tell Jade, but it felt right. They were the two people who'd decided the hat was cursed in the first place, the only people who ever talked about it.

What? Jade asked. *I ordered chilaquiles for us to split.*

Jade had a habit of ordering for the table.

Theeeee hat, I destroyed it. Or not destroyed, but I threw it away. In the trash, Naya explained.

Does C know? Jade asked.

A server with nails filed to sharp points dropped the chilaquiles on their table and hurried away. The patio was packed. Naya found it difficult to filter out all the background sound. Her head thrummed. She reached for Jade's Diet Coke and sipped from it.

Of course not, she said.

She'll be mad, Jade said.

To put it lightly.
Why though?
Naya shrugged. *Thought it might end the curse?*
Throwing things in the trash doesn't usually do that. You could have called up my superstitious Persian mother if you really wanted a curse consultation.
This is serious.
I'm being serious! Also you look like ass.
Thanks, babe.
Naya's phone buzzed. She startled. Hadn't she put it on airplane mode?
A text, from C: *going to Bex's if you wanna meet later*
Naya toggled on airplane mode again. For the first time? She could have sworn she'd already done it.
What's that?
Nothing, just C. She's going to Beeeeexxxxx's. Naya drew out the name while rolling her eyes, and Jade laughed.
She still dating—
Lucia, yeah, I think so.
Of the many things Naya and Jade shared, aggravation with Bex was one of them. C often ingratiated herself with a crew of femmes who insisted they weren't femmes because they wore expensive patterned women's suits from a trendy queer-owned brand and minimal makeup. Bex was their quasi-leader. She was a photographer and a podcaster, but again, it was difficult to parse which was the main gig and which was the side hustle. C, a proper butch in Naya's eyes, had known Bex et al since everyone's closeted Tumblr days.
Gonna go? Jade asked.
Fuck no. Naya crunched the side of her fork against the chilaquiles and scooped some into her mouth. *Well, I don't know, maybe.*
Bex's impromptu day parties usually took place in her backyard,

which had a pool. A pool sounded like an ideal phase two to Naya's hangover treatment. She ate more of the chilaquiles and could feel phase one settling in. Jade ordered another soda for herself, conceding the first to Naya silently.

The text was a good sign. If C had noticed her missing hat, she would have asked about it. Maybe she was drunk enough the night before to feel hazy on whether the hat made it back. Did she even remember punching the man? Naya felt a sudden surge of hope cresting over the curdled mix of shame and sadness she always felt during her worst hangovers.

☙

C's cartoon-character-like consistency encompassed her appearance. The symmetrical face, yes, but also her uniform. C's butch uniform: 100% denim jeans (no stretch, custom made perfectly to fit her by a seamstress ex. It puzzled Naya how C was somehow on good terms with, in fact, her only ex, perhaps because C was a good client, simple as that) and a white T-shirt. Just a plain white tee, but it always was, of course, designer. This bemused, maybe even embarrassed Naya at first and then, later, when she found herself absorbing some of C's more snobbish attitudes, became a point of emulation.

Jeans, overpriced white T-shirt that fit like a glove, and a hat.

The hat was the one thing she liked to switch up, to a degree. Always a flat brim, none of them repping sports teams, because C found sports mundane and emblematic of something wrong with society. Paradoxically, she did enjoy sports betting occasionally. She had about three dozen hats, all organized by color in a custom built-in drawer in her walk-in closet, though not in a rainbow pattern, as C and Naya both found rainbow shit remarkably corny.

The cursed one, though, went on a hook by the front door, too powerful to sleep in a drawer. She wore it when she was feeling celebratory or when she was feeling confident or when she was feeling horny or when she was feeling adventurous or, who is Naya kidding, there is no algorithm or calculation to perfectly predict when C would wear the cursed hat. Curses are constant but not necessarily consistent. Curses, like we all do, have their origins, sometimes difficult to trace. Curses are everywhere if you pay attention.

She was wearing the full uniform, cursed hat and all, when she punched the man in the bar.

Of course she was.

☙

C would like it known she feels incompletely rendered in this telling of what happened. She feels like you might not actually get to know her based on what's presented here. But then again, she was the one who insisted upon being referred to, vaguely, as C.

☙

Do you think she knows? Naya asked Jade.

They'd finished brunch and were sitting in Jade's car in her apartment's parking garage, the engine cut and Naya wearing sunglasses despite the darkness.

About the hat? Jade asked.

About all this, Naya said, waving her hands around. She brought them down too hard on the dash and regretted it. Jade flinched.

You'd know if she did, Jade said.

☙

Of the many things Naya and Jade shared, C was one of them. Jade was C's ex-girlfriend, and shortly after Naya started seeing C, she received a strange DM from a woman she'd never met asking her to brunch to discuss something. It was Jade, warning Naya about C's alcohol-induced rage over vanilla creme French toast. The warning went unheeded, but Naya and Jade found something else instead. A point of connection over the cursed hat. A shared if complicated love for C, who Jade was no-contact with, but it was clear she got *something* out of hearing Naya talk about her, perhaps still in love with her despite despite despite.

After the initial warning, she never told Naya to leave C again.

Of the many things Naya and Jade shared, a special interest in queer history was one of them. Yes, Naya and C were also jointly interested in queer history, as evidenced by their partnership on the newspaper, but this was different. It was distinctly sexual. Naya and Jade were turned on by tales of homo past, especially ephemera like newsletters and journal entries and fliers and personals posted in radical lesbian zines circulated by hand decades ago.

Jade collected these ephemera, a hobby she was able to build out robustly when dating C and benefiting from her enterprises. Now, her collection was self-funded. Naya and Jade were quite literally aroused by these collectibles, by visiting a queer way of being they weren't quite sure how to embody in the digital age they existed in. It's not that they wanted to *return* to the past; they weren't inane white girls romanticizing previous decades and wishing for time travel. But they did want to reconstruct something(s) lost that they weren't totally sure how to put into words. They felt it any time they read about the ghosts of lesbians past.

This was how their arrangement went: Jade would sit on her vegan leather couch, *purchased with blood money*, as Jade put it, which meant C bought it. Naya would lay on the floor. Jade read from her lesbian ephemera collection while Naya fucked herself with her fingers, prone on the patchwork rug. Jade read, and she watched. And that was it. Sometimes they had brunch.

Naya rationalized it all, because they never kissed, never touched during the ritual.

She knew, if the roles were reversed, she'd stab C for the betrayal.

☙

Back in the car, it was getting hot without the air conditioning. *Well?* Jade asked.

Well, Naya said. She took her sunglasses off and placed them on Jade's dash. She closed her eyes and pictured the hat in the trash again. They got out of the car and went up to Jade's.

☙

On a whim, Naya one night asked why C only stole from men, was it something to do with feminism?

She was joking, and C snorted. One of the things Naya liked about C was that she always knew when she was joking. She couldn't say the same for a few of her exes.

The first part of the question was genuine. Why men?

They're caught between ignoring me and trying to figure out what my whole deal is, C said.

It was like the fact of her butchness rendered her both invisible and a threat to them. It was disarming *and* protective.

Sounds like it's gotten too easy, Naya teased. She bit C's wrist, where a watch might go, but C wasn't wearing a watch.

Yeah? C asked. She kissed Naya and bit her lip. Naya bit her back.

Maybe you should try women, Naya said.
That what you say to all the straight girls you hit on?
Tennis bracelets instead of watches.
Okay. Tonight.

☙

Later, at a poolside bar where C had already scored a couple watches a few months before, they were indeed surrounded by women in tennis bracelets. These were the kinds of places—places where women wear tennis bracelets—C and Naya hit up when C had an itch or when they needed money, much of which they spent going out to places like this, places where women wear tennis bracelets. They were unlikely to run into any friends here.

C spent the night talking to beautiful women. Naya watched. In wild oscillations, she cycled between being turned on, jealous of the women, jealous of C, annoyed, bored. She stewed while chewing the straw to her spritz. One woman touched the brim of C's cursed hat, and Naya hoped it meant she'd lose her house in a climate-crisis-induced mudslide. She ordered another spritz. The sun was setting, and everyone looked awash in a devilish glow. This was all a big waste of time.

But it wasn't. At the end of the night, back at home, C pulled a fistful of delicate diamond bracelets out of her jacket pocket. She piled the shiny tendrils on the kitchen bar's countertop, and Naya couldn't hide her surprise.

What? C asked, grinning.
I assumed it wasn't working.
Why?
Those women didn't look through you the way the men do.
Come on, Nay, put it together.

Naya picked up one bracelet. She'd later Google it and balk at its price, wonder what she was still doing working at a community newspaper when she could be living on an island somewhere. No, no, community journalism, the dream archives project, these were her passions. There were so many stories that had to be written down. Don't you see? Even this one.

She knew it was as simple as the women flirting with C and C flirting back. It was actually their devout attention that made it easy for C to rob them, unlike the men and their stupor in the face of a woman who doesn't fit their idea of how a woman should be.

They could feel me on their wrists, and they still let me slide 'em right off, C said, apparently not content to leave it unsaid.

No more women, Naya said. It wasn't often she said no to C or to anyone.

Why?

I was bored. Alone.

You're jealous?

Probably. You'd be!

You want to put one on, don't you?

Put what?

A bracelet. You want to feel like them.

Naya bristled. *The bracelets are ugly, stupid status symbols. They look like something a little girl would wear.*

Too radical and grown for a diamond bracelet?

That's not what I said. They're garish.

I think you want to try.

I don't.

You do.

I don't.

You do.

She did. But she didn't want to admit it. Something about the cursed hat and the look in C's eyes and an echo deep in her mind: *seven*, the number of drinks C'd had. Its echo spelled out rather than in digits, which made the repetition more sinister.

C gripped Naya's wrist not gently, in a way Naya would have welcomed in another context, on another night, when *seven* wasn't looped in her mind, serpentine and sure. Naya briefly attempted to pull her wrist away before letting it go slack. C fastened a bracelet to it and walked away.

Naya fell asleep wearing the bracelet, twenty-seven diamonds lined up like teeth. When she woke up, it was gone. But she still felt its marks on her skin.

☙

After Jade dropped her back off at her car, Naya drove to Bex's house in silence. Everything on the radio sounded wrong, warped. She rolled down the window, rolled it back up. She wished she could make her life into a silent movie.

When she got to Bex's, she parked and sat. She wished she were back at Jade's, but Jade had seemed suddenly uneasy in her own home. Perhaps she was thinking about the hat, too. Perhaps Naya really had fucked it up even more. Could a curse become *more cursed?*

She got out. On the curb, she could hear laughter projecting from Bex's backyard and, from someone, sharp screams that probably only meant someone had shared a particularly juicy bit of gossip with the group. She unlatched the plastic gate, suddenly wishing she'd brought something, a bottle of wine perhaps.

The sun was bright, but it would set soon. She'd left her sunglasses in Jade's car, so she cupped her palm over her eyes and squinted at the group coming into focus.

C beamed as she turned to her, all evidence of the previous

night's violence erased. A new white shirt, no blood.

Naya felt all of her insides clench, but she did not stop walking.

Sitting on top of C's head was the hat.

The cursed hat. Resurrected. Reanimated.

No, extracted from the trash can by C, Naya told herself, afraid.

There she is, said C, as if they'd all been waiting for her entrance.

Your hat, Naya said.

C looked genuinely confused. *Hat?*

Help yourself to drinks over there, Bex said, though she didn't point anywhere.

It's your hat, Naya said again.

My lucky hat? C asked. *What about it?*

The group laughed, bright white teeth shining in the sun.

WILD AND BLUE

AURORA MATTIA

Peach and Sandy were giggling, speeding down the highway in a powderblue Ford Thunderbird at ninety miles an hour.

—I feel like Adriana La Fucking Cerva, bitch.

Coffin-cut pink acrylics clutching the steering wheel lightly, she turned toward Sandy, smacked her Dubble Bubble, then struck a pose (sex eyes, Duck lips).

—Like, get me some snakeskin, bitch!

Tossing her head back, so that the iridescent sequin glued to her upper cheekbone caught the light and glinted:

—Like, Christophaaaa!

Outside the desert was almost past dusk. The air was grainy as a photograph. Sandy held out a vial full of silver powder, into which Peach, without even looking, dipped her pinkie nail.

☙

Later they were in Room 19 at the Eve's Garden off Highway 90. They took no Adderall, drank no liquor, smoked no cigarettes. The ashtrays were empty; the bedside glasses shrink-wrapped. Peach and Sandy were happy. Happier than they'd felt their entire lives, wondering how they'd never felt like this before—wondering why there had been so few nights like this, wondering if it was possible for every night to feel like this? As if their minds had been formed by wonder instead of fear, had been restructured, in one night, in a matter of hours, in a matter of minutes, upon a trellis of pleasure. Because they were worried about nothing, didn't have an anxious thought in their minds, not her and not him, not one thousand and not even one, and in fact felt what Peach always imagined people meant when they said 'at home in the world,' so she took Sandy's face in her hands and wiped away his tears while her own mascara ran down her face.

For some time they didn't speak. Cars rolled by out the window like water. A highway is another way to outrun time. Peach was singing "Silent Night," like this:

—All was calm, all was bright.

And Sandy thought no holy Mother could match her beauty, which was like experiencing a myth in real time. Her lashes, thickened and multiplied by mascara, were like a sunburst, but as if a shadow—as if darkness produced its own glow. Looking into her eyes, he felt like he was falling into another dimension. And the ribbons in her hair, resting lightly on either side of her neck like the petals of a ghost orchid (he had seen photographs on Google, had searched late at night, with his laptop on his chest, 'orchid species,' because he thought maybe if he saw something so strange and alluring just before his eyes closed, then his dreams might be different, might approach heaven): so, the ribbons in her hair, the sense of god haunting the air around her head; the sudden and oscillating depths of her eyes, transparent green tunnels opening and closing like valves, like halls of chlorophyll—

and for both of them, the motel curtains (some polyester imitation of organza, stained and riddled with snags) were as mysterious as a waterfall; both of them were shrouded in its mist, so lightly blue like the descent of a manta ray. And the ceiling (stippled stucco from the seventies) felt ancient, as hallowed as a backwater chapel adrift in a field of gnarled orange trees, heavy with the memory of fruit.

They took a bath together, giggling among bubbles. He ran his hands over her slick breasts. His cock swayed slowly underwater, like a memory of a flower. She thought she saw a string of pearls around his neck, but without a string: just floating together, centimeters apart, levitating above his collarbones. But then it disappeared. Then it disappeared, goodbye…and she saw the cowboy renting a room in the dim recesses of a saloon; the cowboy now lounging in his clapboard tub, rolling a cigarette with a corn husk. So of course she saw herself running away with that man from out of town, the man with a slim scar on his face, riding a speckled stallion, shrouded in a sandstorm—glittering, full of faces, illusions of faces that he carried like a deck of cards, cards made of sand, as elusive as sand, dissolving into the storm he carried with him from town to town, from day to night, from desert to horizon…

Sandy was a man and Peach was a woman, it was so simple. Forever they were a man and a woman, like silhouettes on a high cliff. For a moment it was as simple as 'forever they were a man and a woman, like silhouettes on a high cliff.' For a moment Peach forgot her own name. She felt as glamorous as a woman with memories only of Spring, only of honeysuckles rank and bursting like declarations of love from the vines, as she strolled through the dusk and bells rang and rippled the stillness of the pond in the depths of her mind…

Then came more grain: he was a cowboy (rakish, hair falling into his face, eyes for no one but me) and she was the woman with the torn pink dress, who tore her dress in the creosote brambles, who stole a horse, a blue-haunched mare, from the ranch of another man, a wealthy German stallion breeder with cold blue eyes and the halitosis he attempted to cover with rosewater, which made it all the worse, and who had laughed and laughed at her, because the drug was fading—

she was remembering the man at the little dive bar off the highway where she'd stopped with Sandy that afternoon, laughing because he'd looked at the driver's license, which had said she was a man (she, Peach), which the man, the bartender, thought was so funny because it made sense after all, why else would a woman have such enormous tits, such enormous tits and a voice that didn't quite make sense, a voice that sounded just slightly off-key coming from that face, hers, which he, in an instant, having just imagined slapping it with his cock, now thought ridiculous—

she was remembering (was feeling her fantasy tempered by a blush of rot) because the drug was fading, felt Peach (felt Sandy, too, who suddenly remembered the pearls he sometimes felt levitating around his neck, the pearls he had wanted to forget), the drug, the silver powder which they had stolen together, three days earlier, from the summer ranch of the pharmaceutical mogul who was planning to release it to market, pending FDA approval, as Dysphorable™.

☙

There was one lamp in the room, the type of lamp which no memory would hold. It was hard to notice even when you sat beside it. There was an air conditioner, and a carpet with a pattern. Peach and Sandy lay side by side in bed on top of a brownish floral quilt.

She was beginning to have trouble sensing her own beauty. Her hands seemed suddenly huge, as if her fingers were swelling; her wrists, too, had thickened—they looked like her father's. She winced; felt a contraction of shame, which reached down into her gut like a dry retch. It was an emptiness so profound she couldn't bear to accept it. She flipped open her clamshell pocket mirror. Her chin was too big; her brow ridge too thick; her eyes sunken and sullen. She was a mistake. She was a mistake and it was too late. It was all too late. The air was feeling almost computer-generated, as if it had never held life. Peach was choking on her own breath.

And then her body—which she hadn't seen, because rising from the bath minutes before, she had known better than to look in the mirror—then her body (do you hear me, God?) then her body was no longer the body of—well, of what her body imagined to be the body of a woman. Proprioception split open. Her ribcage was expanding, was prying apart; her shoulders were like great blocks of stone; her head was the head of an enormous baby. Peach was horrified to be buried alive in her own body, buried alive and there was no way out. Help me, I'm suffocating. Help me, please…

Sandy still thought Peach was beautiful, but now her beauty troubled him, made him ache. He wanted it for himself. She was like a disturbance in his mind. When he loved her he did not know who he was. Once, long ago, they had been 'boyfriends' together. They hadn't spoken for years and he had forgotten the violence of wanting to be beautiful. He had simply chased after men who allowed him to pretend that he was only seeking a hot rush of horror, the horror of being alive, of the disgusting fact of pleasure—the totality of degradation. But he had grown tired, too. And the more tired he felt, the brighter the pearls became. The pearls buzzed to life. They glowed with their own light. He needed a means to dim them without destroying himself.

And then one of the men had happened to be a pharmaceutical mogul.

And Peach had always been so skilled at picking locks.

So one week ago he had called her from a payphone. It was good to hear her voice.

☙

Peach was catatonic, staring at the ceiling. Sandy sat up:
—Should we take a little more?
After a while, she replied:
—What are the side effects?
—He didn't say.
—A little more then.

☙

When they woke, they woke with dread. Sandy immediately reached for the vial. Peach dipped another pinkie in the dust. Then everything lustered.

—I love you, baby, he said, kissing her on the forehead.

They were headed for Southern California, where Peach's older sister lived in a small cabin up in the mountains. But before they left Texas, she wanted one last chicken fried steak. As she assessed her outfit in the mirror, striking one pose and then another, she kept muttering,

—Diva at the diner, steak and a Shiner,

in a half-whispered singsong. After tying a handkerchief in a yellow bow around her neck, she patted the pockets of her blue jeans, before realizing she couldn't remember where she'd put the car keys.

—Sugar, have you seen my keys?

But Sandy was realizing he couldn't remember where he'd left his money clip—his grandfather's, wrought from silver and inset with a coldwater agate, the birthstone they'd shared—which, for ten years, he'd always placed on the bedside table each night before he slept. All their cash was rolled up into it. Sandy lifted the mattress and Peach opened all the drawers; Sandy spilled their suitcases and Peach ripped apart the curtains.

—Car's gone.

—No way.

—Gone.

She swung the door wide and sprinted into the lot. Sandy slumped in the doorway, lifting the vial from his breast pocket as Peach rounded the corner of the motel. He tapped some powder into his palm and pinched a bump between his forefinger and thumb. He nodded to an older man in snakeskin boots slow-stepping toward the ice machine. He lit a Marlboro Gold. Then he took a deep breath. Everything would work out. Peach probably had some jewelry they could pawn, and he'd seen her hotwire a car once outside a Target in Abilene. But he was startled awake when the Thunderbird came roaring back around the corner—blue like an act of God—before screeching to a halt in front of him, the air smelling of Hermès and burnt tires, Peach spritzing herself with Eau de Merveilles, dusting her cheeks with blush, yelling,

—We left the goddamn keys in the goddamn ignition,

before tossing the money clip through the window.

—Get in, cowboy.

❧

At the diner Sandy ate two strips of bacon with a side of fried okra. Peach had the best chicken fried steak of her life—crispy, sunk in gravy, sprinkled with fresh diced serranos—and a Dr. Pepper. "Always on My Mind" was playing on the jukebox. When she went to the restroom to reapply her crimson lipstick, he dissolved a heap of silver powder in his coffee. (In the bathroom, tracing her famous cupid's bow, she thought, 'I am the woman in the story I wrote in my head, before I ever knew I was writing a story. I am the woman in the story about love.' Because he had come back, he had come back, and no one could ever say again that he did not love her. He loved her so much that he would even love a woman. He had broken the only law of his desire because he respected the mystery, the inviolable mystery of her face, in which shards, almost runic, of the boy he'd once known remained, glinting like mica, emanating the aura of certain dusks in certain meadows, without disclosing its source—as if these shards were proof of lost time, enshrined and protected by the face of the beautiful woman in which they had been inlaid, as if within a reliquary.) And when she came back, he was pale and wide-eyed, with shaking hands:

—Peach…

—Are you okay?

She slid down into the red Formica booth, taking his hands in hers.

—Hey, are you okay?

—How did we get here?

—What do you mean?

—I mean how the fuck are we at a highway diner in Pecos, Texas.

Now she noticed the vial, next to his coffee cup, on the table and in plain sight. At least a quarter of the powder was missing.

—Baby, she said. Baby, what did you do?

For a moment he met her gaze, shaking his head.

—You are so beautiful.

Tears welled in his eyes. He glanced out the window, blinking.

—What did you do, Sandy?

—The last thing I remember…the last thing I remember is climbing out the window at the Pederson ranch, he said, then glanced back at her, stifling a sob:

—I'm scared, Peachy.

—Hey, she said.

(Quickly, quietly, she slipped the vial into her mother-of-pearl clutch.)

—Hey, look at me, she said, wiping away his tears delicately with the sides of her thumbs, careful with her long pink acrylics:

—When is my birthday?

—I don't remember.

It hurt, it hurt like the beginning of a panic, but she couldn't let it. They were in public. She was a woman in public and she could not panic, so she said:

—Yes you do. What season was it when we first met?

—Autumn. The leaves were on the ground.

—And where did we meet?

—At a party. A house party in Hyde Park.

—Whose party?

—Yours. Your birthday.

—But I didn't know you.

—A boy invited me. But he got drunk too fast and kept telling the same joke, so I went to the backyard to smoke.

—And what did you say, when you walked up to me?

But at that moment they were interrupted by the details of a 'developing story' playing from a handheld radio on the bar counter:

—Police are investigating a robbery at the private ranch of Kevin Pederson, CEO of AmenaCorp, involving an experimental drug, which, the company warned in a press release, is, in its uncatalyzed state, dangerous for public consumption…the suspects…are still at large, but investigators believe they may be hiding out in…

Peach tilted her head, like *let's get out of here.*

—I'll explain everything on the way, she said.

Sandy left cash on the table.

☙

(The waitress had heard the radio and seen the vial of powder, but said nothing to anyone. 'Good luck,' she thought. Later that night, she spent the cash on a few rounds of tequila Red Bulls for herself and her friends and then went home with a man who fucked her well and knew all the words to "At My Window.")

⁂

That night they checked in at a motel in Tucson. Despite a harrowing day of driving—paranoid about Pederson's pigs and both of them in withdrawal, chainsmoking Sandy's Golds, passing a bottle of Jimador back and forth—his lost memories hadn't come back. Peach felt grotesque, sweating her blush off and embarrassed of every word she spoke, like God was subjecting her to her own reverb. She wanted, at the very least, to feel beautiful; at the very least on this last ride, which would never be repeated, she wanted to feel beautiful so she could relax enough to experience a romance while it was happening, rather than in retrospect, rather than losing the instants to her fear that from this or that angle, Sandy would think she looked like a man, which would ruin his love for her once and for all, because she had failed to maintain in every second and from every angle the necessary proof of her womanhood, because if she looked like a man even once, she thought, he would never entirely see her as a woman again, because no matter how beautiful she became, he would never forget the moment when he first glimpsed—with, she imagined, a kind of disgusted pity—the man-failure counterfeiting himself as a woman, humiliatingly, named Peach.

Meanwhile Sandy, who felt a string of pearls clutching his neck, choking him, couldn't stop thinking about the silver powder, which Peach had forsworn the moment she realized that it would steal her memories, because:

—Above all, I don't want to forget you.

And in a motel in Tucson, he promised, crying, his forehead against her forehead, his lips against her lips, never to touch it again:

—I want you to be my wife…

She fell asleep in his arms, while he whispered a plan:

They would mail the vial anonymously back to Pederson, then detour for Las Vegas and get married in a little chapel full of fake flowers, with a faux-Roman fountain spouting water so aquamarine it would seem like liquid candy. And then they would go drink martinis on the top floor of a fancy hotel.

❧

In the morning, Peach woke first. She stared at Sandy's sleeping face, brushed his wavy brown hair behind his ear. She was a woman. It was so simple. She was a woman because she was in love. It could be enough. One day it could be enough because she was a woman and it didn't matter if Sandy was a man or a woman or some kind of secret thing. She was Sandy's woman and it was enough.

—Good morning, baby, she said.

He yawned, blinking.

He opened his eyes.

For a moment he was confused.

Then, struck with terror.

He leapt backward off the bed.

—What the fuck, he said.

—What?

—What the fuck?

—Sandy, what's going on?

—Who are you?

—No.

—Who the fuck are you?
—No. Sandy, look at me.
—Stop saying my name.
—Please. Please, baby. Not like this.
He was moving wildly, grabbing his clothes from the floor.
—Please, Sandy. Please.
She reached out for him, but he stepped back.
—Stay the fuck away from me.
—We're getting married today.
—You're insane.

He took his money clip from the nightstand and slipped it in his pocket.
—Sandy, wait.
He wedged his feet into his shoes without tying the laces.
—Sandy, she said.
He headed for the door.
—That night, she said. When you walked up to me, in the backyard of the house in Hyde Park, what did you say?

(You are as pretty, he'd said, as a peach.)

[Austin, Texas, April 1, 2024]

BAD DOG

ANNA DORN

I HAD A HABIT of digging my nails into my palm whenever Lex spoke.

Lex was my twin sister Poppy's fiancée as of two weeks ago. Lex was insufferable before, but unbearable now that she was "part of the family," as my dad had disgustingly said only a few minutes ago.

We were all seated at a brightly lit New American restaurant, our first dinner as a family since the "big engagement." My parents took Lex and Poppy out for dinner right after Lex popped the question, but I'd been ill that night. Or, I said I was ill. I had no physical symptoms but strong psychological ones. Self-harming urges, sadistic impulses. But when they asked me to dinner a second time, just a few nights after I'd told them I was feeling "much better," and when they knew I didn't have many friends and therefore had no other plans, I felt compelled to join.

I prepared by chewing a pack of nicotine gum on the way to the restaurant. My parents and I lived in the Valley, but we always had to go to Santa Monica where Lex and Poppy lived because Lex refused to drive on the freeway "for environmental reasons." She was insufferable. Did I already say that? Right now, I was glaring at her while she monologued about the same dumb bullshit.

"We always say there are no bad dogs," she said. "Only bad owners."

I'd heard Lex say this exact sentence upwards of five times, and each time she smiled so smugly, as though it was the most original and insightful thing a person had ever said. And my sister and my parents smiled, too, seeming impressed, as though the idea that there were no bad dogs wasn't legitimately inane, as though their firstborn daughter—me—wasn't attacked and seriously disfigured by a *bad dog*.

That bad dog literally ruined my life.

Amber was her name. A deceptively docile name for such a ruthless creature. To this day, I blame everything bad that has happened to me on that dog bite. It was my *Sliding Doors* moment.

In case you aren't familiar, *Sliding Doors* is a 1998 romcom in which Gwyneth Paltrow plays a fancy London ad exec who almost misses her train and the narrative splits, following alternate timelines, one if she made the train and one if she didn't. In the first scenario, she arrives home early to find her boyfriend with another woman. It's a bummer at first, but then she dumps the boyfriend and vastly improves her life. In the second scenario, she arrives after the woman has left and gradually becomes suspicious and miserable.

I was stuck in a second scenario of my own.

The day Amber bit me, Poppy had asked me to jump on the trampoline with her. We'd just gotten the trampoline for our twelfth birthday after begging our parents for it for years. I was about to go outside with Poppy that afternoon when I heard the ice cream truck. I really wanted a rocket pop. It was so hot in the Valley in August. Sweat rolled from my armpit and onto my forearm. I asked Poppy to come with me, but she was already in the backyard, jumping her heart out, and she couldn't hear me when I called.

So I went out to the ice cream truck alone with two quarters from my allowance in my palm. There was no line. I was so excited. I ran up to the truck, euphoric, and just as I was about to ask the nice man for my delicious frozen treat, an unleashed pit bull—Amber—appeared out of nowhere and tackled me.

It happened so fast. I don't remember if I screamed. I think I blacked out or was in shock. I came to in St. Joseph's Hospital with seventeen stitches on my face. I still have a scar. Some people say the scar is "badass." I think it makes me look insane.

Every day I wish I had gone on the trampoline with Poppy that afternoon. Sliding door one, the obviously correct door, the right option that would have taken my life on a completely different and more positive trajectory. In that version of my life, I would have had a lovely afternoon with my sister. I never would have gotten an ugly scar that runs from my jaw to my cheek. I never would have felt like a social outcast and never would have started hanging out with the stoners in middle school, never would have started smoking weed daily, certainly never would have started taking swigs of vodka or Robitussin before class.

If I'd taken sliding door one, like I should have, I would have been popular like Poppy. We would have remained in the same friend group and gotten the same straight-A grades and been on the same sports teams. We would have both gotten lacrosse scholarships to Stanford, where we both would have majored in engineering, leading to high-paying jobs in tech upon graduation.

I would not have nearly failed out of high school, then actually failed out of community college, then gone to rehab shortly thereafter for alcohol and cocaine abuse. I would not have replaced my drug and alcohol addiction with a nicotine and shoplifting addiction, and definitely would not have started drinking again not long after taking up shoplifting, would not have found the combo of whiskey and petty theft irresistible.

In sliding door one, I would have gone to college out of state, or at least outside of the San Fernando Valley, would not have lived with my parents until I was twenty-eight, when they finally kicked me out. I would not have worked at Bloomingdale's at the Westfield Mall and I definitely would not have gotten fired from said Bloomingdale's for shoplifting Chanel bronzer. I would not currently be a hostess at Casa Vega Mexican restaurant in Sherman Oaks, where I routinely get margaritas spilled on me and recently got thrown up on.

I cannot stress this enough: That dog ruined my entire fucking life.

And now my twin sister, with whom I'd become estranged since Amber bit me and ruined everything, was engaged to a woman who ran an organization that rescued pit bulls from dogfighting rings and allegedly rehabilitated them to be adopted by bougie families.

Lex's organization was called Good Dog.

I hated it. Hated her.

Hated her face, which was round and huge and stricken with rosacea, and her mouth, in which her gums were eerily prominent. Hated her astounding level of confidence, the way she spoke as though her words carried so much gravitas, as though she wasn't just some average adult spoiled rotten by her movie producer daddy. I hated the shape of her body, short and muscular like the terrible dogs she loved so much.

Poppy's decision to marry such a person, an advocate for my oppressor, felt like a very pronounced *fuck you*.

And my parents' decision to embrace such a person for Poppy felt like the clearest indication that they preferred Poppy, among many other very clear indications. Such as their elated faces when she entered a room, the way their voices ticked up in pitch when they said her name, whereas when they said my name, it was always *Iris* in the tone of a coroner announcing a body was dead on arrival.

I looked up from my lap and everyone was staring at me, perhaps waiting for me to validate Lex's statement.

I cleared my throat. "The pit bull who attacked me had nice owners," I said, as I'd said the last time, and the time before that. "I think there was something wrong with the dog's brain." I sipped my Shirley Temple—my family didn't know I was back on the sauce—then looked Lex right in her fugly mud-colored eyes. "I think she was just a...you know...bad dog."

Lex shook her head, and before she could say anything else, I put my hand up and excused myself to the bathroom. On the toilet, I vaped and looked at my phone. For a second I wished I had friends, but I really didn't want that. I just wanted someone to make me feel different from the way my family made me feel, which was like a tragic loser.

Desperate, I texted my on-and-off girlfriend Crystal. She was a dancer (exotic) who wore body-con dresses and clip-on hair extensions and smelled like cheap perfume and menthol cigarettes. She broke up with me after I cheated on her. I cheated on everyone, it wasn't personal. I blame the dog.

Hi honey, I texted Crystal, like a creep.

I saw her typing, then stop typing. I flushed. I got up and examined both stalls for anything someone might have left behind: a wallet, a gold bracelet fallen to the floor, an expensive lip gloss discarded by the sink. But the bathroom was spotless. Washing my hands, I avoided my cursed reflection. I didn't need to see it to know what was there: unwashed auburn hair, shoplifted YSL eyeliner smudged around my eyes, ten-year-old American Apparel dress stained with salsa.

The bathroom door opened, and I jumped, spilling water on myself. I recognized the face of the person who entered, as it was my same face. Just cleaner, more hydrated, treated with a twelve-step skincare regimen and Botox and whatever else bougie people who work in tech do to look ten years younger than they actually are. Her hair was blown dry into a silky long bob, a "lob" if you will. Poppy had rejected her natural hair texture, *our* texture, for as long as I could remember, which felt like one of her many rejections.

"Iris," my twin said, in that same coroner voice my whole family used when addressing me. "Behave yourself," she hissed.

Poppy had been so mean to me since Amber bit me, everyone had.

"Sorry," I mumbled while Poppy walked into the stall.

A text from Crystal popped up on my phone.

Fuck off, it said.

☙

The rest of the dinner felt like torture akin to being waterboarded, until Poppy said she was going on a meditation retreat.

When she first mentioned the retreat, I instinctively began to zone out, the way I typically did when someone mentioned any branch of woo-woo Californian culture (see also: reiki, tarot, astrology, crystals…). But I snapped back in when Poppy said she wouldn't have a phone and that she'd be gone for two days. Lex was whining, making a gross pouty face that activated her rosacea. She said she wouldn't be able to survive without Poppy for two days, and my family members made sounds revealing they found this *so cute* and not an obvious indication of toxic codependency, which it most definitely was.

But I got an idea.

A great one at that.

In the reflection of my locked phone screen on the table, I saw my disgusted expression morph into a smile.

☙

I hadn't pretended to be Poppy in years.

It would be harder now, for sure.

She worked out, did Pilates, got expensive skin treatments. But we had the same face.

We were once a single egg in our mother's womb, split in two.

I could easily become her.

I started preparing almost immediately. Poppy was leaving in ten days. I shoplifted a kitten calendar from CVS and pasted it on my bedroom wall just to cross out the days. I jacked a spiral notebook too, and new pens, to document my plans. It felt good to have a goal. I couldn't remember the last time I had one, other than basic needs like making rent and feeding myself and getting laid. But now I had all these extracurricular tasks to accomplish.

I needed to push away Lex, as Poppy. I wasn't sure exactly how this was going to happen, but I'd been alienating people my entire life. I knew if I could just get myself in that house, looking like Poppy and acting like myself, Lex would be gone before the real Poppy returned.

How to lose a girl in forty-eight hours.

But first, I needed to become Poppy.

So I went from gym to gym in the Valley, collecting one-day free memberships and trying out their personal training services, fooling them into thinking I was planning to join. During my first session, I threw up in the first five minutes. But I didn't give up. Poppy and I were naturally athletic. I hated working out, but when I did, I gained muscle definition very quickly. And I carried no excess weight due to my nicotine addiction.

I quit nicotine in preparation to be Poppy. I quit soda and alcohol, too. I drank large amounts of water and exposed my skin to the sunlight in short, timed intervals. I needed to glow. I flirted with a butch dermatologist I'd met at work until she agreed to inject botulism toxin into my forehead for free. I cut my hair into Poppy's exact long bob, a haircut I absolutely hated, but if I was going to do this job, I needed to do it right.

Crystal came over on day eight.

"What the fuck did you do to yourself?" she asked. "You look like my high school principal."

Her menthol scent caused me to drool.

I thought about telling her the truth about why I'd altered my appearance, but I knew that would interfere with my primary goal of the moment: getting laid.

I told her later that evening, though, after I accomplished said goal, when Crystal was lying in the nook of my arm tracing circles on my stomach with the tip of her acrylic nail while Bjork played on my record player.

"What is this crap?" Crystal said, nodding her head toward the record player.

"Bjork," I said.

"Sounds like an alien," Crystal said. She looked up at me and smiled, batted her lashes, which were fake. Did Poppy have fake eyelashes? Did I need to get them? No, she'd probably think they were tacky.

"I'm going to impersonate Poppy," I told her.

"Who is Poppy?" she asked.

I rolled my eyes. The weight of her head was starting to cut off my circulation. I shoved Crystal off my chest and sat up with my back propped against a pillow. I didn't have a headboard or bed frame. Just an old mattress on the floor. My surroundings were spare. The mattress was next to a tiny bathroom which was next to a tiny kitchen with a fridge that was always humming. I had a lamp. A laptop. A record player sitting on a credenza I'd found on the street. Inside were my clothes and my loot, things I'd stolen, things I'd sometimes sell when I was struggling to make rent. My apartment was 375 square feet and situated above a Chinese restaurant, so it always smelled like dumplings. I grew to like the smell. It was home.

"Poppy," I said, "is my twin sister. We have the same face and genes. You've met her." I hadn't introduced them on purpose, but Poppy came over a few months ago to bring me her old TV—a charity act for her sad twin—and Crystal showed up uninvited. The two of them interacted as though they were different species. Poppy with her long bob and freshly ironed clothes, Crystal in a transparent tank dress that revealed her perky nipples. They talked about how sunny it was, how bad traffic was, standard Los Angeles dialogue, but with great physical unease.

"We have the same face," I continued. "And genes."

Crystal burst out laughing. She sat up next to me on the pillow. She was always too close to me, clinging, her body always a little sweaty, her sweat always a little sour. My life was always a little disgusting.

"I thought her name was Polly," Crystal said.

I shook my head. "Always Poppy."

"The fuck kind of name is Poppy?"

"It's a flower," I said. "Like Iris."

"Your parents really like flowers, huh?"

Sometimes I wondered if Crystal had been dropped on her head as a baby.

"Mine like diamonds," Crystal continued, staring at the blinds, which were barely holding back neon light from the Chinese restaurant's huge sign. "My dad wanted to name me Diamond, but he left, so my mom picked Crystal."

"Well, Poppy is about to be my new name," I said, redirecting the convo back to me, and also realizing that Crystal was an exotic dancer and could easily go by Diamond if she wanted to. Why hadn't she? I was too self-centered to ask. I'd yet to see her dance, but she asked me to go all the time. The idea didn't entice me. Strip clubs were for men. Lex might like strip clubs because she was basically a man.

"Why?" she asked.

"Because I need to get rid of her girlfriend." I swallowed. "Fiancée."

"Wait, Polly is gay?"

"Poppy," I corrected her. But it was a legitimate question. Part of my being the *bad twin* meant my deviant sexuality. My parents were old school, Christian Boomers on the precipice of the Silent Generation. They'd had kids late, after selling their successful florist business. Crystal was right, they liked flowers. And they disliked homosexuality, particularly as it manifested in me—early, obsessively, directed mostly at older women with tattoos and drinking problems and sometimes criminal records.

Poppy always had boyfriends until Lex. Nice, quiet, disciplined men who also worked in tech and ironed their clothes. Lex had been a surprise to us all. She and my twin met at Coachella, predictably. Poppy had just broken up with one of the nice quiet men and Lex had gone to USC with one of Poppy's friends. They ended up in the same shared house in La Quinta for the cringe music festival and allegedly "hit it off," and "the rest was history," or whatever else unoriginal people said.

Lex was kind of like the nice quiet boyfriends except she wasn't nice or quiet. But again, she was basically a man. She wore ill-fitting streetwear in bright colors. She was significantly more confident than she should have been given her skillset, appearance, and intelligence level. She held the door for Poppy and bought her flowers every Friday. When I asked Poppy what she liked about Lex, Poppy said Lex "felt like home." I nearly vomited.

"I don't know what Poppy is," I said.

"No labels," said Crystal. "Me too, girl."

I rolled my eyes again, then got a glass of water from the kitchen. I poured a glass for Crystal, too.

"Got anything harder?" she asked after chugging the glass. Water dribbled down her chin. I tried to lick it off, and she shoved me. We were often rough with each other.

I went back to the kitchen—it was very close—and poured her the last bit of whiskey I had in a dusty old bottle. I smelled it but didn't sip.

She offered me the glass.

I shook my head.

"Why do you need to get rid of her girlfriend?"

"She sucks," I said.

"Sucks how?"

"Literally every way," I said. "Name a way."

"Cunty?"

I paused. Lex wasn't exactly nice, but she wasn't mean either. She was too arrogant to be cruel. She had no hatred in her heart, only confidence and corniness. Frankly, I would have liked her better if she was a little cunty, as in my experience, that typically came from a place of woundedness. Lex was too coddled to be vulnerable.

"Annoying, cocky, *huge* gums," I said.

Crystal laughed. "You want to get rid of her because you don't like her gums?"

"You'd understand if you met her." I sat up straighter, leaned over to get another whiff of Crystal's whiskey. She smelled disgusting by a well-adjusted person's standards, but to a dirtbag like me, she smelled like literal heaven.

"Oh!" I said, realizing I'd buried the lede. "*Also,* she rescues pit bulls. That's like her whole thing. Her dad is some Hollywood producer, and he gave her a bunch of money to start a nonprofit, and *that's* what she decided to do! Of all the things!"

"Aww," Crystal said, as though she was under Lex's dumb spell from afar. "That's kind of cute. Pitt bulls have beautiful eyes." She wrinkled her nose. "Like yours."

"Her dumbass catchphrase is, 'There are no bad dogs. Only bad owners.'"

Crystal said nothing. She looked at her lap. "I shouldn't be here."

Oh no, I hoped she wouldn't start crying. Women tended to cry around me, who knows why. Although I guess I'd recently cheated on her. But we'd never exactly defined the relationship, its terms, whether it was monogamous.

"You know I was attacked by a pit bull," I said, positioning myself to be the victim instead of her.

"Yeah, yeah," Crystal said, sniffling. "Like a billion years ago." She wiped her nose with the back of her hand. "You expect me to get over you cheating like a week ago, and you can't even get over a dog biting you when you were twelve."

She stood up. She was probably right, but I felt angry in the moment. Too hurt to respond. I am very sensitive, it's a problem. I went into the bathroom and turned on the sink to drown out my cruel, self-pitying thoughts. Crystal opened the door without knocking. Her purse was sliding off her narrow shoulder.

"I'm leaving," she said. She walked up close to me, her actions betraying her words, and dragged the tip of her acrylic nail against my scar. "Don't forget to cover this up," she said, "when you pretend to be Polly."

I was about to correct her when she said, "Just kidding." She winked. "I always knew her name was Poppy."

Maybe Crystal wasn't dropped on her head as a baby. Maybe she was just fucking with me, the same way I'd been fucking with her.

Crystal turned away from me and left the bathroom. When the front door closed, I was alone with the sound of the refrigerator humming.

☙

Two days later, I used a brush to run the Chanel bronzer I'd famously stolen from Bloomingdale's along my scar.

Poppy didn't wear a ton of makeup, but I'd successfully covered the scar using a combination of products I'd taken from Sephora on day nine. I'd made Crystal come shopping with me, mostly because I knew the shopgirls would be focused on her, the stripper who reeked of menthols, and leave me to do my thing. It worked. I'd taken enough bland outfits for the weekend, mostly from Nordstrom.

I gave myself a once-over in the mirror and felt disgusted and proud. My clear skin, minimal makeup, my "clean girl look." My forehead didn't move when I tried to furrow my brows. It was shiny—not from oil, but because the smooth frozen surface reflected more light. My long bob was freshly blown out, silky and effervescent. I wore an overpriced white T-shirt with overpriced black leggings—clothes I assumed resembled the ones Poppy wore to her retreat. I absolutely hated the way I looked, but I looked exactly like Poppy.

I was prepared to scare Lex right out of their little house of premarital bliss.

The walls of their engagement would come crashing down.

Thanks to *moi*.

I'd be a local hero!

I couldn't stop smiling.

I hope this weekend is super zen! I texted Poppy uncharacteristically.

Are you ok? she wrote back.

Yeah, just in a good mood / overly caffeinated! Are you at the retreat yet?

Like an hour out, said Poppy.

This was all I needed to know.

Have a very relaxing time! I wrote back.

Poppy just put a thumbs up on my text.

My phone said it would take forty-seven minutes to get to Lex's house in Santa Monica, so I waited thirteen minutes and then gathered my things.

Carrying the vegan leather overnight bag I'd stolen from Nordstrom that looked like something Poppy would carry, I made my way to my Honda Fit parked semi-illegally on the street. Inside the car, I reached into the vegan leather purse I'd also shoplifted and took half a Xanax. Crystal's brother dealt pharmaceuticals, so she'd hooked me up with enough benzos to keep myself and the dogs subdued for the weekend.

Traffic moved at a glacial pace as I passed through the Sherman Oaks boutiques, then crawled along the 405 past the Getty Center, by UCLA, then through unnaturally green and manicured Brentwood, then finally tasted the ocean as I approached Santa Monica. I parked two blocks from Lex's house, then grabbed my bags, took a deep breath, and approached.

I'd seen on Redfin that Lex bought her house for $1.9 million, which was insane because it was very bland and fairly small. White walls, pale wood appliances, small AstroTurf yard for the dogs. It was a new construction with zero character. Frankly, I preferred my 375-square-foot apartment that smelled of dumplings. At least it had a vibe. Lex's house was utterly vibeless.

Her car wasn't in the driveway, which thrilled me. This would make things easier. I knew there was a key under the mat, so I let myself in. The house smelled of overpriced sandalwood candles and wet dog, as it always did. I braced myself for their inevitable stampede.

Yesterday I Googled *how much Xanax to subdue a pit bull?* The internet recommended putting 2.5mg inside of a treat. I brought 8 pill-stuffed treats just in case they needed more. Drugging the dogs was going to be the scariest part of the weekend. I currently had four pill treats in my palm because I knew they were going to come at me and probably realize I wasn't Poppy, because dogs always sensed that shit.

Before long, I heard their footsteps like thunder. My heart rattled in my chest as three disgusting slobbery creatures came running at me. I put my palm out and closed my eyes. I squirmed when I felt their gross tongues on my hand and immediately wished I'd taken more Xanax. These dogs were allegedly rehabilitated, and Lex insisted they would "never attack someone." But they were former fighting dogs, and I was technically a stranger in their home.

While they were busy eating the treats, I locked myself in the bedroom, waiting for the Xanax to work on the dogs. I took the other half of the pill and then waited for the Xanax to work on me. Half an hour later, I cracked open the door and did not hear the dogs. I crept into the hallway, where they were all passed out on the floor. They seemed to be breathing, their fat, smelly bodies moving up and down with regularity. I exhaled and returned to the bedroom, where I suppose I fell asleep.

❧

I woke up to the front door opening, to Lex's fugly voice and heavy, manly footsteps. I was getting up to greet her when I heard another voice. I'd met Poppy and Lex's friends before, but I never remembered them. They all looked the same, mostly worked in tech or were rich kids with small businesses their dads funded. Whatever, I could fake it. I was on enough Xanax to believe I could do anything; it would all be fine.

Leaving the bedroom, I heard something else. Giggling, a light moan. Wait, was I hearing what I thought I was hearing? Kissing noises? I covered my mouth before I could gasp. God had been so horrible to me, but this was a divine gift. I couldn't fucking believe it. Lex was cheating on Poppy. And I was dressed as Poppy. About to catch her in the fucking act.

God fucking *bless*. I wasn't going to have to repel Lex by being myself. I wasn't going to have to spend forty-eight hours interacting with her. All I had to do was march into that living room right now and watch the relationship crumble before my eyes.

I wiped the grin from my face and did just that.

"What the *fuck* is going on in here?" I said.

Lex and the other woman jumped apart, acting as though I hadn't seen them, hadn't heard what I'd heard.

"What are you doing here?" Lex asked.

"It's my home," I said.

"Hi Poppy," the other woman said. "I'm just here to train the boys." She looked over at the dogs, as if nothing out of the ordinary had just occurred. "But it looks like they're sleepy today."

I tried to suppress the smile that desperately wanted to form on my face. Was this the dog trainer? Was Lex fucking the dog trainer? This was too good!

"I thought you were at the retreat," Lex said.

"I decided to come home," I said. "Because I *missed* you." I deserved an Oscar for this performance. "Because I thought you *missed me*. But you obviously didn't." I glared at the dog trainer.

"Of course I missed you, Pumpkin," Lex said, approaching me. I instinctively recoiled, which worked for the part I was trying to play, a wronged lover.

"Do you think I'm dense?" I said. "You think I didn't just hear you two smooching like lovebirds?" Poppy didn't exactly speak this way, but she was triggered.

Lex laughed in a way that made it so obvious that I heard correctly, that she'd been kissing this butch dog trainer. Rosacea blossomed on her ugly cheeks.

"Don't fucking gaslight me," I said, then shoved her. It felt good. I'd been wanting to shove Lex for so long. I realized at this moment, after catching her cheating, that I had carte blanche to say every mean thing I'd ever wanted to say to Lex. "Don't smile at me with those huge ass gums and act like I didn't just hear what was happening."

"Poppy, are you okay?" Lex said. "You aren't acting like yourself."

I shoved her again, harder this time. "Don't you dare. You aren't attractive enough to get away with this level of psychological manipulation. Clearly your rich dad made you feel very important growing up, but newsflash, honey—your face is shaped like a pie, your personality is grating, you share a name with a corny lesbian dating app, and you dress like Cedric the Entertainer. You make Rosie O'Donnell look like Penelope Cruz—"

"Sorry to interrupt, but," the dog trainer said. I'd forgotten she was here. She was on the floor with the ugly dogs. "I think there's something wrong with Pickle."

☙

Don't worry. None of the dogs died. But I'd be lying if I said a part of me didn't hope they would. Or at least one would. My grand act of vengeance.

But no, it was an epic, comic failure.

As soon as I admitted to giving Xanax to the dogs, Lex knew I was me. She knew Poppy would never do such a thing to their precious animals. Lex was certain and could not be convinced otherwise, especially because she was right. At the animal hospital, she took a disinfectant wipe and removed the makeup from my face to expose my scar.

I was telling Crystal everything in my apartment that evening over dumplings from downstairs. She'd been concerned earlier when I called her from the animal hospital. I still don't understand why people get so protective over these violent animals. I insisted the dogs were fine, I was not. I needed her to come over tonight.

"That's so mean, Iris," Crystal said when I told her what I'd said to Lex.

"She was cheating on my sister!" I said.

Crystal lifted her thin, heavily arched eyebrows. "I never said anything that cruel when you cheated on me."

"Well there's nothing to say because I'm gorgeous and perfect," I said.

Crystal rolled her eyes. "Right." She dipped a dumpling into a plastic container of sauce. "What do you think is gonna happen when Poppy comes back? Are you going to tell her?"

I swallowed my dumpling, then sipped some beer to wash it down. How I'd missed alcohol. I don't know how I got through rehab.

"She's already back," I said. "Lex called the retreat and said there was an emergency with the dogs. Told her the whole thing. Poppy already called me and chewed me out." I shuddered thinking of the chill in her voice. I was the bad twin, but Poppy was so terrifying when she was angry.

Crystal didn't say anything, just chewed. She looked very cute, the light from the neon sign out the window casting a gold glow on her face as her cheeks formed dimples.

"Wasn't she mad at Lex?" Crystal asked finally.

I shook my head. "She doesn't believe she cheated," I said.

"Really? But you saw them, right?"

I shook my head again. "I heard them. Giggling and shit. And I think I heard them kiss." I smacked my lips to imitate the sound. "But by the time I was in the living room, they were separated. Poppy said I was making things up."

"It's true you do lie all the time," Crystal said, then sipped her beer. "And you were on a lot of Xanax, right?"

I nodded. I had to admit, I was having doubts that I'd heard them correctly myself. I suppose it was possible that I just heard what I wanted to hear, an opportunity to rip into Lex and break up her relationship with my sister. I missed how I felt this morning, so determined, like an astronaut on a mission to Mars. And now I was back to being the bad twin—apprehensive, unmotivated, unwashed, Chinese-food scented, sitting on the floor with my on-and-off girlfriend who came from a long line of drug dealers.

Crystal glanced around the apartment, my dingy, cluttered space. "You know, you shouldn't hate dogs so much," she said. "You kind of live like one." She batted her big fake eyelashes at me. "A very bad dog."

I shook my head. "There are no bad dogs," I said with a grin. "Only bad owners."

A breeze shifted the blinds, bathing my apartment in neon orange.

I leaned over, brushed Crystal's hair from her face, lightly kissed the space beneath her eyelashes. Crystal sighed. I put my head in her lap, looked up at her.

"I'm not a bad dog," I said. "But I am the bad twin."

Crystal shook her head. She twirled a lock of my hair in her fingers.

"I actually don't think you're so bad, Iris," she said. "You're guarded."

"Because of Amber," I said.

Crystal laughed. "Sure. Whatever reason." She got quiet for a second. Opened her mouth, then closed it, then opened it again. "I don't want to say anything mean about your sister."

"Oh go off, please," I said. "Literally no one has ever said anything bad about her—is there something wrong with her? I thought she was perfect."

"She's proper," Crystal said. "But she kind of has scary energy."

"Really?" I said. "I thought she was just like that with me because she hates me."

"You say you have the same face, but you look nothing alike to me," Crystal said. "Your face is sweeter."

"Sweet?"

"Sweet*er*." Crystal laughed. "For real though, I think you have a good heart, Iris. You're definitely fucked up, but no more so than anyone else. Maybe if you stopped seeing yourself as bad all the time, you wouldn't need to act that way."

Crystal sat up and grabbed her dress off the foot of the bed, pulled it over her head.

For a second, I thought about telling her I loved her, which I'd never done before. Not to a love interest. Not even to my family members since I was a kid.

But just when I opened my mouth, Crystal put a finger on my lips.

"I'm going to leave," she said.

I nodded, watching her gather her things.

"Call me if you ever decide you want to be good," she said just before closing the apartment door behind her.

A car honked on the street. Brakes screeched. A neon stripe ran across the wall.

"I will," I said to the empty room.

TWO HUNDRED CHANNELS OF CONFLICT

MAC CRANE

I WAS STANDING IN THE NEIGHBORS' GARDEN watching TV through their window, like I did most nights. I didn't own a TV because I was working on my temper and I thought the best way to do that was to first look the part. I needed to get rid of my frown lines, or 11s as the women inside the Internet called them. But Botox was expensive, so I sold my one and only TV to afford twenty units. I was so excited at the beauty clinic that I could hardly keep still; the happy, wrinkle-free people all over the walls would soon become my kin. I fantasized about how my life would change once I wiped the permanent scowl off of my face. People would begin describing me as *approachable*, starting with the neighbors. The neighbors, who were wife and wife, a little older than me, would finally wave to me, a customary greeting, while they were out working in their garden. They might even invite me in for lavender tea or whatever snobbish thing they made a habit of doing. From there, it would be a piece of cake. We'd become lifelong best friends who went on trips together. Everyone would think we were a throuple, intimidated by our radiant beauty and ability to tend to each other equally; maybe we would eventually become a throuple. We'd make new traditions, bake a lot of bread, get an ornament to mark every year we made it around the sun and didn't explode. I longed for them to find me mysterious and endlessly interesting, more so than I longed to actually be mysterious and endlessly interesting. And Botox would help me achieve this. My life would change, I just knew it.

The Botox doctor told me to sit still and squeeze a ball. He said things like, frown for me, great, just great, wow, you have a really strong glabella, you must work it out a lot, ha ha, okay, all set, don't lie down or work out for three hours after this, it may take one to two weeks to see the full results. I nodded along, thinking all of my problems were solved. And they were, for a little while. The wives waved to me five and a half times. I say a half because one of those times only one wife waved, I don't know why. At the mall, a sales associate asked how I was doing, if they could help me find these jeans in another size. At the bar, the bartender wanted to know what I'd be having tonight. She didn't say, *What's wrong? Are you okay?* which is what she usually said. My best friend, Amp, stopped asking me if I forgot to take my pill today even though I didn't have a pill I could forget to take. I was convinced that because of this newfound royal treatment and its effects on my psyche, I would be equipped with the tools to dig deep down and find a way to stop telling people to fuck all the way off to hell. I would stop regretting nearly everything I said and did. I would find someone I could love thoroughly, with grace and vigor—I would finally stop accumulating exes.

Anyway, no one had told me that Botox wears off—I'd thought it was a one-and-done deal. Imagine my dismay when, just as I was starting to make some progress—I'd successfully de-escalated myself in the Burger King drive-thru when I'd said no pickles, please, and they gave me a mountain of pickles so tall I thought the single patty was actually four—the Botox wore off, and all I was left with was the memory of a better face and a better life. The night I noticed the deep creases between my eyebrows returning, my lamp ended up outside, shards of glass from the window decorating the lawn like seashells on the shoreline. My takeovers—that's what I call my bouts of anger—make me feel like someone has ripped me from my body and filled it with wildfire. I never remember what happens during a takeover. Only after the fact, when I returned to my body, did I put together what happened. A hole in the wall, a red swollen fist. Or, in this case, the lamp. When I returned to myself, I recovered all of the broken pieces and held a proper burial.

I was back to square one, only this time I didn't have a TV, which is why I am standing in the neighbors' garden, watching their TV and wondering what in the hell I'm going to do, when all of a sudden my phone is vibrating in my pocket. It's a text from an unknown number, which, unlike all the other texts I tend to receive from unknown numbers, isn't trying to sell me something or get me to vote for some crook.

Hey, long time no see lol I'm back in town if you want to meet up, reads the text.

I read the message a few more times while the men on the TV walk on walls and ceilings. I've seen this one before. The hero doesn't save the day or get the girl. He doesn't even get a sappy monologue that tricks the audience into believing they've been moved. I've seen this one before because it's the neighbors' make-up movie. I wonder what they've been fighting about this time.

Of course I want to meet up, I text the stranger.

This is my chance to become someone other than me. No, I'm not worried that, upon laying eyes on me, they'll realize I lied. They will be so entranced by me that they will act as if nothing is wrong, nothing out of the ordinary.

Haha, you haven't changed one bit, they say. After a few moments, they send a second text: *I like it that way.*

I nod. Normally I would be upset if someone told me this, considering how I have been embarking upon a personality transplant, but I'm not me in this moment, I am whoever the stranger believes me to be, and thus, I am steadfast and dependable, the only constant in this stranger's topsy-turvy life. I glance in the window, past the wives' heads. The men on the TV become the man on the TV. All the others are dead.

The movie must not be doing its job, because the wives are still sitting a few feet apart by the end, both of them messing around on their phones. Not even this stupid action movie can save them. I imagine them meeting their friends tomorrow night at some fancy cocktail bar downtown. When the subject of what they did the previous night comes up, they will say something like, Oh us? We watched *the most brilliant* indie film interrogating the maternal instincts of clones. Or maybe they'll invent the name of a museum and say, What, haven't you heard of it? We'll have to go sometime. What I'm trying to say is that whenever these two go out in public, they pull their brows up to their hairlines—I've seen it around the neighborhood—but I much prefer them when they think no one, including me, is looking. It's very fortunate that they haven't discovered my little routine: make popcorn, melt a bowl of butter in the microwave, pour it over popped corn, take the bowl and six beers over to their front window, watch whatever they're watching, forget a paper towel every time, wipe my hands on their plants, study their relationship dynamic, then slink home in the cloak of night. How, exactly, would I explain that without escalating the situation the second one of them accused me of being a Peeping Tom, even though they clearly borrow their movie-watching clothes from Bunny Rabbit in *8 Mile*?

Time and place, I text the stranger, feeling more and more powerful by the minute. I'd be lying if I said their texts didn't make me feel special.

Let's do our spot, for old time's sake, they say.

Fuck, how am I going to ask what our old spot is without giving myself away? Already, my new life is foiled. Pissed, I chuck my phone on the perfectly manicured lawn, where it lies and thinks about what it's done for a few seconds before lighting up blue. I get on my hands and knees and crawl over to it, hope propelling me forward.

Betty's opens at 4 tomorrow, let's meet then, says the message.

Can't wait, I say, returning to my bush, my reserved seat in the movie theater of domestic lesbian quarrel.

They are still on their phones, mindlessly scrolling. The one woman, the beefy rugby player, keeps peeking up at her wife, a birdlike lawyer, to see if she's looking before returning to her phone. I find myself wondering what it's like to be other people. Why does our anger present itself so differently? Or were the wives not angry at all, but rather some other terrible emotion that prevented them from reconciling? More than anything, I want them to make up; I want to know there were two people out there who always apologize and always forgive each other.

I pluck a pink flower from the bush and stuff it in my hoodie pocket. I have this idea that I will take the flower to this stranger. I will tell them it's been imported from New Zealand. I will tell them the doctor extracted it from my liver, that it has healing properties. I will tell them plenty of beautiful things. You see, I want to be that person the stranger was texting. I want to be the person they thought of as soon as they returned to town. I imagine the stranger as kind but not too kind. Kind when it matters. Patient but with an edge. Right now, I'm all fury and no patience. But I am trying to change that, I really, really am.

I'd rather not talk about it too much, but I've developed new wrinkles from squinting at the wives' TV in an attempt to read the closed captions, which they always have turned on the smallest possible size as if to punish me, although to my knowledge, they do not know of my nightly visits. I'm lucky their living room is situated in such a way that their backs face me, but sometimes when the screen is black, I catch one of them pointing at the screen where my reflection, however faint, could be seen if I happened to be taking a break from my perpetual squat to stretch my legs.

I am usually very diligent, but the night I make the date with the stranger, I get lazy. I'm so lost in my fantasy world, playing out all the possibilities of the date at Betty's, that I don't realize I'm in full view until the rugby player is tapping the window and holding her hands up as if to say, What the fuck are you doing?

I turn and sprint home across the street, forgetting my popcorn bowl on their lawn. When I peek out my front window, I see both women on the lawn examining my movie-watching area as if it is a crime scene. They start gesturing at each other like the tragic climax of a soap opera. I wonder if I, too, am in the soap opera, or if I've somehow climbed out of the screen and into the real world. I can't be too sure, but what I do know is that I'm too embarrassed on their behalf to keep watching. I lock the door, close the blinds, and dim the lights.

Just as I crawl into bed, I receive another text from an unknown number. I assume it's my stranger, whom I've begun referring to as Betty, but it isn't.

I'm on my way. Be there in 20 ;) says the message.

It takes me a moment to realize it's my Tinder date. I forgot all about her. I check the app: her name is Morgan, 28, and if I want to know anything else, I have to ask. ;)

I'll be here, I say. She immediately texts me back.

I just drove by two people breakdancing on the side of the road, she says.

Are you a dancer? she says.

I stare at the screen trying to comprehend the words in front of me. What does this question mean? Am I a dancer, as in, professionally? I don't understand what she wants from me, so I send her a heart emoji followed by champagne glasses clinking. I have some sparkling wine in the fridge. I'm going to need it.

Hehe sorry, can you tell I'm nervous? says Morgan.

Already, I am annoyed at her self-consciousness, at her use of winky faces and childish laughter. I do what anyone with some sense would do in my situation: I start comparing her to my stranger. Betty would never say something like this. Betty has poise and charm. Betty knows everyone in the room is looking at them.

When I don't respond, she sends me another text: *What I meant was, do you like to dance? That's what I meant when I asked if you're a dancer. I love to dance. Anywhere, everywhere.*

It strikes me that she's going to text me her entire drive here.

Please be safe, I respond, even though I want nothing more than for her to get into a fender bender that ruins the night so I don't have to face her.

Then, because I'm certain that good things will not happen to me, I decide to prepare for the date. I splash some water on my face, then give some to the plants, in an effort to perk all of us up. I throw a few dishes in the trash. I apply copious amounts of deodorant. I stare into the depths of my closet and try to figure out what a non-angry person would wear for a date. My grandpa, the tender man who raised me and used to comfort me by saying sometimes your wires are just born crossed, wears sweater vests and brown slacks, but I don't own those types of garments. I select black jeans and a red thermal crewneck that is meant for better-looking people than me. I do a handstand against the wall to encourage the blood to go to my brain. This date will be good practice for my patience. I will not lash out, I will not lash out.

When Morgan arrives, she texts me from the front porch. I open the door and there she is, all mouth and eyeballs, no wrinkles detected, long black hair hanging down her back, an orange hula hoop in hand. She's more attractive in person, mostly because of the way she holds herself, like she spends most of her time inside of her body. How nice for her. I make note of her smooth forehead, the lack of 11s between her eyebrows. Her smoothness makes her look kind and young and like the type of person one might recruit for life partnership. Not that I want to recruit her for such a commitment, but I'm confident someone will. I just need to get through the evening. I try to smile but I can tell I've overshot it, that I look like a hippopotamus.

There was a note on your door, she says, pulling a piece of paper from behind her back and handing it to me.

I don't say anything, just skim the note, which appears to concern a certain Penal Code 602 PC, something about trespassing, which is a misdemeanor for which I could spend up to six months in jail, one thousand dollars poorer. Morgan twirls her hula hoop in her hand, waiting for me to absorb the threat.

You read it, didn't you, I say.

She makes what I estimate to be a flirty face. A cocked eyebrow, pursed lips.

Don't you worry. This is a matter of sharing resources, I say.

Very socialist of you, she says. Or is it communist?

I don't say anything. Just mess around with my bun and look past Morgan to inspect the wives' house for movement. It is a one-story, ranch-style house, the lit-up windows to the right of the living room window belonging to the bedroom. A silhouette sits on the edge of the bed, hunched over something. The living room lights are off. TV, off.

When it becomes apparent I'm not going to say anything, Morgan tries again.

Do you have any idea how intimidating you are? she asks, still spinning the hula hoop in her hand.

I try to imagine what the inside of someone's mind must look like in order for them to decide on bringing a hula hoop to a first date. I decide on rainbows and unicorns, though the unicorns, for some reason, cluck when they're excited and only run backward.

I try to lead my date straight out to the backyard for drinks, but she lingers in my living room, touching the leaves of my plants with her fingers, which I'm now realizing are unbelievably long, like piano keys. Will they fit inside of me? Suddenly, I am terrified that if we make it to bed, she will be fucking me with just her fingertips. Her first phalanges only.

I don't have a TV, I tell her.

That's okay, I hate TVs, she says, smiling at me.

She makes her way through the living room so slowly I convince myself she's dusting for fingerprints. First, she hovers in front of the sign my grandpa gifted me for Christmas:

TO ALL WHO COME
TO OUR HAPPY HOME
WELCOME

I know what Morgan's going to say before she says it.

Our? she asks.

Another cocked eyebrow. I don't want to tell her the truth, that my grandpa bought it in anticipation of me finding someone very soon, that he believed in wish fulfillment, in behaving as if something has already happened in order to make it happen.

Some baby crickets live here, I say.

I don't know where their mothers are, I say.

Backyard? I say, gesturing through the kitchen.

But I watch her do her thing, ignoring my request. Suddenly, I feel as if I am a figurine on display, the thrift store kind that's so fucking strange you almost can't believe someone would pay money for it until there you are at the register, handing the old bald cashier a twenty. Next, she lands on a picture of my college softball team. She picks it up and inspects it so closely that the end of her nose leaves a grease mark on the glass.

Do I have to ask a question or will you just tell me, she says.

I'm not good at this, she says.

But softball is hella gay, she says.

Yeah, I say.

It is, I say.

I think of Alexis, my college girlfriend and teammate, how she kept me a secret for three years, sneaking out of my dorm at 4 a.m. so no one would catch her. How, the game after our breakup, I was so beside myself that I took it out on the opposition's catcher, bulldozing through her at home plate in a play that ultimately got me ejected from the game.

I don't know how to tell her that I need us to exit the house immediately, that hovering inside my space feels a lot like poking and prodding my brain. Hoping she'll follow, I decide to head to the fridge, grab and pop the sparkling wine, pour two plastic cups, then kick the back door open, the bottle safely in the crook of my elbow. Next to the door, I crouch down and plug in the outdoor lights, the bulbs lining the pavilion turning on simultaneously in one big revelation. I sit on one of the two white Adirondack chairs my grandpa had sent me a few weeks prior in a state of drunken online shopping. It is cold and hard, nothing like I imagine a chair should be. While I wait, I text my stranger, my Betty.

Do you find me intimidating? I say. Immediately, I see that they are typing.

You? Are you kidding? they say.

Remember that time you fed a stray kitten milk from a bottle? they say.

Why? they ask.
No reason, I say.
Just curious, I say.
I get it, they say.
You're thinking of buying a leather jacket, aren't you? they say.
A little image change-up, they say.

Betty always knows just what to say. I think it sounds rather nice, to be the type of person who bottle-feeds baby animals. Everywhere I go, people would say, "There goes Bait, off to sustain more life."

I reply to Betty and tell them I am counting down the minutes until our hangout and they send an ocean wave emoji paired with a levitating man. Does this require a reply? I don't know. I send an ellipsis just in case.

Don't tell me you forgot, says my stranger, my Betty.
I didn't forget, I say.
I love you, I say before I realize what's happening.

I punch my phone screen in an attempt to take the message back but it's gone, into the swallow of the Internet. Morgan comes outside just in time to witness my panicked tantrum. For some reason, it seems to endear her to me. Her adoration is enough to terrify me—what new ways will I find to disappoint someone?

Your profile said you like the outside, says Morgan.

Where do you like to go? she asks, plopping down into the other chair.

The force with which she sits down would have hurt any normal person but something about her seems indestructible. The hula hoop, I notice, is hanging around her neck like the world's biggest glow stick. I think, who is this person and why did I let her infiltrate my life? I'm still panicking about the text I'd sent my Betty. Leave it to me to do everything in my power to ruin my new life before it even begins.

I don't know how to respond to Morgan, so I hand her a cup and tell her about the wives, their garden I hang out in, and their moving brows. I tell her I wish the brows would stay in one place; I crave consistency. She tells me everyone is like this to some extent, that the second you left your home, the white man was in charge of your taste. I ask if she means all white men or if she has one particular white man in mind, perhaps one with a handlebar mustache and combover. She says not to worry about the wives, no one is really who they say they are. I'm not sure we're talking about the same thing. Are the things we like indicative of who we are? What does it mean for me to like plants and studying other people's relationships? Do I actually, on some level, enjoy my anger? Why else would it stick around for twenty-five years? I don't say any of this out loud, but she continues as if answering me.

The wives aren't as interesting as you think they are, she says.

And I think that's because you want them to be your mommies, she says, giving me this look. I give her one back.

Don't worry, it's normal to search for mommies everywhere you go, she says.

I don't see how this night could possibly go on, and yet it does. A headache settles in behind my eyes. I chug my drink then refill it and chug again, anything to sedate my irritation. I'm not yet angry but I feel as if I'm a water-filled pot on a stove set to simmer, the bubbles threatening to break the surface. My date doesn't seem to notice my simmering, and if she does, she doesn't care—she keeps on going, proceeds to tell me about a trip to Belize with her ex, how they'd seen a type of monkey, the howler monkey, whose howl was the same for both a war cry and a sex cry, that context was everything.

Isn't that much more interesting than your wives? she asks.

For some reason, her comment infuriates me. Since when is this a competition? As always, I know my anger is irrational, but that knowledge doesn't do shit for me. I try to breathe my way through it. I feel like a wind-up doll, ready to be set loose.

It doesn't seem like too much trouble to come up with two different cries, I say, steadying my breathing.

She doesn't appear to like my response. She flips her hair over her shoulder, stands up, and performs a few hula hoop rotations. Behind her, tall, sickly bamboo trees lean over my fence, bending it to its limits. Despite their destruction, I like the bamboo for the privacy it provides. No one can see into my yard, and I can't see into theirs. I am free to be as foolish as I wish. To lay out topless and fry my tits to a crisp. I can cease to exist.

Like she's a little kid, I tell her to show me how many hula hoops she can do in a row. She frowns at me, then does it anyway. We're on six hundred and four, the counting soothing me, her hips swaying brilliantly, when Betty texts me back. I need to be alone to take this blow. I tell Morgan I'll be right back and head inside to the bathroom, where I piss out some bubbles and frown into the mirror. It doesn't seem possible that this is the face I was assigned at birth. Weren't any others available?

Leaning over the sink, I take a few deep breaths before reading my stranger Betty's text message.

I'm sorry, I should have been more upfront about my situation when I texted you, they say.

I'm married now. Twins. Van, they say.

You know the deal, they say.

My vision kaleidoscopes, my face a fragmented distortion in the mirror. I collapse onto the fuzzy blue rug before I pass out. I squeeze my eyes shut and try to slow my breathing. If I slow my breathing, I can stay inside my body. What does this mean? Is my stranger married to twins or do they parent a pair of twins? Why have they led me on? I thought I would stroll in there tomorrow to find a confused and casually gorgeous person sitting at a high-top table, wondering where their intended recipient was, but the confusion wouldn't last long because I would woo my Betty with my electric presence. They would be so thrilled for the mix-up that they'd order one of everything, then look me in the eyes and tell me they've been waiting for me their entire life. They would tell me the energy between us feels erotic, that every time I move my body, even if it's only to lift my drink or brush my hair, the entire universe staggers, as if love-drunk. I've imagined it so many times in my head that it hasn't occurred to me it could go down any other way.

Once I recover enough to see my phone screen, I ask if we are still on for tomorrow and Betty says yes, of course, if I am still up for it. I say I am, I very much want to see them, they've been on my mind, and that I didn't actually mean to say I love you but my cat stepped on my phone and sent my text before it was finished. My Betty says they didn't know I had a cat, and I say I didn't know either until about two months ago when I discovered a cat was jumping in my kitchen window and drinking the milk from my leftover cereal bowl in the sink.

Hmph, they say.

You've always been the funny one, they say.

God, how I love that text. And just like that, I am thrust back into my fantasy. Twins, marriage, a carpool van, none of these things are a match for my delicious personality. Feeling confident and refreshed, I march out to the backyard to find Morgan still counting her hula hoop rotations—she is on two thousand—and both Adirondack chairs flipped over like two sad turtles trapped on their backs. It looks suspiciously like a scene I might cause during a takeover. But I hadn't been that angry, had I? Just frustrated, annoyed, a normal reaction to the circumstances before me. I tiptoe toward the scene as if approaching a sleeping animal. I don't want to somehow implicate myself.

I didn't, well, I didn't go anywhere, did I? I ask.

You went inside, don't you remember? asks Morgan, her body fluid like a wave.

I try to explain that I want to know if my mind went somewhere while my body remained in front of her, counting her rotations.

That's between you and your mind, isn't it? she says, smiling. The fucking torture.

This is really important, Morgan, I say, trying to steady my breathing.

I need to know if I flipped these chairs, I say. I right one chair, then the other, focusing on the physical task at hand.

She ignores me and begins to tell me why she loves hula hooping so much—*since you refused to ask me about it*—she says it makes her feel free because her alcoholic ex hadn't let her hula hoop, she'd found it embarrassing. Now she does it on every date, regardless of where it takes place, as a test to see if the person will try to control her. I think, is this what life is? People administering a series of tests to one another? This can't be all there is.

Again, I ask her if she will please answer my question, I need to know that I'm no longer the type of person who flips chairs. I didn't mean to let that last part slip but I'm under a lot of duress, and when I'm under a lot of duress, my mouth tends to disobey my brain. This comment, of course, piques her interest, the phrase *no longer* undoubtedly signaling to her that I once was exactly the type of person who flipped chairs. She makes a face that indicates gastrointestinal distress, or perhaps restraint. But still, she refuses to assuage my fears.

The headache intensifies behind my eyes. I feel a burning that begins behind my sternum, then spreads slowly to my collarbone then shoulders and then to my traps, surging down my back and arms, my fingertips sizzling like sparklers on the Fourth of July.

I think of the white-hot heat of my childhood, of smashing everything—the Nintendo controller, my piggy bank, my softball trophies—against the wall. I banged my head against the wall, too. That part scared my grandfather very much. I didn't know how to tell him that banging my head was the only way to quiet the noise. He would do anything to prevent me from head-banging. Anything except therapy, I guess, because, according to him, therapy was for sick people, and I wasn't sick, I was disoriented. All we needed to do, he said, was reorient my mind, body, and spirit. He took me to church. He held my hand. He said, Can you feel it? Can you feel it? I didn't know what I was supposed to feel but I said yes so that we could go to Dunkin' Donuts afterward.

I return my attention to Morgan, who has put her hula hoop down and is now messing around on her phone. She tells me to follow her on Instagram while I chug the rest of the sparkling wine. She disciplines me with her eyes, so I pull out my phone and do as I'm told. I briefly entertain the idea that I am not real and none of this is happening, but that would be too fortuitous. I am real and I am an angry asshole who is trying desperately not to be an angry asshole. Again, I ask her if I was responsible for the chairs, but she doesn't look up from her phone. She tells me story after story. About everything, and nothing.

Finally, inexplicably, we are heading inside. We are making our way through the kitchen to the living room. We are standing in the doorway. We are saying we had a good time even though we both know we didn't. She kisses me on the cheek before bounding down the lawn to her car. She nearly trips on a cactus and squeals. I close the front door and flop down on the couch that faces the space where my TV used to be. Now, it is just an entertainment center having an existential crisis. I open Instagram and the first photo I see is Morgan's, posted two minutes ago. It is a meme with a photo of a bland white woman pressing her fingers to her temple. The text reads:

ME REALIZING I'M ATTRACTED TO YET ANOTHER NARCISSISTIC ALCOHOLIC

The caption is a bunch of shrugging emojis.

And here I was, thinking I'd been on my best behavior. I want to text her that I'd like a second try to prove her wrong, even though, if I look at the situation objectively, I know I do not want to see this woman ever again. I hate to think this way, but I'm worried about who I will be in her memory, even years from now. What she will think of me, and even worse, what she will say about me? Then I remember how she forced me to follow her on Instagram. She wanted me to see this meme. She'd been planning on it, in fact. Why, if I'm so horrible, is she attracted to me? And why is she broadcasting this for everyone to see?

I don't have much time to sit with her quick judgment of my character, because through the front window I see the light go on in the wives' living room, the silhouette of one of them walking across the room and sitting down on the couch. The TV goes on.

Soon, I am in the wives' garden again, trying to figure out the status of their relationship from the movie the woman, the birdlike lawyer, is watching. It's not familiar to me. I try not to think about meeting my Betty tomorrow, but I can't help it, anyone would be excited about starting their new life.

Will I, against all of my good sense and humanity, become a housewife? I'll wear an apron and make a quiche for breakfast. I'll brush my hair off my forehead with the back of my hand and my Betty, whose name may or may not be Betty, will embrace me in their big, strong arms and kiss me like the little housewife I am. We will, of course, raise the twins, if they do in fact exist. I will be the type of stepmother children can only dream of. When they go to school, they'll open their lunch boxes to find notes that show I listen—nothing generic like *I love you, have a great day*, more like the wishing that Megan, the bully with the braces, gets a D on her math test. The kids will revel in my specifics. *She listens!* they will say. Betty will look at me with these kind, grateful eyes that communicate that there is not a single other person like me on this entire planet. And—

What are you doing here? the wife asks.

She is somehow standing in front of me. She is flapping her arms. It takes me a moment to find my voice. I am, I realize, slurring a bit.

Did you two make up? I ask.

What are you talking about? she says. Still, she flaps.

Earlier, you two were watching your make-up film, I say.

It never fails, I say, nearly choking on my spit.

The woman looks uncomfortable, or maybe I'm just imagining it. She scratches her cheek aggressively as if trying to scrape grime off. She looks up at the moon, consulting its full-bodied wisdom, as if the moon doesn't have enough of its own problems.

It didn't work, did it? I say.

Fuck, I say.

Her eyes fill as she shakes her head no. She blinks rapidly. I notice her T-shirt is wrinkled and stretched out at the neck hole as if she's been trying to loosen the grip it has on her. I don't know what to say, and it turns out, I don't have to find the words, because there is Morgan's car in front of my house. There is Morgan getting out of the car and marching toward us. There is Morgan shoving me in the chest, shouting things I can't or won't hear. I catch a few words every now and then. Not Again. Absent. Commit. She is holding up her phone. She is pressing its cold face to my face. She is showing me my comment underneath her meme.

Who is Betty? she is asking.

Hello? she is asking.

Where do you go when I talk to you? she is asking.

My body, tense, tense, tense, and then free. The wind-up doll marches inside the wives' house, sits down on the wives' couch, and enjoys over two hundred channels of conflict.

"FUCK YOU" MONEY

francesca ekwuyasi

Sharifa has been having a shit couple of years. No, for real, it's been one incredibly irritatingly inconvenient thing after the other. For example, she's just gotten renovicted from her flat. And really, she shouldn't be so frustrated because the place is a mouse-infested, mold-infested, bad vibes-infested dump. It is probably also haunted, considering all the nightmares, inexplicable unidentifiable stains, and the pungent smell of rot emanating from all the drains. Still, fuck, she does not want to be looking for a new place right now, she hates packing, hates needing help, and she *does* need help. And there's the minor issue of the motherfucking housing crisis. Her landlord has only given her a month's notice, and yes, yes, she should take it up with the tenancy board, but there's already so much to do that she has neither the time nor energy to do it.

She's in the hardware store around the corner from her soon-to-be former flat on Beaubien, looking for boxes to make her packing a little less infuriating. It's July and unreasonably humid outside, and the store doesn't seem to have A/C; there's sweat running down her forehead and dripping into her eyes, burning them. She rubs her eyes with balled-up fists, making the burning so much worse. There's also a sharp pain radiating through her right hip, all the way down her thigh. She shifts most of her weight onto her left side to accommodate the discomfort, but now there's a wave of nausea rolling from her belly to her throat. She's doubled over in the packing aisle of the store, hands clutching the ledge of a shelf filled with giant rolls of clear tape. Her stomach has been bugging her for a few days; nothing has helped. Before her stomach and hip, there was a horrible spreading rash—pus-tipped and burning—across her chest and buttocks that was driving her wild. And before that, it was lice! How, you might ask, did she get lice? No idea! Sharifah has no idea how she might have gotten lice, maybe on the metro or at a house party, but no one else she knows has recently gotten lice. She was sure she'd read somewhere that folks with locs couldn't get lice; that's what she thought of, cursing as she cut off her thick locs before taking clippers to her scalp and shaving her head clean. Her hair has grown into a short, fuzzy little fro since then, but she's been afraid to like it in case something drastic, like spontaneous alopecia, suddenly occurs. She supposes it wouldn't be that spontaneous on account of all the stress from these seemingly random slights with which God, or Mother Nature, or the Universe have been spiting her.

The waves of nausea are relentless, fuck the boxes. She needs to go home and lie down and cry or something. She grits her teeth, straightens up, and starts to head for the exit when—

"Shar?" A familiar voice coming from the left of her. "Is that you?"

Sharifa turns and blinks a few times to be sure who she's looking at. A tall, full-figured femme in a tiny white T-shirt and long locs piled high on her head looks back at her. The woman cocks her head to the side, eyes glued on Sharifa. "Oh my God," she exclaims, "it *is* you!"

She walks toward Sharifa. "I've been looking for you for months," she's gesturing wildly with her hands, "no joke, literally months."

Sharifa sighs, exhausted and embarrassed. "Hi, Kemi," she says.

"Hi yourself." Kemi laughs a deep and hearty laugh. "Listen, there's something I did," she says while unzipping the small leather purse strapped across her body, "that I need to undo, so…" She retrieves a card from the purse and holds it toward Sharifa. "Please call me, or better yet meet me at my studio on Friday."

"What?" Sharifa asks, incredulous, annoyed, and on the verge of vomiting.

"Are you okay?" Kemi asks, hand still outstretched with a small silver card between her impeccably manicured fingers.

Sharifa remembers those fingers well. And no, she is not okay.

"Kemi, what the fuck do you want?" she asks.

They haven't seen each other in over a year, maybe two years, yeah, more like two years. Someone lied, someone cheated, someone stormed out in hysterics after a bitter fight and never returned. Someone took that as a breakup and moved on.

"*You're* taking that tone with *me*?" Kemi scoffs. "I'm just trying to fix something, okay, so please come by my studi—"

"I'm actually straight-up on the verge of throwing up right now, so if you don't mind, I'd like to do it outside of this lovely establishment."

"By all means, do what you must." Kemi steps aside so Sharifa can walk past her before she adds, "You've been feeling like shit for the last while, haven't you?"

Sharifa turns around slowly. "I know I'm not looking the best you've ever fucking seen me, but no need to be cruel."

Kemi laughs that laugh again, a sound that used to make Sharifa smile, but today, it is a horrid cackle grating at her already frayed nerves.

"Seemingly random inconveniences have been eating up most of your time, right? Flea infestation, mice, broken phones, stolen wallet, and the like, yeah?"

Sharifa is silent, glowering at Kemi. The fluorescent lights above her flicker and something from a shelf behind her falls and shatters, splashing some chemical cleaning liquid on the back of her legs. She jumps and swears.

"What the fuck, Kemi?!"

"Yeah, well," Kemi shrugs and continues to wave the card towards her, "you fucked me over, so I cursed you, okay?"

Sharifa has no words for this nonsense. She shakes her head and wonders why this is happening to her.

"I'm serious, but you don't have to believe me. I'm doing this for me as well," Kemi says, walking closer to Sharifa and slowly tucking the card into the front pocket of her loose jeans. "I'm getting married in a few weeks and I want a clean slate. I'm clearing all my curses, and you're the last one I have to make right."

"You're getting married?"

"Yes, and I'd rather start that journey clean, you know?" She starts to walk away, then turns around to add, "Please come to my studio on Friday; the new address is on the card, okay? It will be good for you." Then she disappears down the bathroom fittings aisle.

∽

At home, nausea having subsided after some sips of cold water—bottled because the stink from the taps is unbearable—Sharifa takes Kemi's silver card from her pocket. It is a small metallic thing, about a square inch, with a QR code imprinted in a deep maroon. She runs a thumb over the raised texture of the code, then takes her phone out and scans it.

The link brings her to Kemi's online portfolio. The landing page is a moving image, with closeup shots of a glossy brown landscape that Sharifa instantly recognizes as Kemi's body slathered in glittering oil. In slow motion, the camera travels across familiar curves and valleys of her hips, the dip in her lower back, her clavicles. Sharifa scoffs, rolls her eyes, and navigates to the contact page. She finds no address, only a calendar and text box requiring her email or phone number to schedule a studio visit. She selects a slot for Friday morning, two days away, and types in her email address because her phone is broken, and even if it wasn't broken, her credit card information has allegedly been leaked on the dark web, according to an alert from her bank. So she's had to cancel it and has been waiting for a new one for weeks. Also, her bank card had some trouble, so she's been using cash to avoid more deeply frustrating hiccups.

Afterwards, she scrolls through Kemi's portfolio. Her ex has been busy building an impressive body of work: photographs, films, sculptures, and installations, all with a distinctly sensuous signature, deep colors, and dim lighting, all subtly, and at times overtly, erotically charged, in true Kemi fashion.

Sharifa doesn't want to recall how they met. They were different people then. She's trying hard not to sink into the nostalgia of that wretched winter almost four years ago. When ice storms ravaged the city every other week, she'd escaped to Lagos, intending to stay at her cousin Fisayo's duplex in Lekki for three weeks. But Fisayo's husband had no manners to speak of. He kept commenting on Sharifa's appearance, his tone oscillating between mocking and abrasive—of her freeform locs, "So what do they call this kind of dada?"; of her oversized T-shirts and button-ups, "Is this how they dress in Canada? Women wearing men's clothes?" and "Do the men dress like women, too?"; of her paired nostril piercings, "All these accessories are on your face; what is the purpose?"

Sharifa felt too old to explain herself to anyone, particularly some guy—even if the guy in question was her beloved older cousin's older husband. There were reasons she no longer visited her parents in Abuja. So, with gritted teeth, she changed her flight and left after the first week.

She met Kemi during a fifteen-hour layover in Casablanca because Royal Air Maroc offered the least-expensive flight between Montreal and Lagos. And, though she'd sworn time and time again never to fly that airline on account of the shitty treatment she'd often received at that airport, that was where she found herself, complaining on a call to her friend Adanna about how much more unbearable anti-Black racism was when it took place on the continent.

"Do they hate us because we're Black or because we're Nigerian?" Kemi had asked Sharifa after she got off the phone, having overheard her lamenting. Sharifa was tucked away in a corner of a scarcely occupied café in the airport terminal, slowly sipping on a too-hot Americano, stewing in rage. She hadn't noticed Kemi just one seat over with a mint tea. She turned toward Kemi's voice and saw her draped in a casual and elegant floor-length dress.

Sharifa smiled because Kemi was beautiful; she nodded and replied, "Yes."

"Yes, because we're Black? or yes because we're Nigerian?" Kemi asked, cocking her head to the side. She had a massive, blonde-tinged afro back then; in it, tiny crystal flowers glittered.

"Yes," Sharifa repeated, "both,"

"Ha! Benefits of a foreign passport, huh?"

"I mean, I have one; I just don't have the 'fuck you' money required to show these people shege."

Kemi laughed at that. She threw her head back and cackled with a force that shook her breasts and shoulders so that one of the straps of her dress fell to the side. Sharifa had tried and failed not to make that strap and that bare shoulder her business. She'd snorted in a nervous chuckle.

"Well, I don't know if I have 'fuck you money,' but I have enough for lunch if you'd like to join me? There's this restaurant I've been dying to check out in Ancienne Medina."

Disappointment, the sensation of something sinking in Sharifa's chest; this woman was clearly a scammer or something. Fine as Kemi was, Sharifa was really not trying to get taken in Casablanca.

"What's that face?" Kemi asked.

"I guess," Sharifa cleared her throat, "I guess I'm not used to random gorgeous women asking me to lunch."

"Aw, thank you, I *am* gorgeous." She smiled a devastating smile that left Sharifa reconsidering; perhaps she could be open to being taken in Casablanca.

"Well," Kemi continued, "I'd rather not go alone, and you seem safe enough. Also, we were on the same flight from Lagos." She stretched her hand out towards Sharifa. "I'm Kemi."

"Sharifa," she replied, taking Kemi's small, soft hand in her own, "It's nice to meet you."

"Likewise," Kemi replied. "So, are we going or what?"

༶

"Anyway, turns out he was cheap as shit," Kemi said between bites of saffron chicken.

They were seated by ornate jali windows that left geometric patches of sunlight across them, the table, and everything upon it.

Owing to Sharifa's Canadian passport and Kemi's British one, customs had been a breeze. Kemi got them a taxi to the restaurant, where she'd ordered both their meals in fluent French. Then she launched into a story of the fifty-seven-year-old father of three she'd been seeing. She was planning on ending their affair because his assistant booked the wrong airline for the second time. Of course, it was a first-class ticket, but she hated the long and awkwardly timed layover because it didn't even allow for an overnight stay in the Four Seasons, where she had a reservation. He should have booked British Airways or KLM, but as she told Sharifa that afternoon, "he was cheap as shit."

Sharifa had listened, stunned, wondering if Kemi was a high-end escort.

"You're wondering if I'm a runs girl," Kemi said suddenly.

"What?"

"An ashewo."

"No," Sharifa stuttered, "I mean, maybe, yeah…?"

"I'm an artist."

"Right, yeah." Sharifa shook her head. "I'm not judging…"

"I know you're not; you're in no position to judge anyone. What do you do for a living?"

"I'm a data analyst."

"What does that mean?"

"Well, I work at a tech start-up."

"What's that like?"

"It's interesting actually—"

"Is it?" Kemi asked, interrupting with a mischievous grin and her eyes simmering to slits.

Only then did it occur to Sharifa that Kemi might've been interested in her, in a homosexual manner of speaking.

"Oh," Sharifa blurted out.

"You're catching on?"

☙

It wasn't until after they'd fucked in a most feral fashion on nearly every surface except the outrageously luxurious king bed in Kemi's hotel room, a premier suite with an ocean view, that Sharifa asked, "So what kind of art do you make?"

"Conceptual." Kemi smiled. She was lying on her belly, her feet making lazy circles in the air behind her.

"Yeah, but like, what does it look like?"

"I'm actually working on my portfolio right now."

"Yeah? Can I see any of it?"

"Maybe eventually. We've just met, it's too…intimate."

"*That* would be too intimate?! I just had my whole face in your cunt, and I don't know your last name."

"Exactly." Kemi turned around on the bed, her soft body jiggling with the motion.

Sharifa started to get dressed and pulled her T-shirt over her head. "Okay, well, I think I'm going to head back to the airport."

"What do you really want to know, Sharifa?"

Sharifa sat down, disoriented by the whole thing. "Am I like a mark or something? Because," she looked around the room, "I don't have this kind of money, I don't know this game…"

"*This game*," Kemi mocked, "you think we're in a movie?" She sat up, then shrugged. "I saw you at the airport and wanted to spend some time with you…I just think you're hot, like I'm attracted to you. Why is that confusing?"

"So you saw me at the airport?"

"Yes, in Lagos and again here, in Casablanca."

"How about this married guy you're fucking?"

"Well." She walked to the tan leather chair where she'd dropped her black, crocodile-skin Birkin and fished out a slender silver case. She opened it and pulled out one credit card from a collection of several. "I may or may not have some videos of him in some…mmm, unorthodox positions. He wouldn't want those leaked, so I get to keep this." She waved the card and popped her lips.

"Shit," Sharifa said.

"I know, right?"

☙

Usually, Kemi lived between Toronto and London but spent some time in Montreal for an artist residency at Dearest Judas, an art center in the Old Port. The stipend was measly, but as she told Sharifa, she wasn't doing it for the money. It was a six-week residency, during which Dearest Judas put her up in one of their large lofts with attached studio space. Spots in that residency were highly coveted; Sharifa knew that from her artist friends. The residency ended with a group show, and Sharifa finally saw Kemi's work. By then, she was utterly smitten and had only praises for Kemi's installation titled "The Daddies," a multimedia body of work featuring looped videos of older men with their identities obscured by AI-generated emoji masks and voices altered—slowed and low-pitched with resonant basses—detailing the things they desired to do to her or have her do to them. They were mostly, but not always, sexually explicit and would mostly, but not always, be considered deviant by the average Nigerian, or North American, for that matter. Beneath each video was the total amount of money, listed in the currency of their country of origin, that Kemi had "theoretically" *earned* from them. Years later, after their bitter breakup, Sharifa would recall that exhibition with a small fury.

But before then, in stereotypical dyke fashion, Kemi moved into Sharifa's high-ceilinged two-bedroom in Little Italy. She kept at her art practice and kept at her compartmentalized short-lived dealings with the wealthy men she quietly scammed. Other than the details that were absolutely required to ensure some measure of safety—locations, patrons' identities, and what time Kemi was expecting to return home—Sharifa made sure to mind her own business. They enjoyed each other thoroughly until, until…

Until one of Kemi's patrons hit her. That's what she told Sharifa when she returned home at nearly 4 a.m. She stumbled into their place, wobbling in her heels, unaware, at first, of the bruise purpling on the left side of her face until Sharifa woke up and turned on the lights to bring Kemi some water. She saw Kemi's bloodshot eyes, cupped her face, and gingerly touched the bruise.

"What happened?" she'd asked.

"Oh," Kemi waved it off, "we got into a bit of an argument."

"What the fuck happened?!"

"It was just a slap." She shrugged. "you know I bruise easily."

There was something about the way Kemi's eyes refused to settle on Sharifa's that set alarm bells off in her mind, but she didn't want to be an asshole.

"Kemi, that is not okay," Sharifa said, attempting to be gentle. "Can you please tell me what happened?"

"You don't want to know these things."

"I want to know if you're being hurt."

"I'm not *being hurt*," Kemi rolled her eyes, "don't be dramatic. He was just upset about a video I took; he slapped me and asked me to delete it."

Kemi hadn't stuttered; she hadn't paused at any point when recounting the story, but Sharifa knew she was lying.

In a haze of what she knew was utter foolishness, Sharifa stormed out to find the man. She had his name and the location where he and Kemi met; she even had a blurry picture that Kemi had sent once to confirm her safety. But she found nothing because it was incredibly late, and the address she had was just one of the many high-rise luxury condos that populated downtown Montreal, and she wasn't thinking clearly. She drove back home and walked quietly into their flat to keep from waking Kemi in case she was asleep. But Kemi wasn't sleeping; she was on the phone, whispering furiously. Sharifa could only make out snatches of the conversation, something about a bruise, something about a "next time." She shut the door loudly to alert Kemi of her presence.

She couldn't sleep, though. She lay next to Kemi, holding her until she felt her body relax with the weight of sleep and heard her loud, ragged snores. Then she took Kemi's phone, held it before her sleeping face, and locked herself in the bathroom before calling the last number on Kemi's call log.

Someone answered on the second ring, "Babe, I'm so sorry, I'm sorry."

Sharifa said nothing.

"Hello?" The person's voice was soft, effeminate.

Sharifa stayed silent.

"Baby, please forgive me. I just lost my temper. He's my dad. I love you, but I'm not up for this. He's my father."

"Who is this?" Sharifa finally asked

"What do you mean? It's Clo."

Kemi banged on the door just then. "Shar, don't do that! Give me back my phone!"

Sharifa hung up, opened the door, and handed Kemi her phone. She sat on the bed and looked at Kemi, intently trying to *see* her. She didn't actually know who this woman was at all. The realization must have shown on her face because Kemi sighed and said, "Please don't be like this."

"Who is Clo?" she asked, too tired to raise her voice and too disoriented by the potential number of lies.

"What does it matter?" Kemi asked. "It doesn't matter, it's work."

"She's a woman?"

"Obsessed with the gender binary much?" Kemi scoffed, attempting humor, which only ignited a fury in Sharifa.

"You're a liar, aren't you? You're pathological."

"Don't talk to me like that," Kemi replied flatly.

Sharifa's mouth twisted into a sneer. "I'm a mumu, I'm an ode, a big fool."

"Please don't look at me like that."

"How should I look at you?" Sharifa asked, her voice shaking, "when you're really just a lying ashewo?"

"Sharifa."

"What?" She shouted then, "You are fucking this woman, Clo? You are fucking her father for money, or "art", or whatever. You are fucking me for God knows what, you are lying and lying and lying! And this whole time, like a useless fucking idiot, I thought…I don't know, we had a deal."

"Sharifa," Kemi said again and stepped closer.

"I don't know." Sharifa's throat tightened, and a heat unfurled in her chest. She shut her eyes tight to keep tears from spilling down her face. "I thought you loved me," Sharifa shook her head, "but I don't even fucking know you. I love you, and I don't know who you are."

"Sharifa, please." Kemi reached out to touch Sharifa's arm, but Sharifa jerked away from her.

"Don't fucking touch me," she shouted, "don't touch me."

"Okay, okay." Kemi stepped back with her hands up, her expression pained. "For whatever it's worth, I do love you, very much."

Sharifa laughed sharply. "You don't know what love is."

At that, Kemi sobbed quietly, her eyebrows knotted tight on her forehead. "Please," she said. But Sharifa didn't look at her again.

"Fine," she said, then spat at Sharifa's feet, a spray of saliva that also landed on her arms and face. She mumbled something that sounded like melodic Yoruba, but though she spoke and understood the language fluently, Sharifa couldn't understand. Kemi stormed out of the room.

☙

Now, Sharifa is in Kemi's studio at the top of a five-floor redbrick building in St. Henri. She still feels like shit, exhausted in a way that no amount of sleep seems to alleviate. And though she's finally got a new bank card, it still doesn't work. She jumped the turnstile at the metro and was sure an officer would see, but she managed to slip onto the train without getting caught. She's sitting on a tall stool with a sunset-orange backdrop behind her as if posing for a portrait. And Kemi stands before her, lovely in white painter's overalls stained with splotches of colorful paint and a yellow lace bra underneath.

"I'm grateful you're here," she says to Sharifa with a smile, "this will be good for both of us."

"I really don't know what you're talking about, but I'm open to anything right now," Sharifa replies.

"And you wanted to see me again," Kemi says. It's not a question. Sharifa shrugs. "Maybe, maybe not."

"I wanted to see you again," Kemi says. "I've been looking for you."

"I'm not very hard to find."

"You are. You blocked me on everything, and you moved."

"My move had nothing to do with you." Sharifa shrugged again. "The landlord died; his son sold the building to developers that renovicted all the tenants."

"That had something to do with me."

"Right, because of the 'curse.'" Sharifa curves her fingers to make air quotes around "curse." She figures Kemi is using her as a prop in some performance art.

"You don't have to believe it for it to be true."

"Whatever, Kemi."

"We met at a pivotal point in my life," Kemi says, pouring a clear liquid from a small glass bottle over the slim blade of an X-acto knife. "I had just started learning about who I was."

"And who are you?"

"I won't utter my own name. It would be unseemly," she replied, placing a plastic guard on the blade before fetching a clean white handkerchief from her pocket, "but I was lost then,"

"Are you still blackmailing your sugar daddies?"

Kemi chuckles. "I've learned that blackmail is beneath me. I never really needed to; now I ask, and it's given."

"Does your fiancé know what you do?"

"Of course."

"Do you lie to them as well?"

Kemi leans forward and places a hand on Sharifa's shoulder. "Is this okay?" she asks.

Sharifa nods.

"I'm sorry I lied to you, but you should know the curse wouldn't have worked if I didn't truly love you." Kemi looks at Sharifa straight in the eye now. Sharifa blinks and looks away. Her chest tightens, and a ringing sound slowly rises in her ears.

"Yeah, okay," she replies, her voice thickening as she clears her throat.

"You don't have to trust me, but you have to close your eyes now."

Sharifa obeys; she's not sure why, but she does.

"Good girl," Kemi says, the smile audible in her voice.

"Girl, stop," Sharifa replies; she can't help but smile as well.

"You know," Kemi's voice sounds like it's coming from all around her. Sharifa begins to open her eyes, but Kemi is tying the handkerchief over them, "the curse wouldn't have lingered this long if you didn't truly love me too,"

"What are you doing?" Sharifa asks, but she's not afraid. There is no spike of anxiety running up and down her spine; there is just the ringing of Kemi's voice, which feels like a soft breeze surrounding her.

"I'm setting you free," Kemi says.

Sharifa feels Kemi smear something wet on her forehead with a finger in one slow swipe. She hears Kemi's all-around voice speaking the Yoruba that isn't just Yoruba that Sharifa cannot understand. Then she feels a searing sensation like something deeply rooted with gnarled fingers coiled tightly around vital things being ripped from her core, followed by an utter blank lightness—a great relief.

Kemi unties the blindfold and hands Sharifa a small plastic bucket, into which she promptly vomits.

"The bathroom is over there if you need it," Kemi says, taking the bucket and handing her a glass of water.

In the bathroom, Sharifa splashes cold tap water on her face; she looks at her reflection for a long time and rubs off a red stain on her forehead. She doesn't want to admit it or allow the words to form in her mind, but she feels better than she's felt in a long time. Limber, well-rested, and free from the twisted knot of anxiety that has lived in her lower chest, right above her belly since, since…since Kemi spat at her and walked out of her life.

Back in the studio, she sees that Kemi has new guests: an older white woman with a mass of red curls and a gorgeous Black man who seems about their age.

"Pardon me," Kemi says to them and walks to Sharifa. "I'm meeting with some curators," she says. "I'm on a tight schedule these days," she smiles, "but thank you so much for coming."

"I don't know what to say," Sharifa replies.

"Call me when you think of something." She touches Sharifa's shoulder. "May I hug you?"

"Yeah, okay," Sharifa says and leans in for a hug.

"You're invited to my wedding, by the way," Kemi says, handing her a narrow cream-colored envelope sealed with a gold wax.

Sharifa takes the envelope. She's in a daze. She smiles weakly and nods, "We'll see."

"No pressure," Kemi says. "You should eat something as soon as you can, and oh, um…now might be a good time to ask for a raise or buy a lotto ticket or something." She winks and walks back to join the curators.

☙

Sharifa tries her bank card at a depanneur around the corner of Place Saint-Henri metro. She selects a pack of gum and a lighter and brings it to the cashier.

"C'est tout?" the older Brown man at the counter asks.

"Oui," Sharifa replies. Then, noticing the Lotto 6/49 signage on the wall behind the cashier, she adds, "Et un billet s'il te plaît."

She takes out her bank card as he rings up her items. He turns the POS machine to face her, and she taps her card, bracing herself for the double beep indicating it has been declined. But her payment goes through just fine. She exhales in relief.

"Eh, tu sais quoi? Le tirage du loto, c'est demain," the cashier chirps. "Bonne chance!"

"Dope, merci."

The train ride is quick, and Sharifa is home sooner than she anticipated. Famished, she wolfs down a bowl of cereal, then prepares a proper meal of steamed rice, a fried egg, and kimchi. Belly full, she falls asleep early.

☙

Sharifa wakes up with the sun pouring into her room the following day. The whole thing with Kemi feels like a vague dream or a distant memory, like it all occurred years ago, longer even. She's feeling so well rested that she goes out for a quick jog to Jarry Park. The cool morning breeze feels good. She sits by the pond to watch the geese for a moment and laughs at how they waddle territorially, harassing the ducks. Sharifa walks to her favorite neighborhood café to get a breakfast sandwich, the kind with a thick hash brown hot between the fried eggs and smoked bacon. She retrieves her wallet to pay, and the lotto ticket falls out. She picks it up before paying, then sits by a window to wait for her order to be called out. She has the Lotto app on her phone; she takes it out to scan her ticket.

The phone beeps, followed by a celebratory jingle; she's unsure what it means. She brings her phone close to her face to get a better look at the result, sees it, and shouts, "What the fuck?!"

Then she bursts out in riotous laughter.

MAKE LIFE GREAT AGAIN

PRIYA GUNS

I WAS MUTE TILL the age of seven years and nine months. I come from a big family. There's nothing I haven't seen or heard before. Six siblings on both sides because, as my father would say, my mother was a whore, and as my mother would say, my father was the most despicable man to ever live. Living that sort of life, you learn when to avoid confrontation. It takes a real toll to care and even more to call a spade a spade. My grandma used to tell me that. In any case, I must've landed my job as custodian because I made that apparent; I had no problem looking the other way.

There wasn't always a public restroom in the President's House—that was a recent addition. Only those with certified doctor's certificates for urinary incontinence or other irritable bowel conditions were allowed access, though. I didn't always ask to verify the required documentation, the shitter passport they implemented. I mean, my job was simple, and I couldn't care for the additional responsibility, of course, I wasn't paid enough. Polish, scrub, scour, disinfect, look ravishing and still, people won't reply "Hello"—I could do all of that, and I did it quite well.

When my yellow maintenance sign was outside the entrance of the only public restroom, which was on the second floor, it wasn't so much because I was busy cleaning. My sign was signaling an invitation for those in high places to experience the morbid "exhilaration" of pissing and defecating into the commoner's loo. Nobody knew it, save for that viral post three years ago, but Mr. President enjoyed shitting in the third stall in the public restroom. After a number one and the more often number two, he'd recite his usual tongue twisters in the mirror as water half-pissed from the calcified sink where he washed his hands.

Joanie Jenkins juggling fresh made jars of jams, money jingling in her back pocket.

Joanie Jenkins juggling fresh made jars of jam, money jingling in her back pocket.

Mr. President often stumbled after the second J on Jenkins, as erudite as he was.

Now, Bindi Boo and Noora Nur-Al Din. I didn't know them by name at first, before November 22. They had PRESS lanyards the first time I saw them. Bindi had smiled at Noora as she washed her hands, counting ten seconds under her breath.

"The 'most exceptional of the country.' Nobody's buying that anymore."

"I'd suffocate him in his sleep if I could,"—and I can't remember which of the two said it, but they both laughed, even I joined in. Mr President was an idiot no matter what you believed. Certified lunatic, and believe me, I've seen him in stall three bouncing marbles, playing jacks, grunting like a chimpanzee. From that first encounter, I knew the women would be great friends.

I caught Bindi and Noora necking in the fourth stall with the door wide open one early afternoon. Maybe they said I was some creep for watching, less than an arm's length away. But what stopped me from functioning for a few brief seconds, was the excruciating question of how could these women open their mouths so wide while a fresh turd sat unawares in the toilet, inches away from them? Believe me, my only intention was to flush and scrub, and see, I've digressed completely.

When Sonny Splash announced the water shortage, I wasn't given any information on monitoring consumption, zero instruction, but I took it upon myself to be a mindful consumer. Some of the other custodians expected a riot. I figured there'd be a little ruckus, a few ruffians, the usual tidal storm of depression and the passing fancy of wanting to burn the world down. I was often preoccupied with the list of cleaning I had to do to pay attention, anyway. Sonny Splash and I went to elementary school together, and he had said, in the third grade, that if we sniffed glue in a hot bath before bed, we'd dream of floating elephants. Blame him for the shortage. Sonny Splash was our senator, and there I was scrubbing. Bindi and Noora, well, they were hens on speed and cognac cracking all sorts of ideas. They mentioned security. Bypassing, circumventing, distracting officers with their bosoms and buttocks. None of it seemed alarming, more tongue in cheek. I wasn't paid enough to care. We've all planned crimes we'd never commit.

There was this one day when Bindi stormed in hyperventilating. It was the day we learned the country was on its last hundred gallons of water per household. They went out and said it. Nonchalant. Point blank. Project Island 47 would proceed imminently, eleven months earlier than scheduled. Amy Salacious, Secretary of State, did lines on the steel countertop that evening. She snorted so much cocaine that she passed out on the floor. I mopped around her. I waited about an hour and then dragged her out before anyone kicked her in the stomach. Noora rushed in soon after, looking for Bindi, who had been sat against the wall in tears the entire time.

"I think about it and I'm flooded with a sense of relief," she whispered.

"But it won't change a damn thing," responded Noora. Then

they hugged, and the women were on their way.

At breakfast that next morning, on November 22, my toast had burnt. There's a saying about burning breakfast, timing, and God's protective hand. How the seconds and minutes taken from re-preparation could be the reason you weren't run over or shot in the head. But it was my last two slices of raisin bread, so I had to catch the 5:45 with the bitter taste of charred crust in my mouth. My stomach felt funny, and I had a cyst under my armpit. The state of the world was beyond repair, and yet, the buses still ran on time.

We were expecting a full house. Press, politicians, police, and a whole SWAT team. Senator Sonny Splash and Secretary of State Amy Salacious would be in attendance too. The public had camped out around the entire periphery of the building. Lucky for us, we had that underground passage and could enter and exit without being seen. Call it High Security. At exactly 6:45, I was where I had to be. Supplies in hand and two boxes of Pot of Gold for our guests on the side table by the entrance of the restroom. By 7:30, every inch sparkled, and at 8:37, I left out my maintenance sign. The conference was set for 10.

I couldn't tell you exactly what was done in preparation. I could only assume. Everyone had an itinerary. Of course, the entire building went through escape procedures weeks leading up to the day. People consciously clenched their sphincters. The daily allowance of available drinking water was 60% less than our body's requirement, or a truth as outlandish as that. The skies were gray, laden with clouds of smoke and smog. People walked around with respirator masks on. I mean, surely you remember. Asthmatics dropping dead at street corners, lying like road kill. Diabetics in food courts convulsing. People carried knives more than they ever had because, well, *the mayhem out there*. Now we were going to die of thirst too.

Mr. President was at the podium. About a hundred people were seated before him, and about twenty stood in the stands. I spotted

Bindi Boo and Noora Nur-Al Din right away, in the fifth row. The reports said the women weren't in any formal relationship, but I saw the sparks when their eyes met. In their nods of affirmation. I see you and I'm so glad you're alive. Can't say I ever had a lover who'd take a bullet for me. Can't say I've ever been loved. Maybe they were just friends.

Mr. President cleared his throat.

"We bore witness to the killing of a hundred thousand children in the Holy Lands and we have since never been the same. I acknowledge that. We stand on stolen land to be given back to the indigenous people. I acknowledge that. People of this great nation, let me get straight to it, the American people deserve better! I'm here to soothe your concerns in assuring radical change today."

Mr. President choked with emotion. He added,

"I have so much to be grateful for today, and all of your continued support, despite bearing witness to mass death in this country. Thank you, America."

Mr. President was an erudite man, but had even less water in his brain.

People called out.

"Mr. President, given our deficit, can we afford our venture on this newly discovered volcano?"

"Absolutely! America always has money for the unthinkable."

"Mr. President, how long will it take for us to have access to drinking water? Should we not be moving in sooner?"

"We'll be working around the clock once we've mapped the exact topography and hydrology of the area and identified possibilities. Thanks to our armed forces, we're looking at no more than five days, ten if there are any setbacks, and a million new jobs available to our citizens in construction, transportation, service, any job, all jobs. Two million blue collar jobs will be posted in fourteen days. We're using this crisis to benefit our economy and provide jobs for the people of this great country. Americans deserve the best, there is no one better."

Noora Nur-Al Din spoke loudly.

"Mr. Malarkey, what are your comments on the video footage seen already by five million people that proves the presence of communities with a longstanding history on what is actually called Jebel Uyar. Those people—no, get your dirty pig hands off of me, I'm a journalist!—those people escaped war and famine in their respective countries and started their own self-governed democracy. They were forced out by the depredations and atrocities perpetrated by our nation. How is Project Island 47 any different from the original Zionist project?—get your fucking hands off me—"

"We celebrate free speech and ideas in this country. There are, young lady, rumors and lies, propaganda and any boogeyman you can name, that's been used to prevent us from progressing toward our full potential. That's all it is."

A young man stood and shouted.

"You goddamn liar! You waited until twenty states saw a massacre to offer free mental health care, five years after This Great Depression. You waited until the 1% lost their access to sanitary water before even beginning to formulate a solution. You don't care about people, Mr. President. What's your explanation for the two million recruited overseas to serve in the national army?"

Mr. President responded. "We've made our mistakes. But we also completed our intensive Decolonial Training and Truth and Reconciliation programs, which we've provided as a service around the third world too. Amy Salacious, our Secretary of State, is a trans woman."

"Mr. President, I've been a longtime supporter and stand by Plan Island 47. However, I'm dismayed by the footage the woman mentioned earlier—there is *verified* footage proving civilization on the island. How can we be sure our team of Americans will be safe from the locals' barbarism, and what will we do to ensure that the innocent children among them have their rights protected too? Thank you."

Mr. President said sternly, "I have it on ironclad authority that there are no people living on the island. For years, Dr. Newman and his team monitored Glacier 47, and our saving grace is this newly discovered land mass. We no longer need to worry about a lack of water with the amount available around its shores alone. Any news about civilization on this island is an outright lie. We have Landsat evidence debunking every circulating story. The American people deserve better. We will overcome. America against the world for the people of this planet. Americans."

There was silence. Sweat ran off Mr. President's forehead and soaked patches through his suit. A fly hovered around his face. Before anyone could speak, as photographers continued snapping and the people in the room processed whatever they could, sweet Bindi Boo stood to her feet and pulled out a nine from under her well-ironed slacks. She raised her arm and, with precision I have never seen, she shot Mr. President in the mouth.

The assassination was all over the news. The story saturated global media. I heard they signalled the news out into space too. Everyone saw that footage—the moment when Noora stood and used her body as a barrier between the public and her friend, Bindi Boo.

"She's on her period!" Noora had shouted.

SWAT shot Noora five times. I saw it. Myself and the other custodians slipped out unharmed. I never thought I'd be witness to what transpired next. A massacre. The police panicked and shot willy nilly buck wild killing nearly every person in that room.

I've overheard all sorts of conversations, read everyone's different take on Bindi Boo. I scrolled and scrolled through all kinds of pages, realizing I knew something no one knew.

At 8:37 on November 22, when I had left out my maintenance

sign, Mr. President strolled right in, directly to stall number three. He hummed and worked his voice in preparation for his oral performance. He wiped vigorously; the brush of rough toilet paper was loud against his skin. He made use of his time. Bindi Boo was washing her hands and adjusting her makeup in the mirror as Mr. President casually walked out of his stall and to the sink.

Joanie Jenkins juggling fresh made jars of jam, money jingling in her back pocket.

Joanie Jenkins juggling fresh made jars of jam, money jingling in her back pocket.

Before he could recite the entire line, he choked on that second J on Jenkins. A drop of spit tickled the wrong pipe. Suddenly, his face puffed. His eyes widened in fear. He held his chest, and then his throat. His face brightened, redder and redder. Without a second thought, Bindi Boo rushed to his side and bent the man over, his veins bulging, his body squirming and struggling, as she performed the Heimlich maneuver.

"You saved my life," he panted, squinting from exhaustion. He looked Bindi Boo right in the eye. She half-smiled and walked away. That was at 8:37, and the press conference was at 10.

Call me a liar, sure, disregard anything I have to say. I'm just the custodian in need of validation and attention. Flood my podcast and give me your ear and a sense of purpose. Come on! If I enjoyed anything about my job, it was the time I had, as I scoured and scrubbed and greeted half-people, to ponder why I was the one on my knees, why people moved the way they moved through this hell we called society.

Bindi Boo never seemed crazy to me, far from it. She had her mind, and I knew that beyond a shadow of doubt from all the times I'd catch her in the bathroom crying, washing her face, moving on, looking taller on her way out. She could've just let the man die. But she didn't. I'd think about this for the rest of my life.

I've struggled to sleep ever since November 22, trying to understand our current times. The entire country slept with an eye open as The Mayhem boiled into worse, and I'm one of the few witnesses from the ground, alive and able to share my story. I'm recording to you today, hand on heart, in paid partnership with a company that saved me from complete insanity. For only ten ninety-nine, you can receive a Make Life Great Again Happy Package when you text HELP from your mobile device. Each package contains fifty benzodiazepines and enough water supplements to wake you up in five different flavors. I wouldn't have been able to work on November 23 if it wasn't for my kind sponsors and my Happy Package. I've remained a custodian in The President's House, and our buses still run on time.

TOOTH FAIRY

MYRIAM GURBA

Nat and her herbivore yawned. Both had just finished eating lunch. Their household's third member, a graduate student named Venus, was on campus. Nat hadn't attended grad school, and so she was clueless about what Venus did there. She imagined that her girlfriend and fellow classmates probably spent their days reading French theory and lying about understanding it. Nat hated theory. She preferred reality television.

Nat stared at the blond rabbit. The unfixed John Doe glared back. His origins were mysterious, but one fact was clear: the testosterone-soaked animal resented his cage. Fashioned from lacquered wire, it was rectangular and about double the little rabbit's size. It occupied the stretch of living room carpet that spanned the gap between the wall heater and a heavy bookshelf. After brandishing his teeth, the rabbit clamped them around wires and tugged. The gesture reminded Nat of a cartoon prisoner rattling bars.

Nat wrapped her arms around her legs and hugged them to her chest. This was a self-soothing activity. The rabbit's frustration was making her nervous. The rabbit shook his cage so hard that she worried he might draw blood. He looked mutinous, ready to riot. Nat hated his captivity almost as much as he did. She also feared his teeth. They were tusks.

Nat stood and scooped her plate off the coffee table. She took after her mother, a condiment packet hoarder, and she'd drowned her lunch, leftover French fries, in rival fast-food-chain ketchups. After depositing her plate in the kitchen sink, Nat circled back to the cage.

She knelt and warned, "I'm gonna let you out. Don't pee on anything."

Nat reached for the latch and unfastened it. She pulled open the door. Its hinge squeaked.

The rabbit stepped out and plunged his paws into the carpet. He stretched and then shook his fur the way dogs do after frolicking in a creek. Ignoring Nat, he set off to explore the living room. He sniffed at carpet, baseboards, books, and furniture, mostly hand-me-downs and scavenged things that still retained the scent of their former owners. The rabbit lingered at a pair of dirty tube socks Venus had discarded beside an end table. His nose never stopped moving. Neither did his other end. It crapped a trail of vegan pellets that Nat didn't feel like harvesting.

The rabbit took a sock in his mouth and tossed it. Nat smiled. A yawn contorted this expression. Nat worked at a nearby adult school, where she taught English in the morning and at night. This split schedule prevented her from spending much time with Venus. Nat often had to remind herself that this was okay; her salary would support them while Venus enhanced her marketability by getting another degree. Still, Nat struggled not to feel resentful about working full time while her girlfriend didn't. Venus promised that once she graduated, the roles would be reversed. One day, Nat would be free to pursue her own ridiculous dreams. Perhaps one day, Nat herself would be initiated into the mysteries of grad school.

Their current arrangement was preferrable to how it had been before. Over and over, Venus had been suckered into forking over large sums of cash to grifters who made promises that were impossible to keep. The couple had weathered an array of multilevel marketing scams, two self-help cults, and a talent agent who'd duped Venus into spending several months' rent on a mountain of unusable head shots. Grad school seemed like another con, but at least Nat knew where her money was going when she paid Venus's tuition. At least there would be a piece of paper called a diploma to show for this investment.

Nat aimed the remote at the TV, turned it off, and reclined on the brown carpet. She shut her eyes, laced her fingers together, and rested her hands against her rib cage. She breathed in and then let it out slowly. Tension left her body. Before turning on her side, Nat opened an eye to peek at the rabbit. He was lounging on a sock, front paws crossed. His pose reminded Nat of a male centerfold, Burt Reynolds letting it all hang out for *Cosmo*.

The rabbit's comfort pleased Nat.

She shut her eyes and let her mind drift.

From the balcony, a pair of pigeons cooed.

෴

A rabbit was the last thing that Nat had anticipated hopping her into life after settling in Playa Roja. It was the sort of community where medical waste regularly washed ashore, littering the town's beaches. Stingrays waited for those foolish enough to wade into the murky water they called home. Nat once witnessed one of these little feminists stab a man. He cried. Nat giggled.

Before the rabbit, Venus and Nat had lived in Playa Roja's gayborhood, in a dark, studio apartment within walking distance of a leather bar. Once Venus started school, they moved to a larger apartment on the sixth floor of a stucco building managed by a former child actor. For an extra two hundred dollars a month, they rented a storage space and parking spot in the property's underground garage. Though their pickup truck was in Nat's name, she didn't have a driver's license. She walked to and from work and asked Venus for rides when necessary. When she felt adventurous, Nat rode the bus.

Playa Roja's top employers were its oil refineries and port. Another big employer was PRSU, the state university. Venus was enrolled there and had taken her first gender studies class, a very easy A, from a professor named Max. This professor was the sort of dyke whom Nat considered a gateway butch, a gently masculine woman whose sexual charisma folded "straight" girls into pretzels. Nat had met her own gateway butch in Catholic high school. Hers had been into horses, hearses, and bones. This butch and Nat had plotted to become graverobbers but broke up before they could realize this dream.

One day, after lecture had ended, Max asked Venus to stay after class. She remained in her seat, her heart racing. She watched her classmates file out of the room until she and Max were alone. Then the professor said, "I'm headed to my office. Please walk with me."

They didn't have far to go. Max's office was just upstairs. Once they arrived, the professor unlocked her door and held it open.

Venus stepped inside. Max shut the door behind her.

"Sit," urged the professor.

Venus obeyed and faced Max. With a sheepish grin, professor stared at the student from across a large clean desk.

"Venus," she said. "Could you get me some marijuana?" Max blushed. A grinned showed off her crooked teeth.

These were those dangerous days of yore when cannabis was outlawed for most Californians. Some could smoke the plant for medicinal purposes, but most people still had to buy their weed from "criminals." Now Venus would be joining their ranks. She didn't have much choice.

When she got home, Venus told Nat about her coerced entrepreneurship.

Nat said, "That bitch better give you an A. Where are you gonna get her weed from?"

"I thought you could ask your cousin."

Nat sighed. Of course Venus's drug dealing was going to create more work for her.

Nat called her cousin Monique and arranged for her to deliver a Ziploc bag bulging with sticky, stinky indica. The night her cousin brought it, Nat sat at the coffee table dividing up the product, placing pinches of weed inside small cellophane baggies that she tied shut with green ribbon left over from a throuple's baby shower. Venus charged Max exponentially more than what Nat had paid for it. The professor never complained about the quality, quantity, or cost of her purchases, and so Nat was surprised the afternoon that Venus called her from Max's house to discuss a crisis.

"What's going on?" Nat asked in a panic. "Did you get in trouble? Did you get arrested?"

"No, no. It's that I'm at Max's and…" Venus's voice trailed off in a way that was concerning. "And she found a rabbit! He was in the alley! Hiding behind a trash can! And she saved him and put him in a box in her garage! She got him a cage and stuff, but she can't keep him."

"Why? Why can't she keep him?"

"Her dogs will kill him if he stays here! They won't stop barking at him! They want to eat him!"

"Uh-huh."

"Can we keep him?"

Nat wanted to throw her phone. Instead, she kicked the sliding-glass door. It was more of a tap really, but she hit it hard enough to make the pigeons roosting in a nearby palm tree shoot her a dirty look.

"No."

"That's not fair! I've wanted a pet for so long! A rabbit would be perfect! The landlord will never know! They don't make any noise! And I'll take good care of him! I'll take such good care of him that he'll sit at my feet like a hound!"

It was true that Venus had wanted a pet for some time. It was also true that their landlord would probably never know they were harboring a rabbit in their apartment. But what was most true was that the animal would probably become Nat's chore. This was Venus's pattern. She would become very interested in a person, place, or thing only to become bored by it after a month-long obsession.

Nat knew that no matter how hard she put her foot down, a rabbit would be joining her household. If that was the case, she might as well try to squeeze something practical out of the situation.

"I will agree to the rabbit coming to live with us on one condition."

"What?"

After a dramatic pause, Nat said, "You have to get rid of *that* chair."

That chair was a torn corduroy thing that'd been travelling with them from home to home for the last six years. Its seller claimed the chair had belonged to a famous stand-up comic who'd written his best material in it. Nat didn't believe the story. She thought it was probably a jack-off chair. Unfortunately, Venus swallowed the tall tale. That was why she'd paid two hundred and fifty dollars for the eyesore. Nat had been scheming for years, trying to come up with a plan to get rid of it or destroy it. She never anticipated that a rabbit would become her ally in this project.

"Fine."

"Okay. I'll start getting our place ready. See you soon. Bye!"

Nat made a beeline for the chair, grabbed it, and dragged it across the living room carpet to the front door. After heaving it outside, she pushed it down to the elevator, stuffed it inside, and rode to the ground floor. Dragging the thing through the lobby and garage left scuff marks, and she shimmied it out a side door, dragged it several yards through the alley, and abandoned it where it belonged, by the blue dumpster. She thought about covering it in garbage so Venus wouldn't be tempted to sneak it back upstairs, but Nat decided against this move. She didn't feel like diving into the dumpster that afternoon. A legion of flies was circling it. She could smell rancid bologna.

Nat returned to the apartment and waited. An hour passed. When Venus arrived, she threw open the front door and marched into the living room. She set a cage down on the coffee table. The lesbians and the lop sized one another up. He was extremely fluffy. He paced.

"I want to let him out," said Venus. "I want to see him jump!"

Nat sighed. At least the chair was gone.

Venus set the cage on the floor and opened the door. The rabbit sprang out and hopped about the living room. Venus watched with delight. "Look at him! Look at him! He's better than a dog! Dogs can't do that!"

She was right. The rabbit was a talented acrobat. He jumped, flew across the room, and while in midair twisted and turned his body. It was entertaining until Nat felt something warm hit her face. Her eye burned.

"Ah!" she screamed. "What the fuck is that?"

Nat raised her hand. Felt her eye.

It was wet.

She sniffed the liquid.

Urine.

The rabbit had given her a golden shower.

"I'm gonna wash my face," said Nat. "When you get a chance, can you please put him back in his cage?"

Venus nodded but didn't move.

Nat went to the bathroom and ran the faucet. She splashed her eye with cold water, washing away the rabbit's baptism. She hated being peed on, especially by creatures with testicles.

※

Nat thought she was having a nightmare. Then, when she realized she was awake, she thought... *Earthquake?* The sensation that she was experiencing was not tectonic plates shifting beneath her. It was the rabbit. He'd crept over while she slept. After placing both paws on her ass, he'd begun thrusting his loins against her right buttock. Yes, he was humping her. Nat had seen other humans be humped by dogs, but she never thought that something as quaint as a rabbit would take advantage of her. She pushed him away, but he returned for more.

"No!" she yelled.

The rabbit panted, and Nat started chasing him. He ran away and dove through his cage's open door. Nat slammed it shut.

She spent the rest of the afternoon prepping for class, and at five o'clock, she walked back to work to begin her second shift. Her classroom was in a building that had once housed medical offices. A whiteboard, folding tables, and folding chairs furnished it. Most of the students enrolled in her classes were Mexican migrants. She also taught a smattering of Central Americans and one very hairy Macedonian. That night, her students practiced interviewing one another for a job. They also practiced small talk, which Nat believed was a skill that could be learned and refined. That evening, the small talk category was weather. Given what had happened to her that afternoon, Nat decided that for the next class, their small talk subject would be house pets. That would be fun.

Once class ended and her students left, Nat slung her backpack over her shoulder and headed for the stairs. She waved goodbye to Mr. Habibullah, the school's security guard. She cracked her knuckles.

"Miss Garcia! You are walking home alone, yes?" asked Mr. Habibullah.

"Yes. As usual!"

"You don't want escort?"

"No! I'm good! But thank you!"

Mr. Habibullah always offered to walk Nat home and Nat always refused. She knew that people thought her penchant for walking alone at night was dangerous. She didn't care. Playa Roja felt more alive at night. During spring, it was delicious to walk through neighborhoods while flowers perfumed the dark. Nat would play guessing games, trying to identify the scents. Wisteria. Rose. Magnolia. Gardenia. Sage.

When Nat got home, she found Venus sitting on the living room floor, eating chicken wings at the coffee table.

"Did you let the rabbit out?"

Fuck, thought Nat. She'd forgotten to vacuum the poops.

"Yes. I let him out for a little while. He's so miserable in that small cage. He needs something bigger. A lot bigger. We could also litter box train him. I was reading that you can do that with rabbits. They're kind of like cats that way."

"Really? I let him out when I got home and the first thing he did was start shitting everywhere."

"Yeah, they're really prolific poopers. But before we try to train him, we need to get him fixed. If he keeps his balls, then he'll also keep his bad toilet habits. He'll douse us in golden showers forever."

"Can you take him to the vet?"

"It makes more sense for you to take him. You're the one who controls the car. And the credit card."

"Fine."

"Do you think they'll let us keep his balls?"

"That's disgusting!"

"Not any more disgusting than keeping baby teeth for the tooth fairy."

"No. It's definitely more disgusting."

"I'll call the vet and make an appointment tomorrow."

Venus returned her attention to the game show she was watching. Nat headed to the hall closet with the rabbit trailing close behind her. She grabbed the vacuum cleaner, wheeled it to the living room, and plugged it in. The noise terrified him. He hid behind the corduroy chair that Venus had dragged back upstairs and reinstalled in its corner.

As the vacuum started to suck up the rabbit's poops, Venus screamed, "NAT!"

Nat jumped. "What?"

"What's wrong with you? I'm trying to watch TV. I've had a long day!"

"You need me to vacuum later?"

"Duh."

"Okay. I'm sorry. I'm sorry. I'm sorry."

Nat had learned that the best thing to do when Venus got this way was to give her whatever she wanted. Usually, this meant making herself as small as possible. Shrinking.

She returned the vacuum cleaner to the closet and went to wash her face. Nat was trembling, but she didn't want to cry. Showing she was upset only made things worse. To keep the tears at bay, Nat distracted herself with potential rabbit names. After putting on her pajamas, which consisted of boys' boxer shorts and a sports bra, Nat crawled into bed and fell asleep thinking about litter box training.

She dreamt of smoking a blunt with a very pretty rabbit.

☙

Nat was on hold with the Playa Roja Animal Clinic. Smooth jazz played. When the receptionist returned, she asked for Nat's name and contact information. Then she asked for the patient's name.

"Patient?"

"Yes," answered the receptionist. "You said you were calling to get a rabbit neutered. What's his name?"

Nat panicked. She blurted the first rabbit name that came to mind. "Harvey!"

"Okay. Harvey Garcia is scheduled to be fixed this Friday. We'll send you an email confirmation." Before Nat could ask to keep his testicles, the receptionist hung up.

The surgery went smoothly. Harvey Garcia healed in no time. Wanting to be a responsible bunny caretaker, Nat bought two books about how to keep a rabbit as a pet. To better understand Harvey's culture, she also purchased the novel *Watership Down*. She read aloud from this book to the animal that was quickly becoming her best friend.

One day, during her lunch break, the 1950 film that had inspired the rabbit's name came on TV. Lop and lesbian watched it together. *Harvey*'s plot hinges on a human-rabbit relationship, one involving Elwood P. Dowd, a drunk, and his púca, a Celtic shapeshifter. Dowd's púca takes the form of a six-foot three-inch rabbit that only he can see. Nat's Harvey too was invisible to some. After two weeks, Venus lost all interest in him, just as Nat had predicted.

Over the next few weeks, Nat and Harvey spent hours litterbox training. They also watched a lot of reality television together. It got so that Nat didn't mind Harvey at all. In fact, Nat now looked forward to coming home, and she noticed this while walking home after teaching night school. Instead of feeling her usual trepidation, she caught herself wondering what Harvey was up to.

Nat noticed changes in Harvey, too. It seemed that sometimes, he was trying to serenade her. He pranced around her feet and ankles, making soft honking noises. He also ran in spirals around her, creating turd necklaces that encircled her body, marking Nat as his.

The lesbian wanted to know what her rabbit was trying to communicate through this behavior. When she read about the meaning of his actions, she blushed. Harvey was courting her.

Venus was going to be pissed.

☙

It was the most important day of the year for rabbits. Easter Sunday.

Nat and Venus were celebrating at home. They planned to binge on movies that starred Jesus or rabbits. For supper, they would dine on duck, corn, mashed potatoes, and asparagus. The couple had already exchanged Easter baskets filled with chocolates and jellybeans. Harvey had received a small basket too. His contained banana chips sprinkled across a bed of timothy hay.

Everyone had breakfasted and Nat and Venus sat in the living room, sipping their umpteenth mugs of coffee. Venus perched on their velveteen sofa. Nat sat on the carpet. Harvey lounged beside her, allowing himself to be stroked from ears to rump. His teeth chattered with delight.

"He's supposed to be my rabbit!" accused Venus. "But he likes you better!"

"That's only because I spend more time with him. You're away all day, selling weed to scholars. I'm here with him. I play with him.

I hang out with him. I talk to him. I clean up after him. He knows me. Let him get to know you."

"How?"

"Feed him! That's the quickest way to a man's heart."

"Okay. What do I feed him?"

"He loves carrots. Just like in the cartoons. There are some in the fridge. I'll go get one."

The carrots rested on the fridge shelf beside a glass jar filed with sativa buds. Nat fetched one of these root vegetables and brought it back to Venus. She accepted it and held it in Harvey's direction.

"You need to get closer. So he can smell it."

Venus crawled closer to Harvey. The rabbit didn't budge.

"He hates me!"

"No, he doesn't. Just get a little closer."

Venus took the instructions to heart and moved to tap Harvey on the nose with the carrot. This was a rabbit no-no. A great way to terrify them is to touch their nose. Their stereoscopic vision is interrupted by a blind spot right between their eyes and tapping it makes rabbits murderous. Harvey panicked, bared his tusks, and sank them into Venus's hand. She let out a horror movie moan and tried to wrench her hand out of her assailant's mouth. Harvey remained attached. He flew as Venus swung her arm back, struck the wall, and became dislodged, sliding along the stucco until he landed on the back of the sofa. Venus was screaming, "He bit me! He bit me! He bit me!"

"He didn't mean to hurt you! You tapped his blind spot! He thought you were trying to kill him."

"HE BIT ME!"

Venus ran to the bathroom. Nat heard the faucet running. She rushed to the bathroom with Harvey close behind. Both were scared. They found Venus rinsing her wound. They approached to comfort her, but when Venus saw Harvey, she screamed, "Get him out of here!"

Nat squatted, scooped up the rabbit, and took him to his cage.

"Wrap your hand in a clean towel!" yelled Nat. "We're going to the hospital."

Into Harvey's ear, she whispered, "I'm sorry. I'm sorry. I'm sorry."

☙

Nat had panicked during the ride to the hospital. She was speeding without a driver's license and transporting a wounded drug dealer. At the entrance to the emergency room, Venus hopped out of the truck and ran inside. The parking lot was being renovated so Nat pulled up to a red curb. She shut off the engine but left her keys in the ignition.

Squirrels skittered up and down a nearby pine tree. Nat cried. She was always crying. Her tears usually had something to do with Venus, but a text dinging on her phone put a stop to her blubbering:

We have to get rid of Harvey. Today.

Nat's body tensed with rage.

She wasn't going to lose Harvey. He had become her friend, one of her only friends. Venus had chased Nat's other friends away. Nat was done compromising. She was done paying for everything. She was over having to put not just her life but herself on hold. Venus wanted nonstop sacrifice from her. Harvey's teeth had lain bare what Nat had known but didn't want to allow herself to even think: Venus was an asshole. Venus was hell.

First, Nat whispered it: "I'm breaking up with Venus."

She thought the world would end when she uttered it, but nothing happened.

The squirrels continued to skitter. The clouds continued to

shroud the sun. An ambulance siren continued to wail.

Nat repeated: "I'm breaking up with Venus."

Each time she said it, she felt stronger. More confident.

Finally, Nat said, "Fuck this shit. Venus can figure out how to pay her own bills. Why do I always have to be the grown-up? Venus is older than me anyway."

Nat began to fantasize about new apartments. She fantasized about how much money she would have being single. She fantasized about how much less work she would have around the house. She was excited.

A hawk perched on a pine branch. She watched squirrels dart through the grass. Nat watched the hawk and called her cousin Monique. After wishing her a happy Easter, she said, "Prima, I'm done with Venus. I can't anymore."

"OH MY GOD! You don't know how long I've been waiting to hear you say that!"

The cousins laughed.

"Really?" asked Nat.

"Yes! Oh my god, I can't *stand* Venus! No one can."

"Well, why didn't you say something?"

"I didn't think you were ready to receive it."

"Well, thank you for backing me up now. Can I stay with you 'til I figure out what I'm going to do next?"

"Of course."

"Can I bring Harvey?"

"Yes. But on one condition."

"What?"

"I've never been comfortable with Venus selling my product. I want you to take over selling it."

"I can totally do that. I love you. I'll call you later when I'm done with the hospital."

"Why are you at the hospital?"

"Harvey attacked Venus."

Monique laughed. "Good for him. Come over when you're done."

The cousins hung up. Nat felt lighter. Unburdened. She still had her eyes on the hawk, who still had his eyes on the squirrels. He spread his wings and dove toward them. The two saw him coming and took off running in opposite directions. He continued straight, soaring toward a bunny rabbit nibbling at a hedge. Nat braced herself. The hawk released his talon, ready to snatch the mammal, but the rabbit bucked its hind legs, knocking the hawk back. The startled hawk limped away. Nat and the squirrels laughed.

BLACK JESUS

VENITA BLACKBURN

After school I arrived at home, took off my shoes at the door, kissed the 8x10 photo of Black Jesus in the hall, ate Froot Loops over the sink so Nana wouldn't scream if I spilled milk on the carpet, and then watched TV. I used to watch this cartoon with beasts that turned to stone in the daytime and came alive at night. This was my ritual, my afternoon ceremony of duty, love, and magic. The previous Christmas, my nana came to live with us, my mother and I. In Los Angeles Christmas can be deceiving, but I loved it anyway. I dreamt of cotton snow and the oily smell of plastic holly. Authenticity never made much sense really. All that is real is what is in front of us, if the satisfaction is absolute. Aluminum icicles over the porch satisfied me deeply. Nana, not so much. I killed her, so she says, but she says everything killed her even though she's as alive as a dog bite.

Nana was smaller than me even then, a granddaughter of slaves, and knew life without electricity and frozen waffles. She knew other things too, especially about cows, not just milking them, I'd done that at the LA County Fair; she could deliver their babies and cure their sicknesses. When Nana first entered the house, she had nothing but her long-strapped leather purse, a brick-thick Bible, and that photo of the darkest Christ I'd ever seen. She didn't have a suitcase or anything. I asked my mother, "Why did Nana have to come?" She said, "Your grandmother lived with my sister, and now she lives with us." That was that.

"Mama" really is God in the mouth of a child. To her I often prayed on bent knees in the kitchen with knuckles under my chin, "Please, please can I have money for the ice cream truck?" The delicious music of sweet dairy bliss grew louder. She told me she'd given me enough change the day before, which was true, but I denied it. I pleaded. "No," she said, "I don't want you buying anything from that musky Albino." God stirred her pot, and the song passed. When Nana caught me prostrate on the floor, she pulled me up and told me to honor my mother.

Nana and I spent a lot of time together while my mother worked. Well, I spent a lot of time with Nana's rules. One morning she caught me kissing the photo of Black Jesus on my way to the bus stop. With her wet bony palm she slapped me downward on the left temple. I didn't know that much pain existed in all the world. She cursed me dizzy with words I didn't know yet. Then she sat me down and read the Ten Commandments to me in more words I didn't know. I did understand that there were primarily just ten, just ten laws not to be broken. That finite sensibility meant everything to me. I may not have made it through the school day without that number, having been poked with such an emotional ice pick as only my Nana could.

In class I stared at my teacher and wondered. Electricity crackled in my blood and out my ears. She had skin like fabric, a suede eel with really great breasts. I knew what I had to do. When I got home I found Nana's mammoth bible and turned to the Book of Exodus and skimmed the commandments. I had to choose one, so I picked "Thou shalt not bear false witness against thy neighbor." My White-Out pen in hand, I blotted out that commandment and taped another over it: "Thou shalt not kiss Black Jesus." It was specific. I was contented. In exchange for the freedom to lie, I would no longer kiss

Nana's Black Jesus.

Several weeks passed before the alterations to this particular holy text were noticed. Christmas left reluctantly and the Southern California rains came in lackluster sprinkles or vigorous downpours. I'd also discovered a few more transgressions that needed to be included in the commandments. Now I was free to lie at will, covet my neighbor's ass, and completely ignore the Sabbath day as needed. The day Nana found the Post-It note that read "Thou shalt not drip milk on the carpet," she roared like a car crash.

"The Bible is God's word," she said, "and God is His word. That's like trying to cover up the Lord Himself. You can't put White-Out on God!"

"Then they shouldn't have put God on paper!" I told her.

Nana belongs to the generation of obedience as success and atonement as failure. I belong to the generation of choose your own adventure. Life means adaptation and renewal. I may convert to new faiths. I may travel to foreign communities. My arm may end up in some witch doctor's stew. I may taste like soy sauce and tears. Each cell of the planet may be lovely and terrible, but we aren't afraid to look and see.

Nana calmed a little, and we spoke like women. She told me Jesus had copper skin and hair of wool, which sounds a lot like my uncle Sheldon. I confessed my reason for kissing Nana's Jesus. For good luck, I said. I lied. The truth I didn't know how to say then. I'd never kissed a man yet of course, not a father or a brother or a lover. Kissing that photo meant kissing the best of all men because the best of all men is the one very carefully imagined.

Nana made me fix her Bible for the most part. So the commandments were returned to stone, and I had my ritual. Several winters later, Nana isn't able to walk on her own anymore, so I stay by her most afternoons and read. She says I killed her with my defiance.

I think I might be stealing her size. I grow bigger, and she grows smaller. When morticians remove organs and weigh them, does anyone measure the tare of the body? What does one weigh without the heart? I'd guess as much as the dead, almost nothing. I read to her from the Bible or magazines or Christmas stories that Nana approves of, but they're never the same when I say them. My mood changes and so does hers. Tonight I tell her, "The crucifix hung from the chimney with care, and Santa's reindeer stood on two hooves with hips jutted to the side in the universal manner of disbelief. Jingle your bells for me, baby; we are all angels." When she is gone I will miss her forever.

DISTRACTION

MAAME BLUE

It wasn't a particularly fancy denim jacket, but it reminded me of my mum's; she told me once that she stole it from my aunt's closet when they were still teenagers. My dad would tell her to throw it on when he was taking her out, and she wore that jacket especially because of how it made her look, and feel. That was back when my parents were still happy. The jacket I found was slightly more modern but it had a similar cut and the same deep blue denim color. Plus, it was on sale. I handed over my cash to the sharp-faced lady behind the counter and wore the jacket out of the shop.

I was going to wear it to the party because I never went to parties, and I needed to do more than just sit in my room, worrying about what was happening at home. But sitting in Ben's living room—a neighbor from first year who had since become an acquaintance with a big social circle—turned out to be not much better. Everyone was already wasted on shots by the time I arrived, or trying to outdo each other with balloons. I, on the other hand, was committedly stone-cold sober, after finding out about my dad's secret drinking last year. I needed to think of something else, and that's how I found myself talking to Ben.

"I love her, ya know? She's just…everythin'?" I wasn't sure if I should answer or just let him continue his drunken rant about his girlfriend, Serena. He looked upset. His body suddenly folded in on itself as he started to sob, and I desperately wanted to look away but couldn't. He shook for a few seconds and then looked up at me, snot dripping from his nose, which he made no attempt to wipe away. "She's hurtin' right now man, 'cos of the thing, but SSSHHH! SHETHINKSIDON'TKNOWBUTIDOOO!"

He followed up his shout-whisper by eyeing me conspiratorially and then dropped his gaze to look for another drink, bringing empty bottles left by other people to his lips. That was my cue to leave. I considered how many times his girlfriend Serena might have had to deal with him in this state. I only ever saw her when Ben was around, and he was usually attaching his face to hers in a way that made everyone present uncomfortable. She seemed untouchably cool and inexplicably amused by him. I suspected she was trying him out, like a new pair of jeans you're not entirely sure suit you yet.

I noticed her just as I was leaving the party. She was standing outside, leaning like a smoker. But she didn't have any cigarettes, just her fingers down by her sides, tapping against the concrete wall as she stared into the night. I decided to be brave and stand next to her. Maybe she could be a more interesting distraction.

"I think my boyfriend might be an idiot."

She spoke without looking my way, and I stifled a laugh. I twisted a finger around one of my dangling curls, trying to think of something to say. Serena turned to face me.

"So you agree, Clare—it's Clare, right?"

I was surprised she knew my name. Every time we found ourselves in the same group, she barely said two words to me.

"Yeah, kinda…Serena?"

I pointed at her as if I didn't know full well what her name was. But I didn't like how my face suddenly felt like someone had pressed it against a radiator as I looked at her. She nodded and turned away from me.

"Okay. So what should I do about him then, my idiot boyfriend?"

I shrugged, even as the words were ready to tumble out.

"Dump him? But not tonight, he won't remember it."

She didn't react immediately to my joke; instead, she tilted her head slightly and looked up into the darkness of the sky. Then she chuckled, like I was the echo for her feelings. Turning her whole body toward me as if she owned everything around us, she tugged at my jacket sleeve.

"I like this, where'd you get it?"

"Er, charity shop, the posh-looking one by the supermarket?"

She nodded again, seriously. "I can't go in there anymore. Shop owner followed me around last time, as if I walked in wearing a balaclava. It was long."

"She *was* intense, actually. I'm also not convinced it's affiliated with a charity, think it's just her private collection."

Serena frowned, still stroking the cuff of my jacket. It felt intimate.

"Wish I was good at shopping in places like that. Knowing how to find the good stuff, not caring who was watching."

I smiled in agreement and dramatically flipped my hair, in a way I later recalled with embarrassment. I'd never done that before that moment, but I fully committed to it, running my hands down the jacket afterward, trying to straighten out imaginary creases and simultaneously calm my growing nerves. She just watched me, shaking her head and releasing a small laugh; I wasn't sure if it was with me or at me.

"We should go shopping sometime. I don't have enough girlfriends to do that with at uni."

"So, you're recruiting me?"

"Hell yes. You can be Girlfriend Number One, which will make more sense once I recruit more female friends. What d'you think?"

"Do I have a choice?"

Her face dropped a little, like she wasn't sure whether I was seriously asking or not. Her eyes got really soft, and it felt like she'd moved closer to me without actually moving.

"Of course you do. You seem cool. And I'm sick of hanging out with idiots."

She gestured toward the front door, where the party was still raging, and then gave me this warm smile that I felt in my toes.

Don't fall for this one, just don't.

The voice in my head was always warning me of potential danger with pretty women. I smiled back because I couldn't help it and didn't want to. She was magnetic.

"I'm on board, as long as we just call me Clare. I'll also accept Cool Clare, Fun Clare, Nice Clare even, but definitely Clare for short. Girlfriend Number One just feels too impersonal."

"Well. You said your name a lot of times just now, so I'm guessing it's important to you. Just Clare it is."

I laughed, embarrassed, enamored, and nudging her shoulder with my own, our lips inches apart for half a second. After that she wrote her number down on my palm like in the movies, and I wasn't sure what was happening. I waited a few seconds and then pulled out my phone. I held it up to her, and she threw her head back in laughter, apologizing for writing on me. I shrugged, attempting nonchalance, and started copying her number from my palm into the phone until she stopped me, the tips of her fingers grazing the back of my typing hand.

"Just Ren, not Serena. I feel like we can skip straight to nicknames."

"We can?" I asked, deleting the extra letters in her name.

"Yeah. You seem like a real one, Just Clare."

We shared a look I couldn't articulate, and then our friendship began.

☙

We started learning bits and pieces about each other, in a gradual way, even though I was in a rush to know everything about her immediately. We were both twenty. She was studying Black British History. I told her I was studying Politics and Philosophy. She frowned briefly, as if it were offensive to her. I didn't ask why; we didn't know each other well enough yet. But I wanted to know why she was the way she was. Why she always hesitated for a few seconds before coming into my share house. She would knock on the door, I would answer, and she'd stare at me, as if she was surprised to see me and she had just found herself outside my door. Just a few seconds of standing, staring, and then she would enter. I didn't get it.

I wanted to understand her, in a desperate way sometimes. Maybe I tried too hard. I once brought up my home life, how my parents were divorcing and my dad was moving back to Ghana, where both of Ren's parents were also from. I thought we could bond over it, that she would be interested in our cultural commonalities and differences. I wanted to tell her that since my parents had split, there was a divide between the English and Ghanaian sides of my family, and that maybe it had always been there, but I was only now seeing it. I needed to tell someone that my mother was having a hard time; that she hadn't slept in weeks as far as I could tell; that she only answered the phone to me; that things seemed to be breaking. But Ren didn't engage with conversation like that. It wasn't that she didn't care, just that she seemed disinterested in getting too deep.

Don't fall for this one. Not this one.

The voice lingered, and I continued to ignore it.

She never really talked about Ben. They broke up a month or so after the party, but she only slipped it into conversation weeks later.

"He cried."

"He did?"

I wasn't remotely surprised, but I thought she probably wanted me to play along.

"Of course he did. At first I felt bad; I was gonna give him back his favorite hoodie that I stole, as sort of, penance? But he didn't want it, kept saying I should keep it for the memories. Although I'm not sure why; it's not like we were in love."

I paused, biting my nail as we sat on my bed playing cards. I felt like I should say something, since the poor guy wasn't around to defend himself.

"I think, maybe, *he* loved *you*."

She looked up at me, eyebrows raised into a question.

"How do you know that?"

"He told me at that party, when he was wasted."

"Oh. That doesn't mean anything."

I discovered she could be dismissive of things she wasn't ready to accept, and this irritated me. I wondered when she was going to dismiss me. I sulked for most of that afternoon, and she couldn't figure out why. She began writing things on her hands and arms in biro pen, holding the words up to my face, trying to uncover the reason for my bad mood.

Hungry?

Tired?

Itchy?

In pain?

Me?

I shook my head at all but the last suggestion. Instead, I shrugged, and she poked me repeatedly in the back, under the arms and in other upper body pressure points that eventually caused laughter to burst from me.

The next day I brought her Post-It notes, telling her she needed to stop writing on herself. She seemed touched by the gesture, even though I got them from the pound shop. When I got home that night, I found a folded, green Post-It note in my denim jacket pocket.

Sorry bout Ben. I did care bout him, wasn't trying 2 be mean. Don't want u 2 think of me that way.

It was accompanied by a click-top biro pen, with the outside possibly made of bamboo. It reminded me of one I'd seen in my Ethics class, on the lecturer's desk. I reread the note, wondering why my stomach was flipping, why it meant anything to me. She cared that I cared. I went back over the words slowly, looking for more meaning than there was, in her choice of which words to shorten, in her scribbled handwriting. I wrote her one back, slipping it under her door in her halls of residence, on my way to lectures.

I would never think of you as mean. Plus, breakups are hard, I get it.

This was how we began to communicate. Replacing the ease of text messages with brief Post-It notes about real stuff, things we had to think over before committing to paper with permanent pen, not easily erased and rewritten in a digital text box. One day she slipped a note into a book I'd left at her place that she returned to me the next day. This time there was a freshly sharpened yellow and black pencil with it, with the letters BS inscribed on the side. I recalled her complaining about a classmate in a recent lecture who was a bit of a know-it-all and only wrote in pencil, which sounded to Ren like nails on a chalkboard. I took a second before I unfolded the note this time, apprehensive about what I might find.

There's something I want 2 tell u next time we hang. Friday?

My stomach turned to stone as I read it. I felt dread and excitement. Wasn't it just another meetup, like we had been doing all year? Why did it feel like more? The voice in my head continued warning me to keep away. But all I saw was Ren, waiting for me, with Friday on the horizon.

☙

We met up in the park and sat on a hill overlooking the town, at a picnic spot without much of a picnic. All we had were sandwiches and crisps from the local bakery. We sat chitchatting about nothing much for a while, and then she slowed the world down and told me that she had an abortion at the start of second year, and I knew I had no idea what to say before the words had finished leaving her mouth. Instinct took over and I shifted over to her, taking my denim jacket off to place it on her shoulders, wrapping my arms around her. And then she started to cry, and I took deep breaths to stop myself from crying with her.

She told me Ben didn't know. I didn't correct her this time, or fill in any gaps; it didn't matter. She pulled herself back slightly and looked at me with her sad, awful eyes and told me that she just couldn't bring herself to tell him. I said it was her choice to make, not his. Then she cried some more.

Later, we ate our sandwiches. The sky was overcast with thick gray clouds, and the air smelled of thunder. Ren stared into the distance and said:

"I feel safe with you."

"Good."

It was all I could say, because I, in turn, felt so vulnerable in her hands.

"I haven't told anyone else."

"I know."

We didn't wait for the rain to find us. We headed down the hill and walked the fifteen minutes home, and she held my hand the whole way there. I felt guilty for feeling so much joy in her moment of pain.

We went back to her halls and she put cushions on the floor at the foot of her bed for us to sit on. She switched the TV on to some comedy show we weren't paying any attention to. It felt wrong. I could see her out of the corner of my eye, wiping her face every so often, trying to hide her tears. I took the remote from her and put the TV on mute.

"We can talk, if you want. It doesn't have to be about…you know."

She was staring at the floor, picking at the carpet as if irritated. A moment passed before she said something.

"I don't know what to say."

"Okay. We can just sit here, then."

She scrunched up her face, like she was thinking.

"I don't know what I'm *supposed* to say."

"What do you mean?"

She lifted her head and then leant back to rest it on the edge of the bed, so that most of her face pointed toward the ceiling.

Beautiful.

I shook my head, trying to refocus.

"I feel like…like I'm supposed to have this deep and meaningful reflection about getting knocked up and exercising my right to choose. But I don't have the words for it. It's sad, no big deal."

I hesitated, considered saying nothing, but once the words came to my mind, I could rarely stop them.

"If it's no big deal, why did you tell me?"

She shrugged, and then closed her eyes, a faint smile lingering on her face.

"Do you think I'm a bad person now? 'Cos I did that?"

"I think you're a brave person."

She smiled again, properly this time. I could tell she didn't believe me.

"There are plans and things expected of me. Graduate, get a good job, get married, have kids."

"But it's not *your* plan?"

I knew the expectation well.

"I don't know what my plan is, but kids aren't in it. And even if they were, *my* kids in a post-Brexit Britain? No thanks." She placed her hands on both cheeks and then looked up at me and gasped. "God! Can you imagine Ben as someone's dad? I think I did the world a favor."

We both burst out laughing and then shook our heads, feeling mildly shameful. She pulled her knees up to her chest, her voice a little lighter.

"Do you want kids?"

I took a moment to think about a thing I'd spent hours, days, years pondering.

"Absolutely. Just, not right now."

"Wow. You're so sure."

"Some things are just that way for me. What I want the future to look like, who I want to be with, where I wanna live, stuff like that."

She was giving me that look she gave when she was really listening. Sometimes I couldn't take how intensely she watched me.

"So…who do you want to be with, then?"

She was resting her chin on her knees, no longer looking at me, but I felt like I was under a spotlight.

"I just mean, I know the kind of person I want to be with, eventually. That they should be kind and smart and driven and—"

"So all the things everyone wants in a partner?"

She scoffed. Her assessment of my words read as: *what a cliché*. So I countered.

"Is that what you want? Because Ben was…not that."

She raised her eyebrows at my quip, but didn't seem offended.

"No, I guess not. But I'm not those things either."

"Yes, you are. And more."

I couldn't help it, dancing around the elephant in the room was wearing me out. She wouldn't look at me, instead remaining focused on the wall in front of her.

"I'm not a good partner for anyone. I'm too self-involved. I take too much from people."

I felt it then, finally. A firm rejection of the premise I was trying to introduce into the conversation. So I corroborated, standing up and sitting on the bed.

"No arguments from me on that."

She feigned amused shock and then came to sit beside me.

"Let's have a sleepover? Your house is ages away."

"It's like a ten-minute walk."

"Yeah, but if you stay here, we could watch a film and drink the vodka I've got in the freezer."

She grinned at me, winning and persuasive, knowing she would drink the vodka alone and she just wanted someone there to witness it. I got changed into a T-shirt and shorts I'd left at hers the last time

I was there. Who knows what we watched, but we lay together in her bed that night, and she wrapped herself around me as we fell asleep. I didn't know what to make of it, why it made me feel so sick and thrilled all at once. To hear her breathing in my ear, to feel her heartbeat as a soft rhythm against my back, was to feel happier than I had in months. And I knew I was in big trouble, because this would be over soon, and then what would I do?

※

The parameters of our friendship were becoming more unclear, fluid, moveable. My housemates thought she was my girlfriend, and I didn't correct them straight away. Things began to change in that painstakingly slow way that makes you want to tear your hair out because it feels like nothing is happening. I was learning tangible things about her. Most notably that she had light fingers for very small, insignificant things. Paper clips, thumb tacks, and most of all, pens. She had an extensive collection from all manner of places. Each was branded with a different shop or design.

"I'm a collector, of sorts."

She said it in a fancy-pants voice when I inquired about them, running my fingers along the edges of the five beer glasses that were full of pens, displayed on a shelf in her room.

"Some of these look expensive."

My eyes lingered over a gold-rimmed pen with a fat body.

"Not for me. Five-finger discount and all that."

She laughed to herself and didn't see my eyebrow raise in judgment. I don't think it actually mattered to me, I just wanted to seem less agreeable than I was becoming.

She had started calling things out in a jokey way, when we blurred the lines of friendship, saying they were "romcom moments."

She'd stop mid-sentence to remove an eyelash from my face. Or our hands would brush and then linger as I handed her a cup of tea. She constantly wore my denim jacket home to her own halls, always returning it a few days later, until it began to carry her scent. It belonged to the both of us now. We skipped parties and group outings to the pub to spend our evenings together, huddled under a blanket watching films. I would feel her shoulder pressed against mine like a strong wall, still and warm.

Those moments, though, began to matter so much to me that imagining what they might not mean for her terrified me. I made a foolish attempt to distance myself from her for a couple of weeks. She'd want to hang out, and I'd tell her I was busy, and then after canceling a couple of times, I would agree to meet up. Then I'd drop into conversation the names of a few girls from my course that I knew, just a hint that I was wanted by other people. Even though I wasn't paying any real attention to them because she was constantly on my mind. She heard their names and laughed awkwardly. Then she would say something dripping with sarcasm.

"Sounds like you're popular. How do you even still have time for me?"

I would feel bad and spend the rest of the day giving her all my attention.

෴

As second year came to an end, I told her I was deferring my final year, that I needed to go home, to help my mum get back on her feet. Ren was sadder than I had anticipated. And angry.

"Why didn't you tell me what was happening with your mum?"

"I dunno. It's hard to talk about."

"But I told you about—" She stopped short, sighing and frowning at me. I stayed calm. "I thought, you know, we were closer friends than that. Aren't we?"

"Are we?"

She just looked down at the floor when I threw the question back, leaning against a window to a seminar room. Her words came out clipped.

"*I* thought we were. You mean something to me."

"Something."

The word just fell, like another slap in the face.

Told you so.

I hadn't listened to the voice in a while, and its re-emergence jolted me a little. I stood opposite her, holding the cold radiator behind me. We were underneath the student union, music blaring upstairs, right above our heads. She straightened herself up and looked around to see if anyone was coming. They weren't. Even her anxiety pissed me off. I scoffed at her, and she just sighed. Then she took a step forward and kissed me on the mouth. It was a soft brush of the lips that I didn't expect to take my breath away, but it did, because she did.

She moved her head back to look at me, her eyes asking if it was okay. I placed my hands on her waist, clutching tightly on both sides like she belonged to me. I wanted her to be mine, but I didn't believe that she was. She kissed me again, deeper this time. I let my tongue explore her mouth, feeling her hands on my face, in my hair. I let the fantasy play out. Then I pushed her back to the other side of the wall, taking control. She clutched my back, and I felt her fingers digging in, silently telling me not to stop.

For a while we kept going, and I pressed myself against her, and then, and then she…laughed. At first it was just a small sound that escaped her lips in between kisses, but it quickly erupted into loud guffaws. I pulled my face from hers slowly and took a step back, letting the space between us take over. She was hysterical, doubled over, holding her stomach, saying through breaths of laughter:

"I'm sorry! I'm sorry!"

After a few seconds, she managed to stand up straight and look at me, crestfallen and suddenly aware of what she'd done.

"Oh my god I'm sorry, I just—this is a lot, isn't it? We should slow down because I think, I think it's a lot."

I could still feel her fingers on my face, the traces of them on my back, the taste of her in my mouth. I put my fingers to my lips, wondering if they were still there. I needed to make sure she hadn't managed to take everything from me. My tongue felt heavy with what had just taken place. My face felt hot, too hot, and suddenly all I could think of was the cold outside air, how desperately I needed to breathe again, to get away from the suffocation of my feelings for her. So I ran.

She called after me, but didn't follow. She was frozen in her same position, making no effort to chase me, only wanting me to come back to her. I felt stupid. Like, the kind of stupid where you see a hot pan and know it's a hot pan, but you touch it anyway and then feel angry for getting burnt. I headed home, broken, embarrassed, and still a little turned on, which just made me angrier. I slammed my bedroom door shut behind me and heard the rustle of material against the door. My denim jacket. It still smelled of her. It was shoved into a backpack in seconds, and I practically marched all the way to the town center with it. The shop owner seemed surprised to see me, and then annoyed when I handed her the jacket back.

"We don't do refunds."

She handled the jacket with the tips of her fingers as if it was dirty.

"I don't want it anymore, or your money."

I turned on my heels and exited before she could say anything else.

Two weeks later, my car was packed up. I hadn't responded to any of Ren's text messages. In the preceding days, my flatmates would tell me I had post, and I'd find three pens of various sizes and colors, thrown together in an envelope with a Post-It note saying ***I'm sorry*** or ***Plz talk to me.*** Soon I had five envelopes' worth, and I gathered them up into an old pencil case I had planned to throw away. It was ultimately all I had left of her, of our friendship, a collection of things that didn't belong to either of us. And then she came by as I was leaving. I was maneuvering a bag into the boot, and she stood across the street, holding something. She didn't wave or walk toward me, she just stood there, looking at me. She was only about ten feet away, and I shouted at her with little feeling.

"Are you gonna cross the road or what?"

She nodded and crossed immediately. She had a forlorn look on her face, like she'd just been given really bad news. As she came closer, I instinctively moved backward. She noticed and gave me an awkward smile, and then placed her hand on the now closed boot.

"How long's the drive?"

"About four hours, if I only make one stop."

"Cool. Clare, I—"

I turned to go into the house, couldn't take the small talk that was leading to a bigger conversation, some dumb apology weeks too late. And she looked phenomenal too, even though she was dressed how she always was, but not seeing her seemed to have made her effect on me more potent. I returned a minute later with another bag, which I threw into the backseat. I pulled the passenger seat back to its original position, and she came round to that side of the car, blocking my exit before I could close the door.

"Wait."

She held up one hand in front of my chest. In the other was a plastic bag. She pulled out something neatly wrapped in brown parcel paper and threw it into the passenger seat before I could protest further.

"A goodbye present."

I didn't look at the parcel. I wanted to ignore the heat from her body that was mixing with mine as we stood so close.

How can I still taste you in my mouth?

I shook my head slowly, realizing I wanted to kiss her so badly I thought I might have to push her out of the way just so I could flee. Luckily, she did it for me, stepping aside so I could close the car door.

As soon as I did, she wrapped her arms around me from behind, pressing her face into my back. I was frozen, unable to move or respond. I just let myself be held. And then she was gone.

I left ten minutes after that, driving away slowly, trying to shake the fantastical thought from my mind that she would be in my rearview mirror, flagging me down and begging me not to go. I turned up the radio, letting other voices fill my head.

After two hours on the road, I finally took a comfort break. I reluctantly brought her gift with me into the burger place, where I ordered and then placed the package on the table, staring at it until my food came, and then watching it some more as I slowly ate my meal. I wiped my hands when I was done and finally opened it up. My denim jacket was neatly folded and pristine inside. I held it up to the light, and a Post-It note dropped out.

> ***Dear Just Clare,***
> ***Couldn't imagine you without it. Don't worry, got a good price: five-finger discount :-)***
> ***Ren x***

I laughed out loud as I put the jacket back on. It smelt of washing powder; clean and fresh, almost brand new. I hoped my mum would like it.

GRAND BEAVER CABIN

EMILY AUSTIN

I'VE BEEN ENTERING CHILDREN'S COLORING CONTESTS. I sign my name "Abigale, age 6." I write the g's backwards to fool the judges. My artistic ability is weak for a thirty-one-year-old; however, my fine motor skills blow most children out of the water. There is rarely competition. So far, I've won:

One five-foot-tall chocolate rabbit.

Two child-sized bicycles.

One coupon for a free bucket of Kentucky Fried Chicken.

I ate the chicken, sold the bikes, and dismembered the rabbit. He's chopped up in my freezer. When I'm hankering for something sweet, I gnaw on his frozen remains.

One hunk of his face has a white fondant eye adhered to it. The eye has no iris or pupil. It looks like the rabbit has suffered some sort of macular degeneration, or like he's seen a ghost.

I'm saving that piece. I'm going to eat it when something special happens.

☙

I had to draw a self-portrait in middle school. I toiled over it. My pencils were nubs by the time I turned it in. I worked on it for weeks and stayed up way past my bedtime, painstakingly pressing pigment into paper. I pressed so hard, I hurt my fingers. I could barely make a fist the morning it was due.

※

"Am I speaking to Abigale's mom?" a woman in my phone asks.
"This is she," I lie.
I'm holding my phone to my ear with my shoulder. My hands are occupied, coloring in a picture of a worm. It's for a contest hosted by a greenhouse. If I win, I get a free trowel, pruners, pots, and wildflower seeds. I live in a high-rise apartment with no access to a garden, but I felt drawn to the worm. He's wearing sunglasses and eating dirt.
"We've got big news for your little one! She won our coloring contest! What a talent. Is she really only six years old?"
I smile. "She's almost seven."
"Her work really stood out! She barely draws outside the lines."
I put my pencils down and massage the palm of my hand. "That's kind of you to say. She'll be ecstatic. What did she win?"
"A three-night stay at the Grand Beaver Cabin. Have you folks ever been?"
"Never," I say.
I remember seeing commercials for it as a kid and asking to go; however, my parents preferred to spend their money on my brother's interests. He had hockey tournaments. Expensive sports gear. Going to weird beaver-themed hotels was too aligned to me.
"Well, you're in for a treat. You'll have to tell Abigale there's a big swimming pool. It's all beaver dam themed, of course. It looks like a marsh. It has two waterslides and a diving board. There's even an arcade."
"What a generous prize. Thank you so much. Do you know if

adults can ride the waterslides?"

She laughs. "Yes. Why? Does Mom want a go on the slides?"

I look down at my worm picture. "She might."

She laughs again. "You must be a kid at heart."

&

When I was a kid, I wanted to be an artist. I pictured myself standing at a bay window beside an easel. I envisioned paint stains on my smock, rainbow globs on a palette, and oil paint under my fingernails. I collected clippings from magazines and newspapers. When I spotted a picture I liked, I cut it out, and planned to recreate it on a canvas someday. I still have most of the clippings. They're in a box somewhere. They're mostly toothpaste ads. Pictures of people smiling with enormous white teeth.

&

"I'm sorry. Something is wrong with the booking. There's only one bed."

The hotel host is tapping on his computer. I'm standing in front of him with my girlfriend Susan.

"I'll try to move you to one with two beds," he says.

"Why?" I ask.

"Because there's two of you."

Sue sighs. "There's no need, sir. Thank you."

"It's no trouble," he continues to tap on his keyboard. "I know we have other rooms available—"

"There's no need, sir. Thank you," Sue repeats.

The patrons who were behind us, who were greeted by other hostesses, have already left with their room keys.

There's a stack of brochures on the counter. My eyes are drawn to the text: COLORING CONTEST. I pick one up and flip it over. There's a picture of a beaver dam on the back. In small text below the illustration, it says: FOR CHILDREN AGES THREE TO TEN. WINNERS WILL BE DISPLAYED IN THE ARTIST ALCOVE GALLERY AND WILL RECEIVE $300 WORTH OF PREMIUM ART SUPPLIES.

"We want to sleep in one bed," Sue says finally, annoyed.

I put the brochure in my back pocket, then drape an arm over Sue's shoulders.

"Oh," he says.

"Oh," he repeats.

☙

I don't have any artistic talent. I got a C on that self-portrait I did in middle school. My teacher wrote: TAKE YOUR HOMEWORK MORE SERIOUSLY. THIS DOES NOT DEMONSTRATE EFFORT.

I put significant effort into that assignment. I was tempted to ask Ms. Randall to expand on her feedback, to give me more useful criticism, but I was too ashamed.

I did take liberties with the assignment. I didn't draw a realistic self-portrait. I drew myself with oversized teeth and pupils shaped like spiders.

I guess it's hard to tell how much effort someone puts into art. There were kids in my class who put less effort into their projects and earned higher marks than I did. They just happened to be more talented, I guess.

Art isn't really about effort. I'm not sure what it is about. I don't have the eye for it. I don't see things the way artists are supposed to. I wish I did. I feel really drawn to artsy people. I love to visit galleries. I like touching paper. Smelling paint.

GRAND BEAVER CABIN

✧

Susan and I are carrying our bags to our room. I didn't tell her I won our stay. I said I booked us a six-month anniversary getaway on a whim, thinking it might be a fun backdrop for her art. She's a photographer.

The center of the hotel is a large pool. All of the rooms have balconies facing it. The entire place reeks like chlorine. The pool is beaver dam themed. The slides are made to look like logs. The water is surrounded by fake plastic shrubbery, and the tile is brown like dirt. At the center of the pool is an enormous plastic beaver. He's the size of a minivan. His face is pointing toward the ceiling and his arms are outstretched. He looks euphoric, like he's about to be beamed up into heaven.

"What a hilarious animal theme to pick," Sue snorts. "There's so much sexual innuendo. Do you think the person who designed this place picked beavers to be funny? Or do you think they're really sheltered, and have no idea this place is named, like, the Vagina Lodge?"

"Hey. Sorry. This is a family environment," a woman behind us says.

We both look over our shoulders. The woman has a baby strapped to her chest, bags hanging off her shoulders, and a little girl clinging to her arm.

"Sorry," Sue says before discreetly rolling her eyes at me.

✧

The walls in our room are plastered with swamp-themed wallpaper. It feels like we're inside a deep, cartoon forest. If you look closely, there's tiny woodland creatures hidden in the pattern. Wood ducks. Marsh wrens. A deer. The bed is shaped like an enormous hollowed-out log. There's a desk in the corner that doesn't match the theme. It's just a basic black desk paired with an ergonomic chair.

"Hey," Sue says.

I look at her.

She takes my picture with flash.

"This was such a sweet idea," she says.

I can't see anything. The flash blinds me.

She kisses me. "Thank you for planning this."

☙❧

While Sue showers, I take my pencil crayons out of my bag and locate the brochure I took from the front desk. I inspect the coloring contest on the back. It's an illustration of a contented beaver lounging in a pond. He's lying on a log like it's a pool float.

I run my hands over the picture to flatten it while I consider what colors to use. I test several shades of green on the notepad provided by the hotel. I land on *Mountain Meadow* for the grass, with notes of *Goldenrod Yellow* for dimension.

I use *Sea Green* for the lily pads.

Cornflower Blue and *Pearl White* in the water.

Burnt Sienna and *Raw Umber* for the beaver's fur.

Robin's Egg Blue and *Linen White* for the sky.

☙❧

Sue has dressed me in a dead woman's clothes. She got them from an estate sale. It's for a collection she's working on. She raids dead people's closets and takes photos of me dressed in outfits she assembles.

I'm lying by the pool in clothes that smell like their previous owner. There are notes of iris, talc, and BO. I'm wearing a heavy circle skirt, stockings, and a collared lace blouse. Sue has also painted my face with vintage makeup. My lips are burgundy and feel like they're coated in melted crayon.

Children are splashing in the water nearby. Most are playing sharks and minnows. Some are cannonballing into the pool. Screaming. One little girl keeps practicing her diving in the deep end. She seems to be taking it very seriously. She takes a deep breath before taking deliberate steps along the board.

"I wish we had an old bathing suit," Sue says. "Like a one-piece with a skirted bottom, and boning, or something with a belted waist."

She's posed me in a lounge chair with one arm under my head, and my other arm raised, wrist limp. I'm trying not to move because she's picky about how I'm positioned.

She snaps another photo. "I think I have bloomers in my bag. Would you wear bloomers?"

"Sure."

She smiles. "You're such a good sport. Okay, I'll be right back, then."

I remain posed while she runs past the NO RUNNING sign.

I stare into the water. I look into the eyes of the giant beaver.

"What are you doing?"

I blink. The kid who was diving is now sitting in a chair beside me. She has a juice box.

"Nothing," I say.

"You have your arm up weird, and you're dressed like Anne of Green Gables."

I breathe air out of my nose. "I'm not dressed anything like Anne of Green Gables. She's from, like, the 1880s."

She slurps her juice.

"This outfit is from the 1950s," I explain.

"Whatever," she says. "The point is your clothes are weird. Are you, like, a pervert?"

"What? No, I'm not a pervert—"

"How old are you?" she asks.

"Why do you care how old—"

"I think you're like eighty."

I frown. I don't like children.

"Thank you," I say. "I'd kill to look eighty. I love how old ladies look. Sometimes I scrunch my face up on purpose, hoping to make the lines in my forehead deeper."

She makes a face. "That's weird."

"Everything's weird, honey. Leave me alone."

༄

"I figured we'd buy food," I explain.

We're back in our room. Susan is complaining about the snacks I brought. I packed two Ziploc bags of chocolate rabbit hunks and one jar of bread and butter pickles.

"These are the worst kind of pickles." She holds up the jar. "And I'm sorry, but I'm sick of this rabbit. What possessed you to buy an eighty-pound chocolate rabbit?"

I didn't tell her I won it. She doesn't know about my coloring contest habit.

"It just looked good," I lie. "And it was fifty percent off."

She snorts. "You're nuts, babe. I'm going to go down to the cafeteria to find us something better to eat, okay? Are you craving anything?"

"I'm good with whatever," I say.

༄

Sue returns with a large pizza and an old lady.

"This is Eunice." She nods at the woman.

Eunice smiles. She has a buzz cut.

"Get this, they won't sell pizza by the slice." Sue puts the pizza down on the desk. "Eunice here just wanted one piece, but they wouldn't sell it to her. They only sell it by the pie. Isn't that ridiculous? I invited her up here to have a slice of ours. I told her you wouldn't mind."

"Of course," I say, even though I do mind. I'm in my pajamas and I didn't expect company.

"This place is built for a specific kind of family," Eunice says while settling into the chair at the desk. "You can only buy pizzas by the pie. The deals on their website are all for families of four. Did you notice? And all the signage is of a mom, dad, and their kids. God help you if you're anything different. Did you know you can't sit in the Log Lounge unless there's at least three people in your party? Get fucked if you're a single parent, I guess. This place caters to certain kinds of families—if you catch my drift."

"Are you a single parent?" I ask.

"No. I'm here with my grandson." She takes a slice of pizza from the box. "He's playing with a horde of boys in the arcade. He had chicken fingers for dinner. I'm not a big chicken finger aficionada. I thought perhaps pizza, but like your Susan here said—they only sell it by the pie. I was this close to buying an entire pizza for one slice, just to throw the rest out. Isn't that awful? I had my gallbladder out a few years ago, so I struggle to digest fatty foods. I can't eat more than one piece or I'm in trouble."

She cuts up her pizza with a plastic fork and knife.

Susan hands me a slice and says, "The world was built for people with gallbladders, wasn't it, Eunice?"

"Ain't that the truth," Eunice says with her mouth full.

We all chew for a moment.

Eunice puts her fork down, and says, "Hey, did this room come with a bible in it? Ours did, and I made them remove it—"

She opens the desk drawer, and I choke. I hid my coloring contest entry in there.

"What's this?" she asks. "A drawing?"

"Uh," I say. "I, um, colored that in for fun. It was just silly."

She holds the picture with her greasy fingers.

Sue squints. "You did that? When?"

"Yeah," I say, "just earlier. When you were showering."

"Oh. It's nice," she says.

"You think so? Really? Thank you."

☙

"Did you always want to be a photographer?" I ask.

Sue and I are lying alone in our log bed, facing each other. We're falling asleep.

"No." She yawns. "I wanted to be a stay-at-home mom."

"Really?"

"Mhm. I wanted six kids. A white picket fence. The works. What about you? Did you always want to be an HVAC technician?"

"Definitely not. What made you change your mind about being a stay-at-home mom?"

She rolls on her back. "I guess I never *really* wanted to be one. I just believed it's what I was supposed to be, you know, because of my family."

Her family is religious. Her parents taught her birth control was created by the devil and that women shouldn't wear pants.

"I still might like to have a kid, though," she says. "I haven't decided. What about you?"

"I don't think so. I don't really like kids, and I had a bad childhood. I don't want to be responsible for someone else's unhappy upbringing."

She rolls back on her side. "Why was your childhood unhappy?"

I shrug. "I don't know. I felt sort of unloved, I guess. Like I was nothing special. I remember finding drawings I made as a kid in our kitchen garbage. They were splattered with tomato soup, lying beneath chicken bones. My parents cared a lot more about my brother."

"That's sad." She touches my face.

※

Sue and I are sitting with Eunice by the pool. Her grandson, Joon, is jumping off the diving board. The little girl who accused me of being a perverted Anne of Green Gables is practicing her dives again. Every time Joon lands in the water, she dives in shortly after. She is very deliberate about how she dives. It seems like she's training. I wonder if she's in swim classes. She seems to know what she's doing.

"DON'T RUN ON THE DECK!" Eunice shouts at Joon.

"Excuse me." A woman with a baby in her arms approaches us. "My daughter Wendy is playing with your Joon." She points at the girl. "I need to take my son up to our room. He's not feeling well. Could I bug you to keep an eye on her for me?"

There are lifeguards here, so we aren't being asked to watch Wendy in terms of her swim safety. Our role has more to do with reminding her not to run, fight with kids, or hog the floaties.

We all nod.

"Thank you. I won't be long," she says.

After she's out of earshot, Eunice says, "That mom keeps asking me to watch her kid."

"Really?" I lean in, interested to hear hotel gossip.

"Mhm. She hardly pays attention to her. The kid is constantly asking her to watch her swim, but she barely looks up from her phone or that baby. She'll be up in her room for over an hour, you'll see."

"Yikes," I say. "Does she just expect us to stay here?"

"I guess so." She leans back in her chair. "I'm trying to give her grace because I know it's hard to be a mother, but boy she's testing me. Are either of you moms?"

"No," we both say.

Her eyes are glued to Joon. "I just had the one. Joon's mom, but even that almost killed me. They didn't tell me what I was signing up for, that's for sure. It's a lot of work being a mother."

"Did you have help? Are you married?" Sue asks.

"I was," she says. "But he wasn't much help, to be honest."

"Did you divorce?"

Sue doesn't mind asking people prying questions like this. I always find it a little uncomfortable, but I'm usually interested in hearing the answers, so ultimately, I don't mind.

"No. He died decades ago."

"I'm so sorry," Sue says. "Forgive me, I hope this doesn't offend you, but I thought you might be gay."

Eunice is styled very butch. She has a shaved head, and she wears masculine clothing. There's a tattoo of a nautical star on her wrist.

Without looking at us, Eunice says, "I had a girlfriend who passed away too."

Sue and I look at each other quickly.

"I'm sorry," I say.

"Can you tell us about her?" Sue asks.

Eunice barks at Joon. "YOU'RE GOING TO CRACK YOUR HEAD OPEN! I'M SERIOUS! DON'T RUN!"

She turns back to us. "Her name was Angela. She was a fiercely intelligent woman. A scientist. Being with her felt like coming home. Isn't that nauseating? She was a true partner. My biggest supporter. The absolute love of my life. We were together for fifteen years, but I lost her three and a half years ago, and I miss her every day."

Sue puts a hand to her chest. "Oh God. That's so sweet."

I open my mouth to speak, but I don't know what to say.

"Do you have any of her clothes?" Sue asks.

☙

"I think it was weird to ask for her clothes," I tell Sue back in our room.

Eunice lent us her girlfriend's scarf. She brought it to the hotel. She brings it everywhere.

"Everything's weird," Sue says, while holding the scarf up to various jackets she packed for the hotel. "I think it goes well with this one," she says, holding it against a dark blue velvet blazer. "Can I take your picture in it?"

☙

"What do you do with these pictures?" Eunice asks.

We're back at the pool. Sue is taking photos of me in Angela's scarf.

The pool is loud. Wendy's mother is back. She's sitting on the other side of the deck.

"Watch me, Mom!" Wendy shouts before diving.

"I sell prints," Sue says while I watch Wendy's mom turn away from the water, uninterested. She adds, "And I've done a few exhibitions."

"She's really good," I say, still watching Wendy. "She's very talented. Really has the eye for it."

"She's talented too," Sue says.

"Me?" I ask.

"Yes, you. You're a very gifted model." She snaps another picture. I grin.

☙

I'm inspecting the piece of chocolate rabbit that has an eye. Sue is beside me. We're back in our log bed.

"Are you going to eat that?" she asks.

"No. I'm saving it," I say. "It's a special piece. It has this candy eye."

She looks at it. "Do you think the candy will taste good?"

"It's just white fondant. It's strange it has no pupil or iris, though, don't you think? It makes the rabbit look blind."

She squints. "I think it makes her look wise."

☙

Sue fell asleep. After lying in bed beside her for hours, I get up and take my drawing out of the desk drawer. I turn the lamp on and take my pencil crayons out. I try to color over the pizza-finger-grease stains that Eunice left.

I pause to stretch my fingers and frown at the drawing. It still looks dirty. It's impossible to hide the stains.

Maybe I should start over. I could sneak down to the lobby and take a new brochure.

☙

I'm in the lobby, clutching my ruined drawing. It's 2:07 a.m. There's no one manning the front desk.

There's a large box in the center of the lobby that looks like a ballot box. It has a large slit in the top.

I approach the desk to grab a new brochure but notice a sign above the box as I pass. It says, in bold letters: COLORING SUBMISSIONS DUE TODAY.

Fuck. They're due today?

I look down at mine. Maybe it isn't so bad. Maybe the stains make it look more like a kid's. Children always have sticky hands. Their submissions are probably coated in jam.

I can hear someone in the room behind the front desk.

I eye the box.

☙

I'm eating a waffle shaped like a beaver's face. His eye and buck teeth indentations are pooled with butter and maple syrup. Sue and I are at breakfast. She ate her beaver's eyes first. Her plate is just a mouth.

Wendy and her family are at the table beside us. I'm eavesdropping. Wendy keeps talking about diving. She's impassioned. She says, "You know, you have to maintain speed and rhythm. That's very important. And I'm getting better at that, don't you think?"

Her parents aren't interested. Her dad is reading something on his phone, and her mom is tearing a waffle into pieces for the baby.

"A clean dive has minimal splash," Wendy says. "Do I splash a lot?"

"Mom?"

"Hey Dad, did you know a thirteen-year-old diver won a gold medal in the Olympics once? Isn't that something?"

☙

At the pool, I think about my coloring contest entry and the prize I've likely missed out on. *Premium art supplies and a spot in a gallery.*

I've never had premium art supplies before. I asked for art supplies for Christmas one year, but my parents got us a basketball net instead. It was for my brother. I never used it.

The spot in the gallery is nothing, obviously. Why would I want that? Though, I would have liked that if I were a kid. That would have really meant something to me then. I'd feel really special, having something I made on display like that.

☙

"Joon and I leave tomorrow," Eunice says. Sue and I are in the lobby with her. "And we're never coming back. This place has been a total shit show. Are you two ever returning?"

"We leave tomorrow too. I think this was a one-time thing for us as well—" I say.

"Hey. Isn't that the one you did?" Sue says.

"What?" I look at her.

"You submitted that?" She points at the wall.

I look where she's pointing.

My drawing is on display with two others. There's a sign above them. It says FINAL THREE.

Sue furrows her brow.

My face feels hot.

I try to keep talking to Eunice. "You know, uh, we actually won our stay here. I wouldn't spend money here now that we've been—"

"What? We won our stay?" Sue says.

Fuck. I wasn't thinking. I was just talking, trying to change the topic.

"Excuse us," Sue says, pulling me away from Eunice.

☙

"What the fuck?" Sue asks as she shuts the door. She marched me by the arm to our room. I spent the walk trying to come up with something to say. "What do you mean we won our stay?" she asks.

"Why did you submit that drawing? What's going on?"

I open my mouth.

"Why would you enter a children's coloring contest?" She raises her voice. "That's unhinged. You're, like, stealing from kids."

"I don't see it that way," I say.

"How do you see it?"

"I'm just trying—I just…" I stop.

I guess that is what I'm doing.

"It's just a coloring contest," I defend myself. "It's meaningless."

"Exactly." She frowns. "So why do it?"

The first time I did it, I thought it would be funny. I didn't expect to win.

"It's an art project," I lie. "It's like performance art."

When I won, I felt this little hole in my chest healing.

"Who's your audience?" she asks.

I'm still avoiding her eyes. "I don't need an audience."

"You're lying." She raises her voice. "This isn't art. You don't know the first thing about art, do you?"

My chest pangs. "Fuck you," I say.

I start to walk toward the bathroom.

"What the fuck?" she shouts.

I lock the bathroom door.

She knocks twice, but I don't answer.

❦

When I leave the bathroom, Sue is gone. There's a note on the desk written in *Burnt Sienna*. It says, I LEFT.

I was inside the bathroom for over an hour, sitting in the tub, looking at my fingernails. I was thinking about oil paints and the little hole in my chest.

☙

I fell asleep with the lights on, woke up at 4 a.m., and ate every pickle and hunk of chocolate I packed, excluding the piece with a fondant eye. This was a mistake. I wanted to stay locked in the room until checkout at noon, but now I feel so sick I have to emerge to find stomach medicine.

Before falling asleep, I cried. My eyes feel swollen. I'm ambling down the hall, clutching my gut, feeling nauseous and sad.

When I reach the lobby, I glance at the wall my picture was on yesterday and frown. It's no longer there. There's a new sign. It says WINNER above someone else's submission. I walk up to it. It's the worst of the final three. The artist used yellow and brown pencil crayons exclusively. A significant portion of the submission is not colored in at all. Moreover, the page has been torn, and there's a concerning red smudge in the upper right corner that I worry could be blood.

"Why did this win?" I ask the host behind the desk.

He looks up. "I'm sorry?"

"Why did that win?" I gesture at the wall. "I saw the other submissions. They were much better—"

"It was a draw," he says. "It was randomly selected."

☙

"Where's Susan?" Eunice asks.

I was directed to the arcade to buy medicine. They sell it at the prize counter. I'm parked in front of the pinball machine, sipping Pepto-Bismol.

I look at her. "She left. She's mad at me."

"Oh." She sits at the machine beside me. "Why?"

"I don't want to talk about it."

"Is it because you've been entering children's coloring contests?"

I look at her.

She's laughing. "What possessed you to do that? What a strange crime."

"I told Sue it was an art project."

She snorts. "Was it?"

I shake my head.

"What was it, then?"

"I just—I don't know. I'd never won anything before. I—" I pause. "I think maybe I was getting revenge for my child-self."

She tilts her head. "I see."

I sip my Pepto. "Do you think Sue will forgive me?"

"I hope so. You make a nice couple." She reaches into her pocket and pulls out her cell phone. "She sent me a preview of that portrait she took of you in Angela's scarf. Have you seen it?"

She passes her phone to me. The screen is magnified because of her old lady eyesight.

I'm grinning in the picture. My mouth looks enormous. Behind me is the beaver. My face looks just like his.

I love it.

She takes her phone back. "You know, Angela and I argued quite a bit. Mostly about her family. They didn't know we were together. When she died, I couldn't see her in the hospital. I made a big stink about it, but nothing could be done. We weren't married."

"Jesus," I say. "That's terrible."

"Mhm." She nods.

"Things were harder for you," I say. "Do you resent younger people like me for how easy we have it? Arguing about coloring contests?"

"No. Of course not," she says. "I want it to be easier for you."

☙

I exit my room and haul my bag down to the pool. Checkout is at noon; however, I can stay by the pool until it closes. I plan to stay until I've figured out how to apologize to Susan.

I sit by the diving board. Wendy is practicing, as usual.

While I place my bag down, I watch her perform a perfect twisting dive. She rotates her body midair. She maintains a straight line throughout the dive. There is minimal splash.

When her face emerges, she shouts. "Mom! Did you see me? Were you watching?"

I look for her mom and see she's talking to someone. Her head is turned.

I look back at Wendy.

"I saw," I shout.

Wendy looks at me.

"I was watching." I pull the rabbit's eye out of my bag and bite into it. "It was amazing. Barely a splash."

OPERATION HYACINTH

SAM COHEN

It wasn't like we all thought it was so great, or anything, before the developers came. To the contrary, as Avi, our resident academic, might say. We'd moved in in our twenties and didn't anticipate still being here twenty years later. We had imagined real houses, two bathrooms with those rectangular white sinks, partners, living rooms with Christmas trees. Time had seemed abundant, and then, while we were falling in love and breaking up and looking for gigs and making our art and talking about the world and what we wanted from it, it narrowed and disappeared. We were still here.

Donita had been complaining for years about hearing Avi have sex through the walls and Pearl complained about Donita's film screenings that turned into late-night karaoke sessions and Stef complained about Pearl's passive-aggressive notes reminding everyone not to let friends' dogs pee on the pollinator garden or to please keep bottles separated for Bosco, the unofficial super and brother of their landlord, Vero, who liked to return them to the store. Chicken was the only one among us who had always seen this as a kind of utopia, a forever home, who complained about nothing. We didn't complain about Chicken either.

In addition to no laundry hookups and dyke drama, we had Doña Carmen, Bosco and Vero's mother, crawling to our door, or else hobbling on knobby skeleton legs which didn't support her weight even though she was a sack of loose yam skin over fucked-up bones. When she arrived here ten years ago, she was old but could walk fine, and her probing and gossipy lucidity was interrupted only by short afternoon spells of other-world inhabitation. The first few Christmas Eves, she had even made tamales and delivered them to our door, but now, to traverse the eight-foot distance to Donita's or Pearl's, Doña Carmen employed all four limbs, grabbing a tree branch, a bamboo stalk, a rain gutter. She used her full upper-body strength to hoist a foot and swing it forward, land it. Her eyes these days made us think of psychic witches and ancient madness, the way they focused on the world beyond. But the scary part was when she'd refocus, bore those eyes into one of our doors, which she'd then rattle. "*Llevame a casa!*" she wailed in a voice that sounded like it came from the pre-birth, beyond-the-grave world. Bosco came over to feed her breakfast and dinner, and Vero came over a couple times a week to give her a bath, but mostly, we were the ones who were around in the daytime, left to usher Doña Carmen to the big bungalow at the front of the property.

"This is your home!" we told her with that condescending cheer you use on toddlers. We knew she didn't mean this home, though, but the other one, the place she lived before she was a La Llorona bag of not-fully-connected bones. The body of Doña Carmen made us wonder about our own bones, which now seemed magically lubed up, with seamless, almost plastic hinges, and her wailing made us shudder at the horror of wanting to return to a home that no longer existed, waking up daily to the belief that your husband and kids and garden and cats are all there waiting and you are somehow stuck in an otherworld.

We tried to adjust her to this world so that she'd stay—we feared that once she died, Vero would sell. Pearl brought her floral teas sprinkled with just a half of one of Chicken's mushrooms powdered in a coffee grinder. Stef propped her up in a lounger in the yard while she sawed planks of wood with goggles on. She put sunglasses on Doña Carmen with a baseball cap that said LA DYKE DAY and stuck a La Croix in the armrest of Doña Carmen's lawn chair. Sometimes Donita would come out and give her a swipe of lipstick or paint her nails. If we made fish tacos on the grill, we gave her some. We wanted to convince her she was one of us, that she belonged here.

The feral, haunted feeling that Doña Carmen brought to the complex was amplified by the menagerie of wild animals that had appeared ever since Avi started feeding the cats, which they named Ursula, Octavia, Audre, and Karl and referred to as "outdoor pets" if anyone dared to utter the word *stray*. The bowls of kibble Avi left on the patio table attracted possums and skunks and raccoons, and the complex became a preserve of freaky nocturnal wildlife.

Plus there was a mean Chihuahua named Kendy who lived in the back bungalow with Bosco. We all thought her name was Candy with an accent until she got a dog tag one day. Kendy did that terrifying Chihuahua bark-and-run any time someone's door opened. She'd lunge at your feet and never stop. Even if you gave her a little piece of cheese, she'd snatch it from your fingers and snap her teeth, keep barking her nasty demon bark.

Sometimes we'd look at Trulia rentals or call a number on a For Rent sign and learn that Los Angeles one-bedrooms really were $2400 now, and then the crawling woman howling for a nonexistent home and the late-night screaming of Hole and the Cranberries and the cats and their attendant spooky night mammals seemed okay.

Donita watched the hummingbird. It was the new thing she was doing in the morning—meditating, stretching, reading with her coffee, looking out the window. "I'm in my healing era," she'd begun telling people. The hummingbird stuck its long proboscis into a long pink flower, beating its wings. It was in the tree where its nest was, a thimble of spiraled fibers, a teacup for the dolls of wood nymphs. Donita was trying to stop being such a hater, in her healing era, and watching the hummingbird helped. When her morning ritual was over, Donita glanced at her phone. Stef had texted: *burrito?*

Donita checked the time stamp. A half hour had passed.

Still down? Donita asked.

BRT, texted Stef, and two seconds later, Stef was standing on the front stoop. Stef was one of those Tilda Swintony people, willowy and translucent with ashy hair and eyelashes, only she was in a boxy jean jacket, white leather cons, hair hanging from a cobalt beanie. She wore the single triangle earring Donita had bought her in Mexico ten years ago, and her face, however much Donita would never say so, was the only real marker of time passing, the most home-feeling face in Donita's life.

Stef lived in Hyacinth, too, in her own bungalow ever since she and D broke up five years ago. The timing coincided perfectly with Carrie's move to Ohio to take an academic position, and Stef wasn't sure if it was weird to stay in the complex, which we called simply Hyacinth after its gorgeously floral and gay-sounding street, but Donita encouraged her. Already rents everywhere were insane, and also Stef used a corner of the yard to make large-scale artworks, and where else was she going to find space to do that on her tenuous mix of freelancing, adjuncting, and dog sitting?

"Oh hey, come in," Donita said. "Just gotta put pants on."

They walked to get burritos, and Donita noted the bean trees, the scent of jasmine, the urine-soaked tunnel that spit them out at the park. She felt, intentionally, the way the sun touched every part of her and the way her skin responded, each cell opening and then chilling the fuck out. She'd quit her job six years ago to go back to college and study art, and while she wasn't making art as much as she wanted to, this was part of why she quit, too, she knew: to get a burrito with Stef, to feel her body respond to the sun, to notice the bean pods. She'd been going to an office every day for twenty years, starting when she was seventeen and the golden child of Job Corps, a government program designed to get at-risk youth behind desks filing papers and answering phones, and she was resentful of Stef, a working artist, not just for making art but for going outside when she wanted to, for hitting up a yoga class midafternoon if she felt like it, for reading and walking and engaging deeply enough that she could be a genius.

Genius was something people said about Stef—art writers, queer people who cared about art. It was rough for Donita, who would get home at five to Stef in sweatpants in the yard making art—she'd get drunk and yell at Stef that everyone thought Stef was such an art genius but it was privilege that allowed her a genius permission slip. No one had ever told D that she could be a genius. She was treated as remarkable at seventeen for being one of the only Job Corps kids to land an actual job where you got to sit down, a job at Honda answering phones.

D worked her way up to being an office manager, but she quit her office job and here they were, walking in the sun, picking up potato and egg burritos, seeing a flock of green parrots, both free. And Donita had to admit it was hard, being free. Hard to figure out what to do with each hour of your day when you were in charge of it, how to make life meaningful and pleasurable, how to pay rent.

But then Doña Carmen was dead. Bosco told us. And where we had seen open space between the windows and their frames, missing bathroom tile, bad popcorn ceiling, and broken heaters, we now saw an intentional community, a gated cluster of queer-occupied one-bedroom cottages. We saw the pineapple guava tree, the lemon trees, the empty dirt lot between Donita's and Stef's where we grew tomatoes and flowers, where we had a communal fire pit and a barbecue and a picnic table, and it seemed suddenly like something Avi's students would have dreamed up as an ideal—a queer commune where everyone had their own little cottage, but where Chicken would offer you a beer if they were outside in their little foldable lounger, where Pearl was always bringing over tiny wrapped chamomile cakes or matcha cookies she'd made, where we'd hang at the picnic table and talk about the war or who broke up or what vegetables might go in the plot this fall.

Stef and Donita ate on D's couch, sweaty from the walk and craving A/C. Stef was pouring hot sauce into a bite hole and D was shoving a chip into her burrito when their phones dinged simultaneously.

Man on the land!!! Pearl had texted the Hyacinth group text. Pearl was the only trans girl among us and so the only one from whom this joke could be 100% funny. The group was labeled HYACINTH HOMOS with three hibiscus emojis that seemed like a mixup from someone in the group with spotty flower literacy.

Donita spun around and looked out the window. Indeed, two men were measuring, marking the distance between Pearl and Avi's front doors, scratching X's in the corners of the empty lot's dirt.

I also see the men, Donita texted, with a side-eye emoji.

I don't like them here with their measuring tools, Pearl wrote. *Getting my crystals out to ward them off,* Pearl sent, followed by three crystal emojis and three red X's.

I'm going out to play scary latina dyke. Watch me in case I need backup

I've got you, texted Avi.

And then Donita was outside in her short shorts and platform docs going "hola hola" to the men. "Que pasa aqui, que hacen?" she singsonged.

"We're measuring," one man said. "Our boss might buy this property."

Donita felt the ground become wavy, and something dropped in her. The ground was unsolid, she was unsolid, but she clenched her teeth and told herself no: the ground might be unsolid, but she was solid as fuck, she was standing on water like Jesucristo, like a fucking miracle. "Pues, he hasn't bought it yet." She cocked a hip and put her fist on it. "People live here."

"We've been sent here, señora."

No one called Donita señora and got away with it. She'd spent too much of her life queer, too much of her money on nails and botox and cute outfits to be called *señora*. Donita lit a cigarette and stepped behind the men, shooing them with her pointy metallic acrylics. "Eh eh eh," Donita said. She pooched her purple lips as she herded them toward the gate. "Vayense porfaaaa, graciaaaas."

Donita stood at the gate, peering over it all get-off-my-lawn. Pearl came out, drinking something golden and see-through out of a Mason jar. It reminded Donita of shimmery pee.

"Nice work," Pearl said.

"Thanks," said Donita. "Is there glitter in your drink?"

"Petal dust," said Pearl.

"Check this bitch, straight from fucking fairyland."

Pearl pulled her face into a cartoonish smile, then splayed her hands out like a music box ballerina, flapped them like little baby wings. Her outfit was something between sundress and nightgown, raspberry pink with what looked like a piped-out frosting splooge of ruffles around the hem and neckline.

Whereas yesterday she might have found Pearl's whole getup and glitter drink cheesy and annoying, she now saw the whole thing as kind of magical. Where else in this late capitalist hellscape would you be safe and free wearing this semi-sheer housedress with ruffle cum all over it *outside in the sunshine?*

"So what'd they say?"

"Their boss is thinking of buying."

"Fuck," said Pearl.

"Fuck," Donita agreed.

Everything in the neighborhood was transforming. The Mexican restaurant where you used to get $3 margaritas on Wednesdays was now a cocktail bar that served margaritas at half the strength but with a pink sugar rim for $17. The karaoke bar run by the two mean Thai sisters was gone, the sisters gone, too. They had yelled at the basic bitches who sang bad drunken Britney in large groups to respect the two-drink minimum but when anyone from Hyacinth entered, they invited us into the back room for hot dogs and cold noodles. The giant French restaurant with the dark cocktail bar and big 1950s man booths constantly said they were closing and then some group would come and save it again under historic preservation laws. Hyacinth Street itself had a few houses of straight white people now, their *oh my god Becky* conversational sounds threatening to overtake the tinny rancheras the other houses played on Sundays. Horizontal woodslat fences were going up.

We hugged and offered condolences, added flowers and placards to the little shrine outside Carmen's bungalow, but also panic spread through shared glances and speculation on the Hyacinth group text.

I'm scared Vero's only been keeping the property so she wouldn't have to uproot her mother, Stef wrote.

Duh, Donita replied.

"Should we write Vero?" Pearl asked, nervously opening and closing one of her plastic cricket barrettes.

Donita shrugged. "Not right on the heels of her mother's death. I say we wait."

But it turned out that on the heels of Vero's mother's death, developers were knocking on her door in the Valley.

"Veronica Parra?" we imagined them saying in Valley Girl voices, all extended vowels and *rarara* Rs.

"Monsters!" We imagined Vero shouting, with a stronger accent than she has in real life, a high drama voice like she was in a telenovela. "Today is my mother's funeral!"

"A million," they must have offered, because that was the number we heard later. "We can do a million."

Vero sighed, must have thought of her brother Bosco and what he could do with a few hundred thousand. Must have thought of Donita and Chicken, who she had also come to think of as her fuckup children, even though they were only a few years younger. Where would they go? Vero thought it must be a sin to even think about large sums of money on the day you bury your own mother. *But this is a sinful place and time.* The Vero in our minds crossed herself, a move she hadn't done since Catholic school, but it did something, connecting her to God and her child-self, all the earnest Mexican Catholic children and abuelitas everywhere, to her deceased mother.

"Leave the paperwork and go," our imaginary Vero said, in a voice no sane person could respond to.

"I didn't sell to them though," she said, standing on Donita's porch. "Those people were ruthless. But I guess it wore me down. So many people were asking to buy and eventually it seemed inevitable. Just a question of who. It's not a done deal yet, but it's moving fast."

Donita nodded, not speaking out of fear she might burst into tears.

"I'm sorry," Vero said. "I did think about you. But I also thought about Bosco, and my sister. I'm okay with money but they're in a different place. I have to think about my family."

Donita swallowed. Family was the engine of capitalism, that much she was sure of. Fuck everyone else over to support the fucking family.

Chicken put little handmade invitations on our doors—HYACINTH EMERGENCY MEETING! BRING PENS AND PAPER! BRING DRINKS! Chicken was not someone with a lot of organizational skills, but they did have a strong propensity to make flyers, to hand out La Croix and hard kombuchas, and to show up for a fight. Chicken had once been the front person of a band everyone loved, on the East Coast, bopping and screeching and making high-pitched swooping nonsense noises onstage. This felt like the ultimate expression of the essence of Chickenness but now Chicken lived here bopping around Hyacinth, organizing occasional nature walks for kids, sometimes playing with a band, sometimes growing squash in the garden lot, sometimes selling mushroom chocolates. We felt lucky to get Chicken now, and felt like maybe it's okay, and even extremely lucky, to get to be the ultimate expression of yourself only once and briefly and then just be.

When we showed up for the meeting, Chicken was sitting at the picnic table, which was technically Donita's but had become communal, with a six-pack of hibiscus and grapefruit hard kombucha which felt thematic for the hibiscus/hyacinth merge no one had ever verbalized. Next to Chicken was a giant notepad on a pop-up easel, like Chicken was suddenly a character in *The Office*. "We're going to brainstorm," Chicken announced. "There are no bad ideas!"

"Rob a bank," Donita said. "Buy the property from Vero."

"Yes!" Chicken responded, and wrote ROB A BANK in purple marker on the giant pad.

"Get the developer guys to eat a bunch of Chicken's mushroom chocolates and show them that no one owns the land," said Pearl. Everyone laughed.

MUSHROOM CHOCOLATES*!!!* Chicken wrote.

Stef raised her hand.

"Yes, Stef!" Chicken called.

"Really big kickstarter," Stef said. "Like, really mobilize anti-gentrification movements and get national support."

"Oooh, okay," Chicken said, "Yes. Yes. I'm into it." Chicken wrote KICKSTARTER / ANTI-GENTRI ACTIVISM.

"I like Stef's idea," Avi said. "But I think we have to look around and see that people are losing their homes everywhere. Families are being pushed out. If we fundraise, we have to fundraise in solidarity with our neighbors."

"Good point, good point!" said Chicken. SOLIDARITY W NAYBS, they wrote.

"Fuck that," said Donita. "You know what's cool about families? They have a family to move with. If we get pushed out of the neighborhood, we're each alone."

Everyone fell silent.

"Okay okay okay!" said Chicken. "Hear me out. What if we, like. Like. Squat? In a dog grooming place. Take it over. Do a dog grooming fundraiser."

"Chicken," Donita said.

"I mean, no?"

"Dude. If I could make three million dollars grooming dogs before this shit goes to escrow, I'd be grooming dogs right now, believe me."

"Turn Vero into a radical leftist," said Avi.

"Magic spells?" Stef said.

Audre Lorde hopped up on the table in front of Donita then, something she never did really, because Donita was not a cat person.

"Magic spells?" Avi asked Audre, and Audre sauntered down the table to rub her face on Avi's chest. Slowly the animals circled. Two skunks, a possum, and three cats stood like prayer statues with shining eyes around the picnic table.

"Well that's good," said Pearl. "The animals want us to stay."

Doña Carmen started visiting Pearl while she drank her evening tea. Her skin was on tight now, a layer of fat making the bones invisible. Her cheeks had become plump and dewy, her long lashes mascaraed thick, and her body moved sinuously through space in a way that made Pearl think of genies.

"You were so pretty, Doña Carmen!" Pearl says. "You have all your subcutaneous layers back!"

"My brain is back, too, *mija*," Carmen says. "And I can tell you I was more beautiful than every one of those pink flowers you've got in your pollinator garden, more fragrant and more full of nectar. It's wonderful they give you the nectar back," she said, batting her eyes. "You can call me Tía Carmen."

Pearl felt a little pink swell in her chest. Some of her tías could not accept their trans niece and it felt so nice to have this ghost tía to replace them.

"Are you stuck here, Tía Carmen? Do you want help crossing?"

"No, mi amor," she said "It's not really like that. You can come and go, or in a way you can be in both at the same time but *where* you can go is a little bit limited it seems. I can't seem to get off Hyacinth Street. I can go to my old house, this means, but who is living there? Four gringuitos with ridiculous hairstyles. Three girls, one muchacho, and all these stringed instruments from India, all these masks from Africa. It's true what they say about going home again. You can't. I try to haunt these gringos but it doesn't work because no one can really pick up on anything from this realm. You, La Perla, are sort of half-in half-out though, huh?"

"Since I was a little kid." She liked being called La Perla by a ghost. It made her feel like a real trans witch who talked to ghosts.

"I knew that about you. So I just wanted to say hi," said Tía Carmen, and then she was gone.

"Tía Carmen?!" Pearl shouted.

She rematerialized, now with red lipstick on. "Yes, mi amor?"

"Vero's trying to sell the property. We're all really scared. We don't have a place to go."

"Ay, la Vero," Tía Carmen said. "She is seeing in dollar signs. If we can figure out how to get me off Hyacinth Street, I'd be happy to haunt her. No one knows how to manipulate Vero like her mother."

At the next meeting, the animals came right at the beginning. A skunk raised its giant terrifying dandelion tail right near Donita.

"Yo," Donita said, bringing her knees to her chest, "why you always gotta run straight up to me and poof out your tail like that?"

The skunk didn't answer.

"It's scary, girlfriend," said Donita. "I don't like it."

The skunk took two steps backward, relaxed its tail, and sat down. It looked suddenly unmenacing, a stripy chipmunk.

Everyone had eaten a couple mushrooms for this meeting, to

try to connect to each other's brains and also the universe, and was now drinking lavender iced tea that Pearl made from the pollinator garden. "To connect us to the land," Pearl said. It was sweltering.

We held hands and called in the ancestors.

"We have to come up with a down payment," said Avi. "We have to buy."

"Like, how?"

"First of all, everyone throws in their savings."

"I have $13.01 in savings from my Keep the Change account," said Donita.

"I have 3k in my emergency fund," said Stef.

"Of course you do," said Donita. "So responsible."

"I have like almost $70k in savings," said Avi.

Everyone's mouths fell dramatically. A possum inched closer.

"You guys, that's not a huge amount of savings, okay? I'm almost fifty. I've been saving for a long time. I thought I was gonna buy a house one day but it's, like, not possible in this city. So my savings can go in."

"I have a clay piggy bank with hundred dollar bills I've occasionally put in over the years," said Pearl.

"Let's go smash it," said Donita.

It turned out Pearl had $4,200 hidden inside a clay pig which lived among a menagerie of stuffed bears and lions in a pull-out plastic drawer under her bed. Now the pig was a pile of terra cotta shards Pearl was sweeping into a pink dustpan while Donita smoothed the bills.

"You're a fucking freak, Pearl," said Donita.

"I've been putting them in there since I was a kid," Pearl said. "I got the pig from my abuelito for my seventh birthday. Ever since then, I'd save little bills in a jar until I reached one hundred, and then my abuelo would change the money out for a bill that would go in the pig. After he died, I started doing it myself. It was supposed to be my engagement ring fund, for when I met my dream girl."

"Aw, Pearly," Donita said. "This is so sweet of you. What if you still meet your dream girl?"

"I am my dream girl," said Pearl.

Chicken had $19,000 left over from an inheritance from an aunt, Stef sold two guitars, and in the end, we realized we had a total of one hundred and eighteen thousand six hundred and eleven American dollars, including all the loose change from Donita's car floor.

Doña Carmen worked on locating the dream portal. She kept trying to get into Vero's dreams, to tell her not to sell the house, but it was hard. It was hard both to figure out how to flip into the dream dimension, and also Vero felt shut down to the spirit world.

So Carmen talked to her new friends, some old brujas and curanderas who hung out in one of the between-dimensions, and learned it was helpful if the sleeper has a high amount of melatonin, naturally or from supplements or meditation, or even better, psilocybin. These really open the portals to the collective spirit world, the brujas said, get the sleeper out of their own world of repressed anxieties.

Then, they told her, you look for the purple light, try to melt into it. Once you are a part of the purple, you can beam into the dreamer's first chakra. "It's sort of like you become the internet, but without any numbers," said one bruja. "You just feel the purple, become it, and go."

"Exactly," said another. "It's your daughter. It'll be easy to find her."

We went to Vero's with a gift basket. Lush Sleepy lotion, a rose-scented candle, thick socks, and two of Chicken's mushroom chocolates. Our condolences, we wrote on the card. We loved Doña Carmen.

"Thank you," Vero said. "This is very sweet."

"I lost my mom, too," Pearl said. "It's so hard."

"The mushrooms have some psilocybin in them," said Chicken. "It's scientifically proven to help grief and can even connect you to the afterlife a little bit. It shows people their loved ones are okay."

Once we invested our hopes in Doña Carmen's visitation, we felt we'd bought some time. It would fuck her up a little at least, make her wonder if she was making the wrong move, selling. We didn't know Vero's decision-making processes too well, but we felt pretty sure no one could be unaffected by a directive from the mouth of their dead mom.

In the meantime, we needed more money.

"Let's go back to the first idea on the list," said Stef. "Rob a bank." We were sitting outside drinking various things and sweltering. Both Donita and Avi were manually lifting their braless, binder-free tits off their chests to let the pools of sweat that had accumulated there dry.

"I've seriously always wanted to rob a bank," Chicken said.

We all laughed.

But then Chicken said, "It's actually easy and possible, robbing a bank. If you slip them a note that says you're armed, they're, like, legally obligated to give you money."

"There's a good tradition of American bank robbers fighting for justice," said Avi. "The George Jackson Brigade. Rita Bo Brown. Bank robberies to redistribute wealth and power, and as a move toward insurrection."

"Fuck gentrification," Donita said, putting her feet on the picnic table. "I'm in."

Somehow Donita's casualness made it real. We all looked at each other and knew.

Operation Hyacinth was born: the boys would go into the banks, but they'd go in as girls. Chicken and Avi in lace-fronts purchased from the down payment money pot, heels, body-cons, lady gloves with baubly rings over them. Full faces but not drag makeup—regular club girls. It was going to take a lot of work, but they'd get there.

Doña Carmen found the purple light. She focused on it, and as she focused, she realized she did not have a body at all. The body was a projection, a fantasy that she believed in so hard that other people could see it. She wasn't molecules but something else instead, something science hadn't found a name for. The something else that was Doña Carmen focused on the purple and then was in it, or *was* it? And, thinking of Vero in her bed, she whooshed to the world of three-headed dogs, fanged cunts, schoolyard crushes, crumbling teeth. But how to find Vero, she wondered. And then she got it: you didn't find the dreamer, you became the dream. She sat down on a green velvet chair and realized she was embodied again, forty and gorgeous. Would Vero recognize her? "It's your mom," Carmen tried. "Hola, Veroniqui." She imagined stroking Vero's head and it appeared, Vero's head, in her lap. "Ahh. Hi, mi amor."

Vero blinked awake. She smiled. It was dream Vero, and this was nothing out of the ordinary.

"I just came to warn you about these gringos you're supposedly selling the property to."

"They're Mexican-American," said Vero. "Not gringos."

"They're gringos in their hearts," Carmen said. "Bad things will come of this sale. Misfortune not only for las tortilleras but also for your brother. He is happy there. He's a sensitive boy, though, and if you plant him somewhere else, who knows?" She hoped she sounded like a wise ghost. "You think a million dollars for all of you is so much money? It is not so much money—there is the taxes, think of the taxes, and even if Bosco could buy a house with his third, so what? It will be far away, isolated. It will need repairs, expensive repairs."

"It's already in process, Mamá," Vero said. She was teenaged Vero suddenly, her hair gray-less and silky.

"Esas tortilleras belong to that land, Vero. Don't mess with that for some gringo money."

It was a good ghost line, Carmen felt. A line that would haunt.

Avi and Chicken practiced walking in heels across the yard, swishing their hips in cargo shorts, at first too much but then, following Donita and Pearl, just the right amount. In days they went from lumbering T-rexes in stilettos to misogynist-leaning female impersonators to girls, real girls. Avi wore one of Pearl's dresses and Chicken wore Donita's, the girls helping them prop up the cleavage that was normally smashed into binders.

Pearl painted them until new faces painted on their faces, highlighter and contour creating novel arrangements of bones, glossy overpainted lips. Chicken was puckering into the mirror, lined eyes and angled brows inspiring intense glares.

"Look at this ass!" Stef yelped, swatting Chicken's butt in padded Spanx.

"The dysphoria parade," Avi said.

"It's for a very good cause," said Pearl.

We imagined Vero waking up spooked but comforted, too. Had the little nibble of Chicken's chocolate she tried, plus dousing herself in lavender cream, been a kind of supernatural invitation? Probably it was normal to dream about your dead mom.

We can see her sliding into her slippers and padding into the kitchen, pouring coffee from the Mr. Coffee carafe, which was programmed to brew at 7 a.m. She opened her laptop and saw the contract had arrived. Strange timing. What had her mother said? The tortilleras belonged to the land? Please. Donita was from Anaheim and Pearl was from East LA. Was this some kind of Aztlán shit? And then there was Stef, a white girl from Ohio or Iowa or one of those. She sipped her coffee and read the contractual language, harsh and jagged at 7 a.m. It had been good to see her mother, health restored and beautiful, made her feel like she *was* in a better place like everyone said. As words like *premises* and *property* and *purchase* popped into her vision, she thought about her mother slithering along the concrete toward her imaginary real home and she wondered what it meant to belong to somewhere.

A miracle occurred. We could only think of it as a miracle anyway. Stef's uncle in Cleveland was put into a retirement home, leaving behind a nearly untouched black Honda Accord. Stef's mom called to ask if she wanted it.

We were all in the yard watching high heel practice when she called. "I know you love your pickup, but it's always breaking down," her mom said. "I'm just worried about you." Our jaws all dropped. Chicken's face turned into the face of a five-year-old. Pearl threw her arms up in the air and shouted, "Santa Carmen!"

"The Honda Accord is a fucking perfect car," said Donita. "You know why?"

"Because it's common?" Avi asked.

"Yes," said Donita. "But because it's a car rich people's teenaged kids have. We can go to rich people neighborhoods, take plates. Then we drive out to smaller towns, change out the plates between jobs. If they're all from black Accords, it'll throw off the cops if someone does get the plates down." She tossed her cigarette, put it out with an espadrille.

"Jobs," Stef said, rolling her eyes.

We packed different looks for our girls. Crop tops and high-waisted pants. Candy-striped miniskirts and white go-go boots. Lingerie-style dresses. Old-timey dresses with pillbox hats and lady gloves: dazzle camouflage.

We all flew out to Cleveland. Stef and Donita went to pick up the car while Chicken, Avi, and Pearl got two rooms at the Motel 6. We went to the gay bar where the menu was unlike any gay bar menu we'd ever seen. We ordered tater tots and Old Fashioneds, macaroni and cheese and IPAs. We sung to Lady Gaga and Lizzo, watched shy old men sip cocktails on dates and young lesbians in studded belts sway awkwardly in slow dances. We felt exhilarated, we were really doing it. We twirled each other and shrieked and laughed our heads off. The bartender offered us a free round of drinks because we were "a lot of fun."

The next day, our destination was a Huntington Bank in Springfield, Ohio. We picked it in part because it was in the middle of nowhere, because the cops would take a while to come and surveillance technology was outdated, and in part because of the Simpsons, because it felt empowering to imagine we were in an animated world. Chicken looked like a cartoon. Pearl had painted them until they were unrecognizable to their iPhone face recognition. They wore a little schoolgirl skirt and high socks with a crop top, a blonde bob, stiletto Mary Janes. We all admired girl-Chicken as she walked toward the bank, holding a leather school satchel, a tiny sexy naif with too much makeup. Did she tremble? We could not see. She looked calm.

Inside the bank, there was no line. This was not LA and so Chicken could saunter right up to the counter, where there was a lone man who looked reared on whole milk and football. A blond cartoon of a man. "Heeyyyy," Chicken said to the blond man cartoon. They pursed their lips and cocked their head, a cartoon, too. The man smiled. Chicken smiled back. "I need to make a withdrawal." Chicken fumbled with the satchel's buckle to get out our note, a note we'd typed up, printed on lavender paper and laminated, which read: THIS IS A BANK ROBBERY. I AM ARMED. CASH PLEASE AND NO ONE GETS HURT.

Chicken slid the note toward the teller and smiled coquettishly.

The teller's face turned red. His hands made things jangle as he wrestled with keys and made other flailing gestures.

"Is everything okay?" asked Chicken. Somehow Chicken felt born for this.

The man cleared his throat and his head looked like it might tomato-explode but after a series of floppy-handed maneuvers, he slid a zippered green Huntington Bank bag through the Plexiglass.

"Thank you so much," Chicken said. "Have a great day." They tossed their bob and sauntered toward the entrance, kept sauntering until they saw our car in the parking lot and then broke into a crazed smile and leapt toward the car.

When they got in, they couldn't stop giggling. "Drive normal drive normal!" Chicken said.

Donita, smiling with closed lips, her expression hidden behind sunglasses, drove. When she turned onto the freeway we all cheered, screaming, shrieking, giggling, hugging.

"CHICKEN!!!" We kissed their face, shook their tiny shoulders. They removed their wig and Pearl passed them a makeup wipe. They scrubbed until they were boy again. Our Chicken in a schoolgirl skirt. We had done something unbelievable.

That night we celebrated at a Lexington, Kentucky, gay bar. We did tequila shots and belted out karaoke songs. Chicken sang the Thong Song and Donita did Rage Against the Machine. We all danced in front of the stage while Chicken bounced in front of the mic: "Shaking that thing like who's the ish with a look in her eyes so devilish," and Donita metal-screamed, "Rally 'round the family, with a pocket full of shells." There was an electricity between our bodies, like all of our organs were vibrating and our skin was vibrating too and every time we looked at each other it would vibrate harder. It was like someone had flicked our power on and now we were all coursing light. We had felt so low-power forever, we realized, so take-what-we-can-get but now we were taking what we were *due*. We were together and ghost-powered and creating our own future. "Doña Carmen!" Chicken yelled during the bridge. "Fuck the banks, fuck capitalism, Hyacinth forever!" We all whooped.

We kept doing it. We couldn't stop. We became a hive, a perfect machine. We'd get breakfast at a diner while Stef, the white one who was also andro-enough to look generally female took the car to find a new set of plates and come back to the diner.

Once we were full of hash browns and coffee, Avi or Chicken would do an outfit change in the bathroom and Pearl would do makeup. We'd distract the waitresses while we hustled our drag girl out and then we'd drive a few hours to the bank where we'd wait around the corner, Donita curling her eyelashes or smoking a cigarette in the driver's seat, Pearl and Stef in the trunk squeezing each other's hands and praying to Santa Carmencita. Chicken or Avi would get back in the car, and we'd scream once we got on the on ramp, get off at some country road ramp and change the plates, drive a few hours more.

We did Bowling Green, Kentucky, because Stef liked the name and Chattanooga because Pearl kept chanting *Choo Choo Choo Chattanooooga*. We had never been to the south and we loved it. The air was thick with the earth's sweat and made juicy things grow. We ate fried green tomatoes and black-eyed peas and grits. We had some luck in that even if people thought we were a bunch of queer and trans freaks, they were nice to us.

We did somewhere called Murfreesboro, where we all said a prayer against transphobia as we pulled in, AND then we went to Myrtle Beach, where we ran into the ocean and felt our bodies become starfish, become manatee, tentacular and mammalian and something different than when we'd started out. We floated and let the sun soak into our bodies and swam past the break line and bobbed on the waves. Donita had always been scared of the ocean but now she was here, too, eyes closed and sunlit face in an uncontrollable smile. Stef looked over at her and couldn't find a trace of hater. She reached for D's hand, held it while they both floated. Stef thought she saw D's smile grow but D didn't open her eyes.

We took a bunch of plates in Myrtle Beach. There were Priuses parked in driveways of a lot of beachside condos. Rich old people could deal with the inconvenience, we felt. We sent Chicken and Avi because they were able to walk around the quiet streets of pink stucco buildings like they were the gay Jewish niblings of the residents there, because they could unscrew plates with the nonchalance of doing a bit of mechanical work for an old auntie. Then, with a pile of new plates, we all went out to the clubs and danced. By morning we were in Baltimore where we got a motel and went to John Water's favorite bookshop and diner, according to an interview we found online. In the morning, we worshipped at the mural of Divine. We stuck handwritten prayers to the wall with cherry-flavored gum, which we thought Divine would appreciate, and then we left to do a bank in West Virginia.

In West Virginia, Avi went in. Lady Avi was a big lady and we outfitted her as a Southern church lady—hat, gloves, church lady dress, sensible heels. She'd practiced her drawl in the car and become improbably maternal, even grandmotherly as she told us sweet black-eyed peas to have a blessed day.

"I just need you babies to help me with a favor," she told the girls behind the desk, white girls with as much makeup on as Avi, one boxed blonde and one brunette, girls with cakey foundation and fake lashes striving for respectability beyond what their origins promised.

"Sure thing, ma'am," the blonde one, whose nametag read Desiree, said.

Avi unclasped her boxy yellow handbag and pulled out the card, slid it across.

Desiree picked up the card, glanced at it, rolled her eyes. "Um, no," she said. She looked at the brunette, whose nametag said Crystal, beckoning her over. Crystal looked at the card, laughed. They stood over the laminated card together giggling, like Avi was a middle school nerd whose journal they'd found a page from.

"Let's see it," Crystal said.

"See what?" said Avi.

"The weapon, dumbass," said Desiree.

"Yeah, come on, grammaw, show us what you got."

"I don't want to have to do that," Avi said, but their voice was stammery, unconvincing. Crystal clutched the card between pink coffin-shaped nails and laughed.

"I'd call the cops but then my good for shitall ex would show up here and I've promised myself I'm done fucking him and baking him pies and this would almost definitely bring him a similar amount of joy," Desiree said. "I don't think I could bear seeing the smile on his face if he came out here. So, if you want to show us your weapon, and please don't shoot, we can give you a little something. Otherwise, I suggest you go on your way, sugarplum."

Avi felt trapped. They hated that their real cleavage was exposed, that Donita had shoved them into one of her bras and now these scary straight girls were laughing at them while their tits were out. They made a promise to themself to demand $15k back for top surgery. Why hadn't they used their savings for this up to this point?

"I don't want to pull a gun on you," Avi said again.

The girls shrugged. "Then don't," Crystal said.

They all stood there staring at each other.

"Can I have my card back?" Avi said finally.

This incited peals of girl-laughter. For Avi, the most triggering kind of laughter. Avi ran, finally, in low heels, realizing low heels felt like the most disempowering shoe, that wearing the tall spike heels with platform toes felt like a strange kind of badassery, like standing on fangs. Low heels were shoes of pathos. Pathetic footwear.

Back in the car, Avi burst into tears.

Whispers of *what happened* came from the hatchback.

Avi tossed their hat and wig onto the floor of the car. Donita sighed, patted Avi's shoulder, and turned out of the parking lot.

On the highway, there was the absence of the familiar whooping. Stef, Chicken, and Pearl clambered somberly into the backseat. Avi swiped their face with one cleaning wipe and then another, swatting and swatting like there was more they were trying to rub off, even after the makeup was gone.

"Are we done?" Stef asked.

Avi stared out the window.

"Yeah," Chicken said. "We can be done."

We counted the money. $220,220. It felt like an auspicious

number. We went to the Olive Garden, then removed the final $1,000 from our stash to share, took it to the local strip club where we tucked twenties into bustiers and garters. "Karma," Pearl said. "Solidarity," said Donita. We started flying back from different airports. We dropped Avi in Kansas City and put the original plates back on the car. Chicken and Pearl we dropped in Santa Fe—Pearl wanted to see the native architecture in Northern New Mexico.

"Should we ditch the car?" Stef asked Donita.

"I think if they have a VIN and it gets traced to your uncle, you're fucked anyway," Donita said. "Might as well keep it. It's a nice car. Also kind of fucked up to your mom to leave it somewhere."

"Okay yeah," Stef said. "Thanks for looking out for my mom."

Stef and Donita drove back to LA, to Hyacinth. They got burritos, ate them under the pineapple guava tree.

"Bad news or good news first?" Avi said, walking down the concrete path in basketball shorts.

"Always bad," said Donita.

"None of us has the income or stability to be approved for a loan on this property."

"Aren't you a professor?" Donita asked.

"Technically I'm a *lecturer*," said Avi.

"What about combined?" asked Stef.

"We're not a family unit."

"God I mean fuck the family," Donita said. "Can we like *please* work on that next? Like registering adults as households who don't have like the blessings of the lord and don't intend to procreate? It's really causing a lot of problems."

"Okay, good news?" asked Stef.

"Good news is Chicken talked to Vero and she's willing to take the money. She said she'll do a rent-to-own type of thing herself. She was really touched that we somehow came up with so much money, and she said she's done some hard thinking and these developers make her feel sick. We give her the money, keep paying rent, and in like fifteen years we'll own Hyacinth."

"I mean, that's great, no? I'm just happy we don't have to move," Stef said.

"I'm happy we got to take a road trip," Donita smiled.

"Stef and Donita are home!" Chicken yelled at Pearl's door.

Pearl came out in one of her vintage nighties holding a sparkle tea. "Here we are," Pearl said. "Let's toast to our Tía la Santa Carmen."

Chicken came out of their house then. "Anyone want a beer?" Chicken asked. We all did.

EDITORS & CONTRIBUTORS

Alissa Nutting is a novelist, screenwriter, and showrunner, most recently of the Adult Swim & MAX animated series *Teenage Euthanasia* and the MAX original comedy *Made For Love* based on her *New York Times* Editor's Choice novel of the same name.

Anna Dorn is the author of the novels *Perfume & Pain*, *Exalted*, and *Vagablonde*. *Exalted* was nominated for an L.A. Times Book Prize. Her next book *American Spirits* is forthcoming for Simon & Schuster. She lives in Los Angeles.

Aurora Mattia was born in Hong Kong and lives in Texas. Her first book, *The Fifth Wound*, is published by Nightboat Books. Her second book, *Unsex Me Here*, is published by Nightboat Books. Her stories have appeared in *Zoetrope: All-Story*, *Prairie Schooner*, *SPASM*, *Joyland*, and elsewhere; and also in exhibitions at the RISD Museum and the Renaissance society, accompanying portraits by Elle Pérez. She's working on a new novel called *Seven Come Eleven*, and writing some country songs.

Emily Austin is the author of *We Could Be Rats*, *Everyone in This Room Will Someday Be Dead*, *Interesting Facts About Space*, and the poetry collection *Gay Girl Prayers*. She was born in Ontario, Canada, and received two writing grants from the Canadian Council for the Arts. She studied English literature and library science at Western University. She currently lives in Ottawa, in the territory of the Anishinaabe Algonquin Nation.

francesca ekwuyasi is a learner, artist and storyteller born in Lagos, Nigeria. She was awarded the Writers Trust Dayne Ogilvie Prize for LGBTQ2S+ Emerging Writers in 2022 for her debut novel *Butter Honey Pig Bread* (Arsenal Pulp Press, 2020). *Butter Honey Pig Bread* was also shortlisted for a Lambda Literary Award, the Governor General's Literary Award for Fiction, the Amazon Canada First Novel Award and longlisted for the Scotiabank Giller Prize and the Dublin Literary Award. *Butter Honey Pig Bread* placed second on CBC's Canada Reads: Canada's Annual Battle of the Books, where it was selected as one of five contenders in 2021 for "the one book that all of Canada should read." She is co-author of *Curious Sounds: A Dialogue in Three Movements*, a multi-genre collaborative book with Roger Mooking. francesca was Queens University's 2023 Carolyn Smart Writer in Residence, her writing has appeared in the *Malahat Review, Transition Magazine, Room Magazine, Brittle Paper, the Ex-Puritan, C-Magazine, Vol. 1 Brooklyn, Canadian Art, Chatelain* and elsewhere. Her short story "Ọrun is Heaven" was longlisted for the 2019 Journey Prize.

Kayla Kumari Upadhyaya is a lesbian writer of essays, short stories, and pop culture criticism living in Orlando. She is the author of *Helen House* (Burrow Press 2022), a queer horror novelette. She is the managing editor of Autostraddle and the managing editor of TriQuarterly. Her short stories appear in *McSweeney's Quarterly Concern, Catapult, The Offing, Joyland, The Rumpus,* and others. She was a 2021 nonfiction fellow and a 2023 speculative fiction writer in residence at Lambda Literary's Writers Retreat for Emerging LGBTQ Voices. She is a 2023-2024 Tin House Reading Fellow.

MAAME BLUE IS A Ghanaian-Londoner, creative writing tutor and author of the novel *Bad Love*, which won the 2021 Betty Trask award, and was shortlisted for the Betty Trask Prize. Her short stories have been published in *Not Quite Right For Us* (Flipped Eye Publishing), *New Australian Fiction 2020* (Kill Your Darlings), and *Joyful, Joyful* (Pan Macmillan). Maame is a recipient of the 2022 Society of Authors Travelling Scholarship and was a 2022 POCC Artist-in-Residence. She contributes regularly to Royal Literary Fund publication *Writers Mosaic* and her writing has appeared in many places including *Refinery29*, *The Independent* and *iNews*. Her second novel *The Rest Of You* was published by Amistad (US) and Verve Books (UK) in Autumn 2024.

MAC CRANE IS AN author, basketball player, and sweatpants enthusiast. Their LAMBDA-award-winning debut novel, *I Keep My Exoskeletons to Myself*, was an Indie Next Pick and NYT Editors' Choice. Their second novel, *A Sharp Endless Need*, is forthcoming in May 2025.

MYRIAM GURBA IS THE author of several books. Her most recent essay collection, *Creep: Accusations and Confessions*, is a finalist for a National Book Critics Circle Award in criticism. Her writing has also appeared in the *Los Angeles Times, the New York Times, the Paris Review* and *The Believer*. She enjoys solving crossword puzzles and binge watching Real Housewives.

Myriam Lacroix is the author of *How It Works Out*. She has a BFA in Creative Writing from the University of British Columbia and an MFA from Syracuse University, where she was editor in chief of Salt Hill and received the New York Public Humanities Fellowship for creating Out-Front, an LGBTQ+ writing group whose goal was to expand the possibilities of queer writing. She currently lives in Vancouver, British Columbia.

Priya Guns wrote *Your Driver is Waiting*.

Sam Cohen is the author of *Sarahland*. Her fiction also appears in *Bomb, Fence, O Magazine, Electric Literature,* and others.

SJ Sindu is a Tamil diaspora author of two literary novels (*Marriage of a Thousand Lies*, which won the Publishing Triangle Edmund White Award; and *Blue-Skinned Gods*, which was an Indie Next Pick and a finalist for the Lambda Literary Award), two graphic novels (*Shakti* and *Tall Water*), and one collection of short stories (*The Goth House Experiment,* which won the Story Prize Spotlight Award). Sindu holds a PhD in English and Creative Writing from Florida State University and is a co-editor for Zero Street, a literary fiction series featuring LGBTQ+ authors through the University of Nebraska Press. Sindu is an assistant professor at Virginia Commonwealth University. More at sjsindu.com or @sjsindu on Twitter/Instagram/Threads.

Soula Emmanuel was born in Dublin to an Irish mother and a Greek father. She studied at universities in Ireland and Sweden, emerging with a master's in demography. She currently lives on Ireland's east coast. Her debut novel *Wild Geese* was published in 2023.

In 2024, it won the Lambda Literary Award for Transgender Fiction, and the Gordon Bowker Volcano Prize at the UK Society of Authors Awards.

Temim Fruchter is a queer nonbinary anti-Zionist Jewish writer who lives in Brooklyn, NY. She holds an MFA in fiction from the University of Maryland, and is the recipient of fellowships from the DC Commission on the Arts and Humanities, Vermont Studio Center, and a 2020 Rona Jaffe Foundation Writer's Award. She is co-host of Pete's Reading Series in Brooklyn. Her debut novel, City of Laughter, is out now from Grove Atlantic.

Works by Venita Blackburn have appeared in the New Yorker, NY Times, Harper's, McSweeney's, Story Magazine, the Virginia Quarterly Review, the Paris Review, and others. She was awarded a Bread Loaf Fellowship in 2014 and several Pushcart prize nominations. She received the Prairie Schooner book prize for fiction, which resulted in the publication of her collected stories, *Black Jesus and Other Superheroes,* in 2017 and earned a place as a finalist for the NYPL Young Lions award among other honors. Blackburn's second collection of stories is *How to Wrestle a Girl* (2021), finalist for a Lambda Literary Prize and was a NYTimes editor's choice. Her debut novel, *Dead in Long Beach, California* (2024) is about the mania of grief, all of human history and a lesbian assassin at the end of the world. She is the founder and president of *Live, Write*, an organization devoted to offering free creative writing workshops for communities of color: livewriteworkshop.com. Her hometown is Compton, California, and she is an Associate Professor of creative writing at California State University, Fresno.

KRISTEL BUCKLEY IS AN editor, publicist and former publisher from the Big Smoke. She is more than happy to talk your ear off about the unfaithful representation of women in history, and her passion is a more equitable, inclusive future for all stories from all voices.

MOLLY LLEWELLYN IS A twenty-something queer, disabled book blogger and editor from the UK. She previously co-edited Peach Pit: Sixteen Stories of Unsavory Women which was published by Dzanc in 2023. She's a big fan of 'weird women' lit and anything that is the color green.